D0890622

Mason

Remington Ranch Book One
Mason and Gina

SJ McCoy

A Sweet n Steamy Romance

Published by Xenion, Inc

Published by Xenion, Inc.
Second paperback edition 2016
www.sjmccoy.com

This book is a work of fiction. Names, characters, places, and events
are figments of the author's imagination, fictitious, or are used
fictitiously. Any resemblance to actual events, locales or persons
living or dead is coincidental.

Cover Design by Dana Lamothe of Designs by Dana
Editor: Mitzi Pummer Carroll
Proofreaders: Aileen Blomberg and Kristi Cramer

ISBN 978-1-946220-00-4

Dedication

For Sam. Sometimes, life really is too short. Few x

Chapter One

Gina stared out the window of her apartment—at a brick wall. In all the years she'd been in New York, she'd never gotten used to looking out at other buildings. She still felt claustrophobic here. Still missed being able to see thirty miles up to the top of the valley and on to the snowy caps of the Crazy Mountains, another fifty miles beyond that. She sucked in a deep breath. Tomorrow she'd see the mountains again. It'd been too long. She got back to see her dad whenever she could, but this time was different. This time she was going to help him put the ranch up for sale. Help him get ready to leave the valley and move to New York so she could keep an eye on him. She swiped angrily at a tear that escaped and rolled down her cheek. She had no choice! He couldn't make it out there by himself—financially or physically. And her own life was here now. She couldn't move out there if she wanted to. She'd have no way to support them. Her photography sold well in the city, and as much as she'd love to spend her days roaming around Montana with her camera, she had to be realistic.

Realistic. Just as she'd discussed with Liam. In his usual no-nonsense, businesslike manner, he had helped her work through the pros and cons. In his usual manner, he had completely ignored any emotional considerations in his assessment of the practical ones. The fact that her dad had lived his whole life in the valley, as had four generations before him. The fact that he didn't want to leave and claimed he'd rather be six feet under than live in New York. Those were emotional concerns that carried no weight with Liam. They were irrelevant. Gina sighed. They might be irrelevant to him, busy as he was at the gallery, staying safely here in New York. They were going to be all too relevant to her for the next couple of weeks while she was in Montana with her dad.

Two whole weeks. She hadn't been back for that long in years. Part of her couldn't wait to get there. Part of her was dreading being there. She was dreading what she knew this would do to her dad. And she was dreading the possibility that she would run into him. Mason Remington. She'd managed to avoid him for years. They hadn't spent more than five minutes in the same room since she'd left for her senior year of college. Although, good as she was at avoiding him in real life, she couldn't avoid him in her dreams. Not a week went by that she didn't spend at least one night with him. Laughing with him as they rode horses up in the foothills. Splashing with him as they floated the river on hot summer days. Screaming his name as he made love to her on a blanket out underneath the big, starry Montana sky. She felt guilty about it, but even when she was awake, it was still Mason she made love to. In bed with Liam she would close her eyes, pretend he was Mason. Pretend that it hadn't all gone wrong and that she was still there in the place she loved, with the man she loved.

She shook her head. She shouldn't be thinking like that. She didn't love him. She didn't even know him anymore. He'd been her first love. That was all. It was natural that a girl should remember her first. Natural to get a little nostalgic. But she had to be realistic. The future she'd dreamed they would share had turned out to be just that. A dream. She'd been young and naïve, and he'd been just a guy. Not a guy who loved her the way she'd thought, but a guy who had enjoyed her and then moved on to the next girl. It was the way things went. Especially between two young people. She shouldn't be mad at him. Shouldn't still hold it against him. But she did. She'd believed him when he told her that he would love her his whole life. He'd been her first. He'd told her he intended to be her last. That she was his and always would be. It still hurt her heart that while she had loved him with all that she was and had believed she would spend the rest of her life with him, he had just seen her as one of the many girls he'd slept with. Just another girl who'd been fun for a while before he'd moved on. All his beautiful words about forever? The words that had meant everything to her? They'd meant nothing to him.

She pulled her suitcase out from under the bed. She didn't need to be thinking about him. She needed to pack. Get everything ready. She'd be there for two weeks, and she had a lot to do in that time. She'd do her best to avoid him, but if she couldn't, she'd be civil. Chat with him like any of her other old friends in the valley. She smiled now. There was one Remington boy she was hoping she would run into. Shane. Shane who had been her best friend from kindergarten through high school. It wasn't his fault his big brother had turned out to be an asshole! She usually managed to catch up with Shane when she was there and always enjoyed his company. In the early years, he'd quizzed her relentlessly about Mason and why she refused to see him or talk to him. He'd eventually gotten the message though. She didn't want anything to do with Mason, and if Shane wanted to keep up their friendship, he needed to respect that. It would be so good to see him again. She bit her lip. Maybe for the last time. Her cell phone startled her.

"Hi, Liam."

"Gina. Sorry, but I'm not going to make it over there tonight. So, safe travels. I'll see you in a couple of weeks. I thought when you get back we should probably start looking for a ring. We need to go through the calendar and find a date that will work for the wedding."

Gina shook her head and said nothing. He hadn't even asked her to marry him. It had come up when he was helping her go through her books. She was hopeless at keeping on top of her taxes. He'd told her that they would both gain a significant tax break if they filed as married. And that, for Liam at least, had been all it had taken to determine that they should—and would—get married.

"Are you there, Gina?"

"I am. Listen, is there any way you can come with me? Meet my dad?"

"No. You know that. We've got the big opening at the gallery this weekend, and next week is fully booked, too."

Gina was disappointed. It was a crazy idea, but she suddenly wanted Liam to see where she came from. "Well, how about next weekend? There's nothing on then. Come for the weekend? Please?"

He was silent for a few moments. Gina could picture him checking his schedule. "I could," he said slowly, "but you know, it doesn't make much sense."

She laughed. "Come on, Liam. Humor me? It doesn't need to make sense. Just say you'll come?"

She could hear the smile in his voice. He was a good man. "You know I try to humor you."

"Thanks, Liam! You'll love it."

He laughed. "But I'm saying no. It doesn't make sense."

"Okay." He was right. It didn't. But still...

"Travel safely, bye."

"Bye." Once he'd hung up, Gina made a face and stared at the phone. "You love me? Oh, I love you too, Liam! You're going to miss me? I'll miss you so much!" She blew out a big sigh and turned back to her packing. "Or not!"

Was this truly what it was like for grown-ups? Getting married was convenient for tax purposes and needed to be scheduled around other, more important appointments? Meeting your future spouse's family was something you would do just to humor them? She pulled herself together. Yes. This is how things work when you're a grown-up, she berated herself. Real life has to be taken into consideration. It's not all magic and romance. That's how you thought it was with Mason. You were a kid. And the way it worked out with him should have taught you what a fool you were. It's time to grow up.

~ ~ ~

Mason took a slug of his beer and looked across the table at his brother. Shane grinned back at him. Another Friday night here in the saloon at Chico was off to the usual start. Shane had already been flirting with a couple of girls who were standing at the end of the bar. He'd promised to teach them how to two-step when the band got going later. Mason checked out the older of the two. She smiled back at him. Maybe she'd do. She had long dark hair, a pretty enough face.

Long legs, and even if they were encased in jeans that had never seen a day's work, they went all the way up to the kind of ass he liked to fill his hands with. Her friend had played right up to Shane while he'd been talking to them, so Mason would be left with this one. If he was up for it. He wasn't sure he was.

This was getting old. At one time, he'd enjoyed the game, enjoyed coming to the resort on the weekends. Throwing down a few beers and finding a sweet little thing he could throw down on a bed later, even if it was only the bed of his truck. It was a release after a week's hard work on the ranch. He enjoyed women. Hell, they enjoyed him. Coming out here instead of going up to town kept it simple. The women here would be gone by Monday. Everybody won. They got to go home with the memory and the story of the cowboy who gave them a night they wouldn't forget. He got to lose himself in a soft body that helped him to forget. Forget her. It was getting harder and harder to forget her though. To push her out of his mind. He looked up again at the girl who was now climbing onto one of the stools at the end of the bar. She was probably a bad idea. Last time he'd taken a girl with dark hair like that back to her room it had been too much. Too much like her. He'd had that girl under him, bent over the end of the bed panting and moaning as he pounded into her. He'd had a fistful of her hair, but all he could see, all he could feel was Gina. In his head, it was Gina who was taking him so deep, Gina's gorgeous round ass he was digging his fingers into. And it had been Gina's name he'd cried out when all the tension in his body had found its release. He'd felt like an asshole. The girl had been cool about it. Said she wasn't worried, it was just sex. She'd been up for more. She'd even laughed and said he could call her whatever he wanted if he'd stay the night and let her ride him as hard as he'd just ridden her.

She'd been okay with it. But it had freaked Mason the fuck out! He hadn't even seen Gina in years. He'd done his damnedest to forget her. To leave her where she belonged—in the past. But she had some kind of hold of him, a hold that only got stronger with each year that passed. Hell, these days it seemed as if it got stronger with each week that passed. He emptied his beer and slammed the bottle down on the table.

"Sorry Shane, but you'll have to figure out a way to work it by yourself. I'm not up for it tonight. I'm heading back to the ranch."

Shane gave him a puzzled look. "But that one with the dark hair is more than up for it. Have you seen the way she's looking at you? You probably wouldn't even need to buy her a drink, you could just take her straight up to her room. She's squirming in her seat every time you look over there. I think she already came in her panties when you smiled at her."

Mason laughed. "Then she's all primed for you or someone else to finish her off." He stood up and put a hand on Shane's shoulder. "Seriously, little bro. I'm more interested in getting some shut-eye than getting a piece of ass tonight."

Shane shrugged. "Whatever you want to do. I can fly solo." He grinned. "Maybe I can talk them into a threesome, I'd hate to see one of them left wanting."

Mason shook his head. "To anyone else, I'd say dream on. Knowing you, I wouldn't be surprised if you pull it off. Good luck."

"Are you sure you're okay, Mase? Are you losing your touch? They have little blue pills for that these days you know."

"I don't need pills. I'm just bored with it all. It seems pretty pointless, you know?"

Shane looked serious for a moment. "I'm going to say something and then dive for cover, okay?"

Mason laughed. "You can say anything. You know that."

Shane chewed on his bottom lip. "Anything except mention a certain person's name, right?"

Mason gritted his teeth and stared at his brother. He could feel that little pulse in his temple that always seemed to pound when he thought about Gina. "There's no need to mention her name. She's history."

"If she's history, why did I hear you shouting her name in your sleep? You did it last week when we were camped out at Overlook Point, and I heard you again last night when I got up to take a leak."

Mason stared at him. "You did?"

Shane nodded solemnly. "I did. And..." Shane frowned, seemingly unsure whether to continue.

"And what? Spit it out."

"Mom said not to mention anything to you, but I have to. I know it still eats at you. She's back."

Mason sat back down heavily. "Back as in here? In the valley?"

"Yeah. Her dad's never been quite right since that fall he had. Since he broke his hip, he's been struggling to keep the old place going. Apparently, Gina wants to move him to New York to be with her."

Mason let out a harsh laugh. "No way would Al Delaney ever leave his ranch! She must be nuts if she thinks he'd ever move to New York."

"From what she told me, she's desperate, not nuts."

Mason's whole head was pounding now, not just his temple. "You've spoken to her? She's desperate how?"

"I have. She's worried sick about her old man. Hates him being out here by himself and hates that she can't get out here enough to keep an eye on him."

"Then she should move back here, shouldn't she! Come take care of her dad and their land. What the hell happened to her that she'd try to move him like that? That she won't do right by him?"

Shane was stone-faced. "A hell of a lot has happened to her over the last few years, Mase. You don't know the half of it."

Mason slammed his fist down on the table, knocking his chair over as he stood. "I don't know the first fucking thing, do I, Shane? How can I when she won't talk to me?" He turned on his heel and left. What the hell was Gina thinking? She might have been able to leave the valley, to never look back, but she knew how things worked here for the rest of them. It was a hard life, a harsh environment. But for the people who lived here, who were born here, it was their world. The land was everything. They may say they owned the land, but in truth the land owned them. The families who had been here for generations—his own and Gina's included—were as much a part of this valley as the river and the creeks were. Like the junipers that dotted the landscape, they not only survived here, they thrived here. Harsh as it was, this environment shaped them and defined them. And just like the junipers, transplanting them elsewhere would slowly kill them. At least that was how he felt.

He strode across the parking lot and climbed into his truck. Damn, Gina! Apparently she was able to survive in the city. New York fucking City of all places. He would never have believed that of the girl he'd known. She couldn't seriously believe Al would be able to survive there. He turned the key in the ignition and then sat back to take a deep breath and calm himself. And why in the hell did he care anyway? What did it matter to him? He liked Al. Still considered him a friend. Helped him out when things got tough. Always sent him a team over to help—and was usually on it himself—at haying and calving. They managed to steer clear of any mention of Gina though. Damn. He pulled out onto East River Road and headed south. It was none of his goddamned business. He should forget about it, about her. If he wasn't going to be able to lose himself in a warm body tonight, he could at least head home and lose himself in the bottom of a glass of bourbon.

Chapter Two

Gina looked up as her dad came into the kitchen. "Morning. Do you want some coffee? I've got muffins in the oven. They're almost ready."

He scowled at her. "You honestly think a few chocolate chip muffins are going to be enough to sweeten me up?"

"I'm not stupid, Dad. It'd take a hundred pounds of sugar to sweeten up an old sourpuss like you."

He tried to look angry, but she could see the laughter in his eyes. "Well, you can start with the muffins and maybe you can make me one of those apple pies for tonight?"

Gina nodded, relieved. He was angry with her—and she understood why—but he loved her. She loved him. She wished there was some other way they could work things out. She didn't want to sell the place any more than he did. At least if they sold now, he might still come away with a little nest egg. If they waited much longer and things kept going the way they had been with the ranch, he could end up with nothing.

He settled himself at the big table and she poured him some coffee. "So, what have you got planned for the day?" he asked.

"I already told you. The realtor from town is coming at twelve-thirty and the other one from Bozeman is coming at one-thirty. I thought it would do them good to see that you're not sure who you're going to use yet. Make them put forth a bit of effort to be the one you choose."

He scowled at her. "I don't want to use either of them, Gina. I don't want to sell."

"Then what do you suggest we do?" She hated this. Hated making him sell the only home he'd ever known. Hated asking him to leave his life. But what else could she do?

His eyes shone as he looked up at her. It broke her heart to see him so sad. "Can't you come back, love? Come live here. We could keep the old place going between the two of us."

Gina felt tears sting her own eyes. "If I believed for a moment that was true, I'd do it. But you know we can't. Beef prices are still falling. Hay prices are still rising. We could bust our butts and still not be able to make it. You know that. I've been sending you as much as I can these last couple of years and you're still only scraping by. If I were to move here too, I wouldn't be bringing anything in."

He shook his head sadly. "I know. I just... Why don't you get them muffins out of the oven before you burn 'em?"

Gina whirled around and rescued the muffins.

"Are you going to take me over to Monique's birthday party next Sunday?"

Gina's heart stopped. "Monique Remington?"

Her dad gave a low chuckle. "Don't pretend you don't know who I mean, girl. How many Moniques do we know?"

Her hands were shaking as she set the muffins on the rack to cool. Mason's mom was a wonderful lady. No one had expected the sophisticated French lady to last more than a year in the valley when she'd arrived as Dave Remington's new wife. That had been nearly forty years ago. She'd proved them all wrong and was as much a part of the valley as anyone. She'd raised four boys and worked the land alongside her husband whenever she was needed. She wore jeans instead of designer dresses these days and was lucky if she got to go shopping in Portland, let alone Paris. She still loved to throw herself a big birthday party every year though.

Gina turned to set the plate of muffins in front of her dad. "I'll drop you off over there."

"You should come. You haven't been to Monique's birthday bash for years."

"Drop it, will you?" She was having a hard enough time being here at all. She was desperately hoping she wouldn't see Mason. The thought of going out to the Remington Ranch, of willingly being in the same room as him...? No. Just no!

Her dad was staring at her. His eyes boring into her as if he could see what she was thinking. "You're going to have to make your peace with him someday."

"With who?" Gina busied herself at the sink, rinsing dishes and making sure her dad couldn't see her face.

"With the man on the moon! Who do you think I mean? Mason. You stubborn little mare."

Gina determinedly kept her back turned to him. "There's no peace that needs to be made with him, Dad. I don't know why you won't let that go. We dated when we were kids. It ended years ago."

"Gina, I'm not stupid, and neither are you. So I wish you'd stop acting as if you are when it comes to him. I don't know what the hell went wrong between the two of you, but I do know you need to make your peace with each other. I can't mention him to you without you losing it. I can't mention you to him without him walking away. If you're going to marry this

Liam character, you need to let your heart say goodbye to
Mason first. It wouldn't be fair to anyone if you don't."

Gina realized she was scrubbing frantically at an already clean
pan. She rubbed her sleeve over her eyes before turning
around. "I said goodbye to Mason ten years ago, Dad."

He shook his head as he finished his muffin. Picking up his
coffee he stood up and stared at her. "We both know that's
not true. You never said goodbye to him, you just didn't come
back. It broke his heart. It broke my heart. And for all you
refuse to talk about it, I think it broke yours, too. If we have to
sell the ranch and leave here, if you really want to marry this
Liam, I'll go along with it. I'll go along with whatever you say
needs to happen. But I have one condition. Before I will move
off this land, you have to make your peace with Mason."

She stared at him. "I told you, Dad. There's no... there's
nothing..."

He gave her a grim smile. "And I told you, Gina. I'm not
stupid." He stopped in the doorway and turned back. "I'll be
down the bottom forty."

"But what about the realtors?"

"What about 'em? Nothing to do with me." He slammed the
door on his way out.

Gina plonked herself down at the table and absently picked at
one of the muffins. Liam would lecture her if he saw her with
it. She popped a piece in her mouth—he wasn't here. This was
all just one big mess. If she didn't have enough on her plate
trying to sort out her dad and the ranch, she now knew she'd
have to come face to face with Mason before she left. Her dad
called her a stubborn little mare? He was a stubborn old mule!
And she knew he'd dig his heels in over her making her
peace—as he called it—with Mason. Perhaps it was a good

thing. She'd blown it up in her mind all these years. Mason had probably never given her another thought—at least not after his ego had recovered from the number she'd done on him by telling him it was over, by not coming back. She shrugged, what else could she have done after she'd discovered how little she meant to him? After she'd heard him tell Guy Preston, of all people, how he really felt?

She started as her dad popped his head back around the door. "I meant to tell you. The pharmacy called. My script is ready. I told 'em you'd pick it up for me before they close."

Gina raised her eyebrows at him. "You want me to go up to town? What about the realtors?"

"You'll still have time after you're done. They're open until six these days." He smiled. "You could catch up with some of your old friends while you're up there."

Gina blew out a frustrated sigh at him. "I don't want to catch up with anyone, Dad."

He shrugged and closed the door again.

He wanted to make her see people, wanted her to engage with life here again. What did he think, that she'd change her mind? That she'd somehow realize that she wanted to come back and live here? And that she'd be able to make it happen even if she did? She didn't want to see anyone. Would rather no one even knew she was here. She hated making her dad leave, but since she had no other choice, she wanted to do it as quickly as possible and get them both out of here without revisiting the past.

~ ~ ~

Mason pulled into a spot right outside the hardware store. He pulled his hat down over his eyes and climbed out of the truck. He hated coming to town. Everyone always wanted to know your business—and to tell you everyone else's. He wasn't interested. Didn't need to know who was divorcing, who was dating, or who was filing for bankruptcy. He sure as hell didn't want anyone knowing his business. Not that he had anything to hide. He didn't understand why they wanted to know. Well, that wasn't true. He knew why—and he hated it. He was the eldest of four brothers, all of them very eligible in the eyes of the old women in town. In the eyes of the young women, too. His family owned a lot of land in the valley, was well respected and pretty well off, by local standards. Any of the Remington boys would be considered a catch, and as the eldest, he was the most sought after.

"Hey, Mason."

He raised a hand to Iris, who was working the cash register. She'd been a year ahead of him in high school. She was one of the biggest gossips around. He made sure he was always friendly with her, chatting and laughing—and never giving anything away. He made his way to the back of the store. He didn't need anything heavy-duty today, just some outdoor party lights to string around the back deck for his mom's birthday. She loved those lights and he loved to see her enjoy her party every year.

As he made his way back through the store, he saw another familiar face.

"Hey, Mase. How you doing?"

He nodded. "Yeah, not bad. How about you, Cody?"

Cody grinned. "Doing great. Brandy's due next month."

Mason smiled. Cody and Brandy had been together since high school. They'd married as soon as they graduated and this must be baby number four, maybe five. "Give her my best."

"You could come say hi if you want. She's out in the car. We were talking about you the other day. You know Gina's in town? We were wondering what happened with the two of you. Always thought you two would be married with kids of your own."

The pulse was pounding in Mason's temple. He'd thought that, too. It turned out Gina hadn't—and she'd never even had the guts to tell him to his face that she didn't want him. He stared at Cody for a moment.

Cody gave him an apologetic smile. "Sorry."

Mason shook his head. "No need. Say hi to Brandy for me. I can't stop, I need to get back down the valley." He started to walk away but turned back when Cody called after him.

"She was in the pharmacy about five minutes ago."

The pounding filled his ears.

Cody shrugged. "Just saying."

Mason backed out into the traffic on Main Street. The pharmacy was a quarter of a mile farther down. He craned his neck to look inside as he drove by. He couldn't see her. What the hell was he thinking anyway? She'd refused to speak to him for years. Why would that be about to change today? He kept asking himself the question as he pulled into an empty space. As he turned off the ignition, the pulse in his temple pounded even louder. He'd pulled in right next to her dad's old truck. He'd just sit here and wait for her to come back.

A few short minutes later, he saw her come out onto the street. The blood pounding in his temple was deafening now. She was beautiful. Older. She'd been a girl back then, she was all woman now. Her hair was shorter, less wild, but still framed her perfect little pixie face. She'd always had a great figure. Curves that drove him wild. She'd filled out a little, the cut of her jacket emphasized a perfect hour-glass he needed to get reacquainted with. His heart clenched in his chest as he watched her greet Mr. Towson from the post office. Her smile was still all kindness and fun rolled into one. He shifted in his seat as the blood pounded its way to the front of his pants. He was hard as a rock just seeing her bundled up in a coat and scarf at a hundred yards. What was he going to do when she reached her truck?

He didn't have time to think about the answer to that one as she came around to the passenger side to put some bags on the seat. As she closed the door, he went with his gut. His mind didn't have time to figure out what to do, but his body knew what it wanted and acted on instinct. He opened his own door and slid out of the cab, landing in front of her as she turned around.

In the narrow space between the two vehicles, his senses filled up with the feel of her. The memory of her. He couldn't help it. He took hold of her shoulders, and, as her eyes widened in recognition, he pushed her up against her truck and leaned his weight against her.

"Mason! I..." Her hands came up to his shoulders as he wrapped her up in his arms and held her to him. Her lips parted as he lowered his mouth to hers and she opened up to him as he kissed her. She felt so right in his arms. So soft, so willing. So his.

~ ~ ~

Gina clung to his shoulders. The feel of his lips on hers, his tongue mating with her own, and his arms wrapped around her, they all took her back. Took her back to the time when he'd been hers, when she'd been his. The time when all was as it should be and she'd been happy. She floated on those memories as he kissed her, knowing she was back where she belonged. He pressed her back against the side of the truck, and she whimpered at the feel of his hardness pressing between her legs. Nothing had changed between them. Nothing at all.

The sound of a car horn honking brought her back to her senses. She pushed him away. What was she thinking? Everything had changed between them. She looked up into his eyes, those beautiful blue eyes she'd thought she would wake up to every morning for the rest of her life.

"I've missed you, darlin'."

She searched his face. He was straight up serious! She shook her head, panic setting in. "I have to go." She stepped away from him. She needed to get back in the truck, back to the ranch and away from this man.

He caught her wrist. "Gina! We need to talk."

She shook her head and pulled away from him. "There's nothing left to say, Mason."

He stared after her as she hurried around and jumped in the truck. He was still standing there staring as she checked her rearview mirror once she'd pulled out into the traffic. The gorgeous cowboy standing in an empty parking space, hat pulled down over his eyes, pain written all over his face, was Mason. Her Mason. And she was driving as fast as she could away from him? Away from the only man she'd ever loved? What the hell was wrong with her? She started to shake as she joined the highway and headed south back down the valley. There was nothing wrong with her. She was being smart. He'd broken her heart, broken her, once before. If she stuck around even long enough to have a conversation with him, she knew she'd fall in love with him all over again. And he'd break her heart again. She didn't think she could survive that a second time. What was she even thinking like that for anyway? Mason was not the only man she'd ever loved. She was in love with Liam. They were going to get married—when they could work it into their schedule.

~ ~ ~

Mason climbed into his truck and sat back in his seat. He pulled his hat down over his eyes and folded his arms across his chest. Way to go, asshole! He'd hoped to see her. Had been trying to figure out how he could get her to talk to him. And what had he done? He'd grabbed her before she even realized who he was, had her up against her truck and kissed the sense out of her. He shifted in his seat as his hard-on pressed uncomfortably against his zipper. If they hadn't been out in the middle of Main Street, he'd have done a lot more, too. That thought made him tip his hat back and take a peek around wondering who might have seen them and how fast word of it would be spreading around town. He groaned. "What are you doing to me, Gina girl?"

Chapter Three

Gina pulled up at the house and rested her head against the steering wheel. Well, she'd seen him. She'd spoken to him. Could that count as making their peace? Hell no! In the space of a couple of seconds, he'd robbed her of any peace she might have ever known. When she'd closed the truck door and heard someone behind her, she'd been about to apologize. Get out of the way for the driver of the vehicle parked next to her. And there he'd been. The sight of him had knocked all the air out of her. He seemed taller, certainly bigger. Ten years ago he'd been tall, muscular, but still a boy in many respects. Now, he was all man. His face was weathered, there were lines around his beautiful, blue eyes. In those few seconds, she'd been hyper aware of everything about him. The slight stubble on his face, the couple of grays in his sandy hair, the way his hat shaded his eyes—his eyes that held so much pain, so much need. She shook her head. Every little detail she'd seen had imprinted itself on her mind as his lips came down on hers. She should have been mad that he'd pushed her up against the truck. Instead, she was grateful. Her knees had been ready to give out, she wouldn't have stayed upright by herself. But it was all wrong. He was just a guy from the past. No matter how gorgeous a man he'd become. No matter that in those few seconds he'd brought back every feeling she'd ever had for him. He was her past. Liam was her present—and her future.

She jumped in her seat as her dad tapped on the window.

"Are you going to come in and make me that apple pie?"

She stared at him, hauling her mind back to the present.

"Well? Are you going to sit there all night or are you coming in and we'll see about some dinner?"

She nodded and grabbed the bags from the passenger seat.

He opened the door for her and smiled. "You run into anyone in town?"

Oh God! He knew! It would be too much to hope that no one had seen Mason pin her up against the truck and kiss her senseless. Word of it would be all over town by now, and had apparently already raced down the valley to her dad. She slid down and glared at him. "Did you tell him I was going to be at the pharmacy?"

Her dad laughed. "Tell who?"

Gina stomped into the kitchen and slammed the bags onto the table. "You may find it funny, Dad, but I don't. You can count that as me making my peace with him. I've seen him. That's it. It's done. Over. And I'll thank you not to mention his name to me ever again. Do you hear me? Ever!"

He was laughing harder now. "Gina girl, I have no idea what happened up in town, but from the state you're in, I'm guessing you're talking about Mason. You can lie to yourself if you want to, but you can't lie to your old dad. You haven't even begun to make your peace with him, but if seeing him has gotten you this stirred up, then you can't deny that you need to."

Gina scowled at him. "Dad, you don't know what happened. He..." She shrugged. "You know how much I loved him. I thought he was the one. I thought we were forever. But that was a long time ago. It turned out it didn't mean as much to him as it did to me. There's no need to go back over something that ended years ago. Please let it go?"

He put a hand on her shoulder. "I don't want to upset you, love. I only want you to be sure that it's as over as you say it is before you go doing something stupid."

"Something stupid?" Gina didn't understand, then realization dawned and made her mad. "You think me marrying Liam is stupid? Well thanks a lot, Dad! You haven't even met him. You don't know the first thing about him. Why can't you give him a chance and just be happy for me?"

He shook his head sadly. "I haven't met him because he's never bothered to come with you. I don't know the first thing about him because you hardly ever talk about him, and, when you do, it's never anything good. I remember when we used to sit at this table and you would chatter at me for hours about Mason—what Mason said, what Mason did, what Mason thought." He patted her shoulder. "It's hard not to notice the difference. That's all."

Gina closed her eyes, remembering herself how different she had felt back then. How deeply in love she'd been. She opened them again and looked at her dad sadly. "It was different because I was a kid. I didn't know any better. It's not the same when you grow up. You have to wise up. And I have done that. That's all."

"No. What you've done Gina is given up. I hope you do wise up before it's too late."

~ ~ ~

Mason wandered from stall to stall checking on the mares. He'd come straight out here to the barn when he got back from town. He didn't want to go up to the house. Word of his encounter with Gina would no doubt have reached the ranch by now. He didn't want to face the questions. He stopped at Annie's stall and she came and blew gently against his shoulder. He rubbed her nose and rested his head on her.

"You still miss her, too, don't you?"

Annie pawed at the straw and leaned against him. The little sorrel mare had been Gina's. She was a part of so many of the memories they'd made. They'd spent so many weekends riding the ranch, checking fences, camping down by the lake. Annie and his own horse, Storm, had grazed quietly nearby so many nights while he'd made love to Gina on a blanket out under the stars. He tangled his fingers in Annie's mane, remembering the way he used to tangle them in Gina's hair. Dammit! He needed to know why she'd left like that. Why? After letting him believe that she would marry him, after telling him he was the only man she'd ever love, why had she shut him out? Why had she gone off to New York instead of coming home to start their life together? And why had she refused to talk to him all these years? Why? He'd been kidding himself that he'd accepted it. He never had. And now he had to acknowledge that he'd still been hoping. Hoping that someday, they would work it out. The realization that her dad was sell the ranch and they'd be leaving for good had shaken him. He wasn't going to get many more chances.

"You can't hide forever, you know."

He turned around at the sound of Chance's voice. "What makes you think I'm hiding?"

"The chatter up at the house. The fact that half the town saw you kissing Gina and the rest of the town is talking about it."

Mason tipped his hat back and stared at his old friend. He didn't know what to say.

"So what are you going to do about it?"

He shrugged. "What can I do? She still won't talk to me. I still don't know why she shut me out. What should I do Chance?"

"I'm not exactly the best one to ask advice about women, but even I know that grabbing her on the street probably wasn't the wisest move."

Mason blew out a sigh. "Yeah, thanks. I figured that much out already."

"Do you need to do anything, Mase? I mean from what I hear, she's in town for a couple of weeks. Her dad is selling the ranch. Once she takes him to New York, that'll be the end of it. She'll never come back here and you can finally get over it and move on."

Mason shook his head. "I don't want there to be an end to it! The thought of her leaving and never coming back?" He slammed his hand against the wall, making Annie shy away. He patted her neck and soothed her before turning back to Chance. "I haven't been able to get over her in ten years. It gets worse, not easier. If she really hates me, I need to know why. I need to know how what we had could ever turn to hate. I never did a thing to hurt her. I just don't get it. I can't let her leave for good without making her tell me what the fuck went wrong."

Chance shrugged. "There's your answer then."

Mason stared at him.

"Get her to tell you what the fuck went wrong! Get your ass over there and get some answers. Once you know her reasons, you can do something about it or finally let it go. Let her go."

"I don't think I can ever let her go."

"I know. So stop hiding and whining and do something. I was new around here in those days, but even I could see how good the two of you were together. If there's anything left between you, you need to do something about it now. Before it really is too late."

Mason nodded. Chance was right.

Mason pursed his lips when they entered the kitchen and his brothers smirked at him. His dad raised his eyebrows but said nothing. His mom smiled at him, her eyes full of concern.

"I don't want to hear it," he said as he took his place next to his dad.

"I'm glad you two are finally talking," said Shane with a grin.

"Wasn't much talking going on from what I hear," said Carter. Beau gave him a knowing look.

"Leave it boys," his dad silenced them all as he glared around the table. "Let's eat. We don't have to feed you anymore. I keep telling your mother we'd save a fortune if we let you fend for yourselves. But since she insists on having you for dinner let's keep it peaceful, can we?"

Mason was grateful. He didn't want to walk away from his mother's table, but he would have to if the guys were going to keep after him. Talk turned to the ranch and soon what had happened this afternoon with Gina was forgotten. Or at least he thought it was.

As he pushed his plate away, Shane turned to him. "Are you coming out?"

"What...now?"

"Yes now. There's a band tonight."

"Nah. I think I'll pass." He couldn't even think about going out picking up women with Shane tonight. Not after seeing Gina. Not knowing that she was here and that he needed to see her again. Needed to talk to her. Needed...so much more.

Shane grinned. "Don't argue. Just come out."

As Mason started to protest, Beau shot him a meaningful look, which he didn't understand. "You know I don't agree with our littlest brother very often, but this time I say listen to him. Do as he says."

Mason sighed. "All right. Whatever. But I'm bringing my own truck so I can leave when I'm ready."

"I was about to suggest you do that," said Shane.

Mason stood and started to clear the dishes. His mom came and took the plate from his hands. "You go. I can take care of these."

"I'll give you a hand first. You shouldn't have to do them by yourself."

She laughed and with an expert flick of her wrist caught his dad on the back of his head with the tea towel. "Your father will help me. You boys get out and have some fun."

He smiled and piled out of the kitchen with his brothers and Chance. "So what's the deal?" he asked Shane. "You're not expecting me to be your wingman tonight, are you? Because I am so not up for that."

Beau grinned at him. "No. Our little brother is being an interfering little shit, and for once I'm impressed with him."

Shane grinned at Beau. "Why thank you, bro. I knew you'd learn to appreciate me someday."

Beau laughed. "I wouldn't go that far."

Mason exchanged a look with Carter. He didn't seem any wiser than Mason himself as to what they were talking about.

"Anyone want to give me a clue?"

"Oh. Yeah." Shane grinned at him. "When I heard about you and Gina this afternoon, I thought you might need a little more time to talk to each other. I mean you two have a lot of years to make up for."

Mason scowled at him. "So?"

"So," said Beau. "He called old man Delaney and asked him over to Chico for a drink tonight."

"You did what?"

Shane grinned. "Al and I are old buds. I thought he might like to get out for a drink. He won't have many more chances to get over to Chico if he's going to be moving away. He was happy I invited him, too."

Mason stared at him. "So you want me to come out for a drink with Al?"

Carter laughed. "Jesus, Mason! I thought I was supposed to be the dumb one. I think they're trying to get Al out of the house so you can go see Gina."

"Oh."

Chance put a hand on his shoulder. "You said you needed answers. Here's your opportunity to go get them."

Shane grinned at him. "I'm trying to give you the chance to go get a whole lot more than answers, Mase. Don't screw it up!"

Mason stared around at them. This was all wrong. He was the one who looked out for the others. He helped them sort things out when they were messing up. Since when had the tables turned, making him the one who needed their help?

"Go do it," said Beau. "Don't look at us like that, and don't overthink it. Just go do it."

Mason nodded and went to his truck. They were right. He'd waited far too long to get answers from Gina. He didn't have long left. If he didn't do it soon, she'd be gone and he'd never get them. He tipped his hat at his brothers as he drove away.

~ ~ ~

"At least let me drop you off?" Gina still couldn't quite get over her surprise. After they'd finished dinner, her dad had announced that he was going out this evening—to Chico! She couldn't remember the last time he'd been out anywhere, let alone gone to see a band at the resort.

"Don't worry. If I have a few, I'll get one of my buddies to drop me home later."

She stared at him. This was so unlike her dad. "And which buddies are you going with?"

He grinned at her. "Just some old friends. Now quit your worrying. You have yourself a nice evening of your own. Relax, enjoy the old place while you still can. You could take one of those bubble baths you enjoy so much. And don't wait up."

Gina shook her head. "Whatever you say, Dad." If he wanted a night out with some old friends, then who was she to stop him? Maybe she would do as he said, run herself a nice hot bath—try to soak away some of the tension that still gripped her since she'd seen Mason this afternoon.

After she'd waved him off, she headed for the bathroom and set the water running. She found some bubble bath and soon the room was filled with lavender scented steam. She stripped her clothes off and dipped her toe in. Perfect! She smiled as she realized that a glass of wine to sip while she sat there would make it even more perfect. She turned off the water, slipped her T-shirt back on and padded through to the kitchen. She uncorked a bottle of merlot and poured herself a good big glass.

She froze when she heard a knock at the door. The kitchen door! She could hardly go answer it wearing only her T-shirt. She did the only reasonable thing to do and bobbed down behind the kitchen table, hoping that whoever it was would give up and go away.

The knock came again, louder this time. "Gina?"

Oh, shit! It was Mason. What the hell was he doing here?

She crouched down further, hoping he wouldn't be able to see her if he peeked through the window.

"Gina. If you don't come out, I'm coming in!"

Oh no! He would, too. She knew it.

The kitchen door swung open. She'd always loved the way everyone left their doors unlocked out here—until now!

"Gina? I know you're home!"

She peeked out at him. Oh God. He was gorgeous! Why couldn't he have gone and gotten fat? Why did his legs have to be so muscular, his shoulders so broad? Why did everything about him have to be all rough and work worn—and sexy-as-sin?

"Gina?" There was a trace of laughter in his voice when he spoke again. "What the fuck are you doing down there?"

Oh, shit! He could see her! She stood up. She wasn't going to cower. She pulled herself up to her full height and was still half a foot shorter than him. "I was hiding!"

He chuckled. He had the audacity to laugh at her? Bastard! "Why were you hiding, girl?"

"Because I didn't want you to see me. Because I don't want to see you!" Damn him! He was looking her over and making it very clear that he liked what he saw. Her breasts tingled as he ran his gaze over them. The heat pooled between her legs as his eyes darkened. She tugged at the hem of her T-shirt, trying to pull it down, suddenly aware that it didn't cover her, that he really could see her!

He smiled his slow, easy smile as he lifted his gaze to meet hers. "I'm happy to see you, babe. It's been too long."

Oh no! She was supposed to hate him, but as he took a step towards her, she wanted to run to him, throw herself back into his arms and beg him to never let go. She gathered what little sense she had left.

"Mason, I..." He took another step closer and her resolve melted. She needed to kiss him again, to feel his arms around her. "No! Mason, no!"

He was still smiling. "You don't mean that, do you, Gina?"

She backed up. She couldn't let him get too close to her. If he touched her, it would be all over. He kept coming, closing the distance between them. She backed up to the cabinets and had nowhere left to go. "Mason. No." It came out as a helpless whisper.

He nodded as he closed his arms around her waist. "Gina. Yes," he murmured in the moment before his lips came down on hers.

Her arms came up around his neck, her tongue met his, and she melted against him as he devoured her mouth. How had she lived without his kisses? His hands closed around her ass, crushing her against his erection. She rubbed herself against him, needing him, needing him to lay her down, to make her his again.

He ran his hands up her sides, pushing her T-shirt up. His thumbs skimmed up over her ribcage then circled her breasts, closing in on her nipples until his rough skin was tormenting the hardened peaks. She clung to his neck, thrusting her hips against him, needing him to take her, right here, right now.

He lifted his head and smiled at her. "My girl," he murmured.

That broke the spell. She pushed him away. How had she gotten so carried away? "It's been years since I was your girl, Mason. What the hell are you doing here?"

His face clouded over. Uh-oh! He was angry. An angry Mason had always been a scary prospect. "You've always been my girl, Gina. Always will be. And why am I here? I'm here to make you tell me what the hell happened! What changed? You loved me. You were going to come back. You were going to marry me. You were weird when you left for your senior year of college, but I thought we were okay. But you just shut me out and never came home." He pulled her to him, crushed her to his chest as he glared down at her. "I need you to tell me what the fuck changed."

Gina's throat went dry. She'd never told him. She'd managed to avoid him and his questions for all these years. She pulled away from him again. "It doesn't matter anymore, Mason. It ended. We ended years ago."

He towered above her. "Just tell me, G. If this is really it. If you're going to make your dad sell the ranch and leave, what does it matter anymore? Just tell me the truth, babe. Put me out of my misery."

His misery? Ha! After the misery he'd put her through? How dare he! She walked away from him. Keeping her back to him she rested her hands on the kitchen table and stood there shaking. She could tell him a half-truth and have it be over. She took a deep breath. "Okay. The truth is..." She was not going to cry. Would not allow herself to. "I changed, Mason. The way I felt about you changed." She wasn't about to tell him that hearing him tell Guy how little he actually cared about her had destroyed her. Wasn't about to tell him that after giving her a couple of years of happiness, he'd caused her more pain than anyone should have to suffer. "I loved you for years. But that summer I realized I hate the way you make me feel."

He moved so fast she didn't have time to escape him. He slid his arms around her waist and pulled her back against him. She could feel his heart thundering in his chest as his mouth came down next to her ear. "I don't believe you, Gina." Keeping one arm around her waist he slid his hand down over her belly. His fingers found their way between her legs, making her gasp. He nipped her neck, none too gently, then swiped the sting with his tongue. She whimpered as he tormented her clit and pressed his hard-on against her ass. "You always loved the way I make you feel. Even now." He stroked his fingertips over her opening. His other hand came up to cover her breast and his mouth came down on her neck again. "You can't tell me you don't love the way I make you feel. Don't lie to me, babe."

She sagged against him, her head rolling back against his shoulder. Lies or truth, she was incapable of forming any words. He owned her body in the way he always had. He squeezed her nipple hard and in the same moment thrust his fingers deep inside her.

"Mason! No," she begged.

"Yes, babe," he murmured against her neck. His fingers slid in and out, carrying her towards the precipice, he twisted her nipple between his fingertips as he moved his hips against her ass. She was lost. He knew her body better than she did herself. She moved her own hips in time with him. Suddenly he stopped and spun her around. Laying her back on the table he spread her legs wide and covered her body with his own. Damn him! He felt so good! Her arms and legs came up around him as he thrust his denim covered cock between her legs. He slid an arm under her waist and held her to him as their hips found the rhythm neither had forgotten. They moved as one, mouths and bodies locked together. Gina was helpless. All these years she'd dreamed of this, believed that never again would she feel him like this and here he was. He was...the tension was building low in her belly, all her muscles tensed in anticipation. He was thrusting hard and she was going to... "Yes! Mason! Yes!" She arched up underneath him as her orgasm tore through her. He ground his hips into her, working her for everything she had until she finally lay still. She clung to him, her face buried in his shoulder. What had she done?

He cupped her face between his big hands and smiled down at her. "See, that's more like it, G. Now we can talk."

She hated the traitorous tear that welled up and rolled down her face. She hated the sadness in his eyes as he wiped it away with his thumb.

"Talk to me."

She shook her head and pushed him off her, struggling to stand up. "I told you. There's nothing left to talk about. Just go, Mason. Please go."

"I'm not going anywhere until you talk to me." He pulled out a chair and sat at the table.

He was such an obstinate bastard! "I told you. I don't want to talk to you. I want you to leave."

"Well, I don't want to leave." He looked down at the front of his pants. Gina was mortified to see the wet marks she'd left on him. He looked up at her with that infuriatingly sexy smile of his. "I'll restrain myself while you figure it out. But give me one good reason why I shouldn't undo this zipper and try that again. No restraint." His hands were on his buckle and her throat went dry.

He was so smug! He knew what he did to her. And he knew that if he did get out of his pants she'd be all over him. She wouldn't even try to stop him. Hell, she was on the verge of unzipping him herself! She had to stop. "I'm getting married. I'd say that's reason enough!"

She'd never seen so much pain and anger mixed together. He rose from his chair and towered above her. He searched her face and, apparently seeing the truth of her words there, he turned and walked away. He stopped and turned back when he reached the door. "I feel sorry for the poor bastard!"

"What?!"

He shook his head. "You're getting married and you just spread your legs and came for me without me even getting it out of my pants. I can only think of two reasons a woman would do that. She's either a whore or she's marrying the wrong guy."

As the door slammed, Gina sank down into a chair and buried her face in her hands. She wasn't a whore. And they both knew it.

Chapter Four

Mason stared up at the big sky as the darkness faded to gray. He hadn't slept a wink all night and had driven up here to watch the sunrise. She was getting married? He lay back and closed his eyes. She couldn't love the guy. No matter what she said about it being over between them, about her hating the way he made her feel, she was lying. He knew it. Yesterday on Main Street and last night in her kitchen, her body had told him that she still loved the way he made her feel. He sure as hell still loved the way she made him feel. He shouldn't have grabbed her in the street and he definitely shouldn't have grabbed her last night, let alone laid her out on the kitchen table underneath him! His only regret was that he'd kept it in his pants, that he hadn't buried himself balls deep inside her. He blew out a sigh. He should have done it while he still could. If she was going to leave for good, go back to New York and marry some guy, he should have taken her one last time. She wouldn't have stopped him. He knew that. Whatever lies she told him, she still wanted him. She'd wanted him since she was fourteen years old. He smiled at the memory.

He'd always thought of her as cute and feisty. His little brother's best friend, she'd been as much a part of ranch life as any of them. She'd surprised the hell out of him the week before he was leaving for college. She'd come out to find him in the barn one night and told him that she loved him. That she knew what sex was and she wanted him to be the one to take her virginity. She'd even handed him a packet of condoms. He'd been tempted! Even at fourteen she was starting to develop the looks and the figure that still held his heart. He'd been realistic, though, and let her down as gently as he could. Told her she was too young. Told her he was about to leave and it would be all wrong for him to take her most precious gift and then leave her alone. That she only thought she loved him, but she was too young to know what that meant, he was just some kind of hero she'd built up in her mind. She'd been mad at him, told him she was old enough, and that she knew her own mind. Told him she knew the difference between a hero and a lover and she wanted him to be her lover. If he didn't want her now, then she'd wait until he did.

And she had.

He shook his head. That was all a long time ago. He was eighteen then. He'd gone off to college, had his share of girls. She'd gotten to him. He wondered now if he'd ever been with a woman and not thought about Gina. The girls he'd slept with in college had all merged into one. Every time he'd had one underneath him, he'd imagined it was Gina. It didn't matter if they had blonde hair or dark, were skinny or rounded, it was always her face he saw when he came. Whenever he'd come back for the holidays or the summer, she'd been around. She'd taken every chance she could get to spend time alone with him. He'd resisted for as long as he could. He watched her grow from a budding young girl into a beautiful young woman.

Each year it became harder not to take her up on her offer.
She still wanted him to be her first.

 He shook his head again. What was the point in reliving it all?
It was over, done. He'd known that for years. He'd been stupid
to think there might be one last chance before she left. She
was getting married. He should let her go. Stay out of the way
until she was gone. He started his truck up and headed back
down to the ranch. He was meeting with his dad and Chance
this morning. He needed to focus on that and forget about
Gina. Once and for all.

His mom smiled as he let himself into the kitchen. "There's
fresh coffee if you want some."

"Thanks." He needed a shot of caffeine to pick him up. He
took his mug through to his dad's office and was surprised to
see Shane sitting at the big table next to Chance.

His brother grinned at him. "You look like you had a heavy
night. What's up, didn't you get much sleep?"

Mason shook his head. "I didn't. But not for the reason you
think."

Shane pulled a face. "Don't tell me you screwed up?"

Mason took his hat off and ran a hand through his hair.
"There's nothing left to screw up. She's getting married."

Shane looked stunned. "Al didn't mention that!"

Mason shrugged. "Why would he?"

"What difference does it make?" asked Chance.

Mason stared at him.

Chance shrugged. "She's not married yet, is she? Where is the
guy anyway? I'm getting married. Someday. Maybe."

Mason continued to stare after him.

"What are you saying?" asked Shane.

"I'm saying she's not married yet and I'm saying that even if there is a fiancé, he's not here right now. And Mason is."

Shane looked thoughtful. "I'm pretty sure she wasn't wearing a ring."

"You've seen her?" asked Mason.

Shane hung his head.

"What does it matter?" asked Chance. "You need to go see her again. That's what matters."

Mason thought about it. "She made it pretty clear she doesn't want to talk to me."

Chance raised an eyebrow. "She didn't give you any hope at all that she still cares?"

Mason couldn't help smiling as he remembered her arching up underneath him, her arms and legs locked tight around his back as she screamed, yes! Mason, yes!

Shane grinned at him. "That look says she did something to leave the door open."

Mason nodded. She had.

"Then do something about it," said Chance. "You'll only live with regrets if you don't."

Mason looked up as his dad entered the room. Hadn't he been thinking this morning that his only regret was that he hadn't made love to her one last time? That would be a tough regret to live with. If he couldn't persuade her to talk to him, to try again with him, he was pretty sure he could persuade her to sleep with him. He made his mind up at that moment. He wasn't going to let her leave without sleeping with him. And if he could get her to do that, it would open up other possibilities, too.

"Okay, guys," said his dad. "We need to get these budgets settled."

Mason nodded. The ranch was doing great, but only because they had diversified so well. Chance managed the cattle operation these days. Shane had surprised everyone when he'd returned from his stint in the Navy and asked if he could set up a dude ranch on the property. He'd surprised everyone even more with the success it was enjoying. Mason himself was all about the horses. He ran a successful stud operation and also held clinics to train horses and riders. His dad kept talking about retiring, kept threatening to take their mom to Arizona for the winter. It seemed that this year he might actually do it. He kept getting them all together for meetings like this and each time he handed over more responsibility to each of them.

As his dad launched into detailing purchases they'd need to make in the coming months, Mason couldn't stop his mind wandering back to Gina. He'd taken her excuses for years. He should have made her talk to him. He smiled to himself. He wasn't going to let her leave without answering all his questions this time. If nothing else, he wasn't going to let her go off and marry some other guy without screaming his own name one last time!

~ ~ ~

Gina sat at the kitchen table sipping her coffee. She was sitting in the same chair Mason had sat in last night. She could still see him, his hands on his buckle ready to get out of his pants and... She shook her head. He'd asked her for one good reason why he shouldn't. Liam was all the reason either of them needed. Wasn't he? If he was, why had she spent the whole night tossing and turning? Wishing that she'd said nothing and let Mason make love to her?

She took another sip of her coffee. So what, if he still made her feel the way he always had? So what, if he was even sexier now he was older? So what, what? Even if she wasn't about to marry Liam and even if she didn't live on the other side of the country, there was no way she could ever get involved with Mason again. She hadn't lied when she said she hated the way he made her feel. For years, he'd made her feel like the luckiest girl alive. He'd loved her, he'd been so much fun, and he'd made her feel alive. He'd finally given in and made love to her when she was eighteen. He'd taken her from girl to woman and he'd made her feel so much of a woman in the years that followed. They'd been so good together, great—in bed and out of it. But when she'd heard him talk to Guy Preston that night, he'd made her feel like a fool. He'd taken every dream she'd ever had and smashed them all to pieces. He'd made her feel that the best of her life was over when she was just twenty-one years old. He'd broken her heart and yes, she hated the way he made her feel. Even now. She felt stupid. She felt betrayed. And she felt as if she would never love or be loved like that again. She felt as though she had to grow up, stop believing in dreams and make sensible decisions. She hated that the man who had starred in all her dreams was also the man who had killed them.

She pulled herself together. Liam was the sensible decision and she would do well to stop dwelling on broken dreams and remember that. She'd call Liam later and ask him to come. That was the best way to put Mason out of her head. If Liam came here, she'd be able to put it all back into perspective. So what if it wasn't realistic for him to come? She'd beg him if she had to. Tell him she needed him out here. She did!

"Morning, love." Her dad rubbed his eyes as he came into the kitchen.

"Hey. Did you have a good night?"

He grinned. "I did, thanks. How about you?"

She wasn't going to tell him about Mason's little visit. "I took a bath like you said."

He frowned at her. "That all?"

Did he know? Had he set her up? She wasn't going to go anywhere near it either way. "Do you need me for anything today?"

He shrugged. "It's you that's in a hurry to get everything packed up and sorted out. Don't see why though. Like that realtor guy told you yesterday. We can't go expecting a quick sale."

Gina nodded. The realtor had done a lot to dampen her hopes that they might get an offer on the place any time soon. While her dad was pleased about that, she was worried whether they'd be able to keep the place going until they got a solid offer.

"Why, what are you thinking?"

She shrugged. "I'm thinking of taking my camera and going down to the park for a few hours. I want to get out, take some photos, clear my head."

He raised an eyebrow at her. "Anything you want to talk about?"

"No." She thought about it. "Actually, there is something."

He grinned. "What's that, love?"

It seemed he must know that Mason had been here. Well, he was going to have to get over it. The same as she had. And Liam was going to help them both with that. "I'm going to call

Liam today and ask him to come this weekend. Is that okay with you?"

He scowled. "What do you want to do that for?"

"I want you to meet him. I want to show him where I come from." And I want to prove to Mason and to myself that I'm in love with someone else now, she didn't add.

"Well, there's no room for him here."

"What do you mean, there's no room?"

"What I said."

"Dad, there's plenty of room!"

He shook his head with a finality she recognized. There would be no point arguing with him. "Let him stay at the resort, if he can even be bothered to make the trip this time."

"Fine! I will." Gina stood up. If he was going to be all stubborn about it, then let him. "You might not want him to come, but I need him to!"

He gave her a sarcastic little smile. "And why's that, Gina?"

She stared at him. Why did she need him here? If she was honest, she needed him to remind her of her real life. She needed his help to hang on to sensible and to stop herself from getting sucked into life here and everything else. What she really needed was to hide behind him so she wouldn't let herself go anywhere near Mason again. "Because I'm going to marry him, Dad." She hurried out before he had a chance to say anything else.

She called Liam and, of course, got his voicemail. She left him a message begging him to come out for the weekend. He'd probably think she was nuts, but what the hell, she probably was. She had the idea lodged in her head now, that if he came everything would be okay. She'd stop thinking about Mason, stop yearning after broken dreams and be able to hang onto reality.

It was six o'clock by the time she drove out of the park. She'd had a great time, hiking up to the falls and getting some great shots. She was always able to lose herself behind the lens of her camera. It had been way too long since she'd made the time to spend a day in Yellowstone like this. She stopped in the little town of Gardiner to check her messages. She'd had no signal all day. Her dad had called, apparently he was going out again tonight. Whatever he was up to, it didn't matter. There was a message from Liam, too. He sounded a little annoyed, but he was coming. She was surprised that he said Kaitlyn and Ian from the gallery were coming too, but it kind of worked out okay, because he said since there were three of them he'd had Kaitlyn book them rooms at Chico. Perhaps things would work out.

Since she didn't need to rush home for her dad, and she didn't feel like cooking, she decided to have dinner at the little restaurant in Gardiner. She loved to stop here when she could and have an elk burger. It wasn't something you could get in New York. She sat at a booth in the corner and ordered a beer while she waited.

The server had just brought her food when she saw him. Damn him! He stood silhouetted in the doorway for a moment as he looked around. Double damn him! He really shouldn't be allowed to look like that. His cowboy hat was pulled low over his eyes, but she could still see them peeking out at her, that hint of laughter in the creases around them. His broad shoulders were speckled with raindrops. The same buckle as he'd been wearing last night sat at his narrow waist, his muscular legs were encased in work worn Wranglers, brown boots sticking out the bottom. He was sexier than any man had a right to be. His smile told her he knew it, too. He sauntered over and slid into the booth to sit opposite her.

"Hey, babe."

Her heart stopped in her chest. His words took her right back, back to all the times they'd sat here, in this very booth. All the days they'd spent in the park, hiking, snowshoeing. All the times he'd packed her gear around for her when she was determined to get the perfect shot of the grizzlies or the wolves.

"What do you want, Mason?"

"You."

Her heart went from zero to sixty in a nanosecond. If only that were true. If only he wanted her like he used to say he did— forever. But he didn't. He hadn't then and he certainly didn't now.

"We both know that's not true, Mase."

"Never spoke a truer word in my life, G. I want you. You say you don't want me. But you do."

"I told you. I'm getting married."

He stared pointedly at her left hand.

She realized that he was noting the lack of a ring. "We haven't picked one out yet."

He laughed. "We? Isn't he supposed to pick one out himself? What kind of proposal was it if he didn't even have a ring ready?"

Gina felt her cheeks color. She wasn't about to tell him that there hadn't even been a proposal!

He narrowed his eyes at her. "You're not shitting me, are you? Does he even exist?"

"Yes, he does! He'll be here this weekend. You should come to Chico and meet him!" Oh, why in the hell had she said that? Introducing the two of them had not been part of the plan!

Mason was grinning at her, looking way more confident than she could be comfortable with. "That's mighty nice of you, babe. I think I'll do that. Be good to meet the guy." He picked a fry from her plate and smiled as he popped it into his mouth. "You want to eat that before it gets cold."

She couldn't eat a damned thing! She took a swig of her beer. "What are you doing here, Mase? I don't for one second believe that you just happened to be down here."

He grinned and took a swig of her beer before answering. "You're right. I stopped by to see you at lunchtime. Your dad said you'd come down to the park. I figured you'd stop in here on your way home."

She let out a big sigh. "Why did you want to see me? I thought we said everything we were going to say last night."

He held her gaze. "Last night I asked you to give me one good reason why I should keep it in my pants."

Gina swallowed. She wanted to wriggle in her panties, the way he was looking at her. She was getting wet just at the memory of last night in the kitchen. And damn him, and his lazy smile, he knew it.

"I'll be honest. You stunned me when you said you were getting married. But I've had time to think about it." He held her gaze and smiled that smile. "I thought it was only right I should let you know."

"Let me know what?" Even to her own ears, her voice sounded husky, full of desire.

He caught hold of her hand and traced circles on her palm with his thumb. She didn't pull away. She couldn't. She stared at him, mesmerized, waiting for him to reply.

"That I don't consider that a good enough reason."

Now she did try to pull her hand away, but he closed his own big paw around it. "What the hell are you saying?" she gasped.

"I'm saying that you can lie to me if you want. You can marry him if you must." He held her gaze as he lowered his voice and squeezed her hand. "But you're going to sleep with me again before you do, babe. And don't even try telling me you don't want to. We both know that'd be a lie."

"No, Mason!" She wanted to sound strong, indignant, but it sounded more like she was begging.

He grinned. "Gina, last night I took you from No, Mason, no, to Yes, Mason, yes! in just a few minutes. Maybe tonight we should take our time."

"Mason. Last night was wrong. I shouldn't have done that. I shouldn't have let you do that."

"But you did let me do that. For all your words, babe, you let me because you wanted me to. You still want me to. So I thought it was only fair that I should come tell you, before you leave we're going to do it again. Except this time I won't be showing any restraint. When I spread your legs, I'm going to remind you how I make you feel. Remind you how my cock feels inside you, stretching you, filling you, driving you wild until you come for me." He looked deep into her eyes. "Remind you that you don't hate it at all."

Gina squirmed in her seat. If he kept talking like that, she was in danger of coming for him right now!

He smiled, knowing what he was doing to her. "So what do you say, babe?"

What could she say? It was all wrong! But her breath was coming low and shallow and her panties were wet. She'd be lying if she said she didn't want him.

He saw her hesitation. "Gina, sweetheart. If you're going to marry this guy, you need to be sure. You can't tell me you haven't thought about me over the years. Can't tell me you haven't remembered how good we were, haven't wished we could have one more time?"

She shook her head. She couldn't.

"So why pretend you don't want to? You'd have let me last night if I hadn't left."

She nodded. It was true.

"Tell me you don't want me. Tell me and I'll walk out of here right now. Wish you the best and leave you alone."

Gina was shaking. If she could do it. If she could tell him one last lie. It would be over. Finally. She swallowed around the lump in her throat, furious with herself as she felt her eyes sting with tears.

Mason's smiled faded. Hope shone in his eyes. "Tell me you don't love me anymore."

Gina shot out of the booth and fled.

Chapter Five

Mason rested his feet up on the coffee table and looked at his brother. "I need you to tell me whatever the hell you remember, Shane."

Shane pulled a chair out from the dining table and turned it around. He straddled it and propped his arms on the back. "Mase, how many times have we done this whole inquisition thing? I must have told you everything I know at least a hundred times over the years."

Mason stared at him. "But maybe I missed something. Maybe you missed something. I mean when I first realized she wasn't coming back, I wasn't thinking straight for months. Then for the first few years, I was angry. When she wouldn't talk to me, didn't even have the decency to tell me why she broke it all off, I was madder than hell. I'm starting to think that I should have tracked her down and made her explain. This is the first time I've pushed her, and she couldn't bring herself to say that she doesn't love me anymore!"

Shane looked at him. "I don't know what to say, Mase. I've badgered both of you for all this time to just sit down and talk to each other. I never understood why she did what she did and I never understood why you let your pride stop you from going after her."

Mason rubbed his hand over his eyes. "Because I'm a complete asshole! That's all I can think of."

Shane grinned. "I didn't like to mention that possibility. There's no point beating yourself up for what's already gone, though. What are you going to do now? That's what matters."

Mason shrugged. "She said this guy of hers is going to be here this weekend. That I should come meet him at Chico. She seems to think he can put me off. I think I can put him off. I'm definitely going to go. But what the hell I'm going to do when I get there, I don't know. You're going to come with me, right?"

Shane laughed. "You know it, bro."

"What did her old man say about this guy? I don't even know his name."

"Al has never met him, but from the way he talked, he doesn't like the idea of him. You know he's always wanted to see the two of you back together. I'd say he's got even more reason to want that now, too."

"Why's that?"

"Think about it. If you and Gina got back together, she'd come back here. Al wouldn't have to go to New York because Gina wouldn't be there anymore."

Mason did think about it. "You really think there's a chance she'd have me back?" He could hardly dare to hope. But since he'd seen her in Gardiner, he couldn't help but hope. He'd known she wouldn't be able to tell him she didn't want him. The physical attraction and connection they shared had always been strong. Stronger than any other he'd known. The other night in her dad's kitchen had proved it was still as undeniable as ever. What had given him real hope was when he'd seen the struggle on her face, seen her eyes fill with tears. She wouldn't have been like that if she didn't care, if she didn't... And she hadn't been able to tell him that she didn't love him. That put a whole different spin on everything.

There were a few details that stood in the way though. Details like a fiancé who was going to be here this weekend, and a life and career that she had in New York. Still, if she loved him, nothing would be able to stand in the way. He'd driven himself crazy these last few days, thinking about it all, finally admitting to himself that he still loved her. That he always had, and that he'd been stupid to accept that she meant it when she'd said it was over between them.

Chance came in the back door. He kicked out of his boots and hung his hat and coat on the rack before coming through. "What's up, guys?"

Shane grinned at him. "We're making plans to go to Chico this weekend. You coming?"

"I could do. It's been a while. Is there a good band coming?"

Shane laughed. "I don't know who's playing. All I know is that big brother is going to go meet Gina's fiancé and I need to be there for that."

Chance turned to Mason. "What's the plan?"

Mason shrugged. "There isn't one. All I know is that I'm not going to give her up without a fight this time."

"Good. Then count me in."

~ ~ ~

Gina sat by the big fireplace in the Bozeman airport. She shuddered in spite of the warmth. Nothing about this trip was working out the way it was supposed to. Liam had insisted that the real estate market was picking up all over the country and

that she should get her dad's place up for sale. That it would
sell fast. The realtors had told her a very different story—that
it was taking at least six months to a year to sell properties like
her dad's. She'd thought that while she was here, she would
perhaps be able to catch up with Shane and definitely be able
to avoid Mason. She'd only seen Shane briefly and had three
major run-ins with Mason. Liam wasn't going to come at all
and yet here she was waiting for him to land. The fact that he
was going to have Kaitlyn and Ian along for the trip confused
matters more.

When she'd asked Liam to come, she'd been hoping the two of
them would get to spend some time together. That she'd be
able to share the place she loved with him and that, seeing him
here, she would remember what she loved about him. She'd
begged him to come because she'd believed that his presence
would be enough to make Mason leave her alone. Even that
had been turned on its head! She was dreading him coming,
dreading having to spend time with Kaitlyn and Ian, and
seriously regretting the fact that she'd told Mason he should
come out to Chico to meet Liam!

She stood up as passengers started coming down the escalator
towards the baggage claim area. Ian spotted her first and
waved. She waved back and frowned as she saw Kaitlyn
leaning a little too close to Liam, smiling up at him as she said
something that made him laugh. The two of them didn't even
notice her until they were almost at the bottom. She shrugged
it off. Kaitlyn had been Liam's PA at the gallery for years.
They were close. Ian came straight over to give her a hug.

"Gina! I hope this resort we're staying at is civilized. It feels
like we've come to the ends of the earth to find you. We

must've flown over at least seven mountain ranges and nothing that looked big enough to even call a town since Denver."

She laughed and hugged him back. "Don't worry. It may be a little more isolated than you're used to, but Chico is very civilized—and they have a great wine cellar. You'll be fine."

Ian laughed as he let her go. "Glad to hear it."

Liam put his hands on her shoulders and pecked her lips. "Well, we're here. I'm not sure what your plea for help was all about, but we came to the rescue."

No hug. No good to see you. Or I've missed you. And we not I came to the rescue. Gina smiled to cover her disappointment.

"Hi." Kaitlyn smiled.

"Thanks for coming," said Gina, even though she wasn't at all glad that Kaitlyn was here.

A little over an hour later, Gina pulled up in front of the lobby at the resort. "Shall we meet you in the bar once we're all checked in?" asked Liam.

Gina looked at him. Was he serious? He was going to let her go park the car while he and his friends went and got settled in their rooms? He didn't want her to come with him? Didn't want a moment alone with her? "Sure," she replied.

Liam climbed out and helped Kaitlyn down from the truck. Ian seemed to understand. He ruffled her hair as he climbed out himself. "You know what he's like, Gina. He's just doing what he thinks is going to be most efficient."

Gina smiled at him. "I know. I wish he could show a little more interest in me than in efficiency sometimes."

Ian shrugged. "He is what he is. We all know that." He grabbed his bag and closed the door before hurrying to catch up with the others.

Gina drove around the lot looking for a place to park. It looked like it was going to be a busy weekend, judging by the lack of empty spaces. She eventually found one and parked. She was making her way back to the lobby when she saw a very familiar red Tundra coming towards her. Shane!

She stood still, blocking his way and he flashed his lights and revved his engine at her. She laughed and folded her arms, refusing to move. She laughed even harder when he started flashing his headlights in Morse code. Blinking S.O.S. at her. She stepped to the side and he pulled up next to her, rolling his window down.

"You know what that was about, right?" he asked.

"Of course I do!" They'd learned Morse code together when they were ten years old. "Save our souls."

"Nope." Shane laughed. "Scoot over sister!"

Gina laughed with him. He felt more like a brother than a friend. They'd been so close for so many years growing up.

"What are you doing here?" he asked.

Gina was uncomfortable now. Just on the drive over from the airport she'd realized that Liam didn't belong out here. He'd commented on pretty much everything he'd seen—and not in a complimentary way. She was pretty sure the resort wouldn't be up to his standards and he wouldn't hesitate to make that known. Asking him to come had been a bad idea, but it was done now. He was here and she would have to make the best of it. "My fiancé, Liam, and some of our friends are here for the weekend."

Shane cocked his head to one side. "You don't look thrilled, G. And you didn't invite me to come meet him. What's up?"

He knew her too well. There was no point lying to him. "Honestly, I don't think he's going to like it here. And..."

"And what?"

"And I don't think you're going to like him."

Shane grinned. "You underestimate me. I may be a valley boy through and through, but I've been out in the big world, remember? I can make allowances for snooty city shits. I mean it's not their fault. They just don't know any better, do they?"

Gina had to laugh. "I didn't say he was a snooty city shit!"

Shane winked at her. "You didn't need to. Don't worry. I'll do my best not to embarrass you. You are going to introduce me, aren't you?"

She nodded. She hardly had much choice, did she? And besides, introducing Shane to Liam was going to be a lot easier than introducing Mason. She waited while Shane went to park his truck, then walked arm in arm with him into the saloon.

Ian was sitting at the bar, but there was no sign of Liam or Kaitlyn. He waved when he saw them. Gina had to wonder why on earth he'd come. He ran the gallery with Liam, and the two of them spent most of their free time together, but coming all the way to Montana seemed a little much.

He looked apologetic. "They should be down soon. Kaitlyn had a problem with her room and Liam was helping her to get a better one."

Gina pursed her lips but didn't comment. "Okay. I'd like you to meet a dear friend of mine. This is Shane Remington, we grew up together. Shane, this is Ian Rawlings, Liam's partner at the gallery."

Shane held out his hand. "Nice to meet you. Are you a photographer, too?"

Ian shook his head. "No, I'm a business brain, not a creative one. Liam and I simply showcase the talents of people like Gina. And you?"

Shane grinned. "I run a dude ranch on my parents' property."

"That's like a vacation ranch, right? Where people stay to ride horses and pretend to be cowboys for a while?"

Shane laughed. "Yeah. Pretty much. The way the economy is going, it's tough for any of the ranches to survive. So we take in paying guests and give them a taste of the Old West. Usually, it's more like picnic rides exploring the back country, but some of them want to try real ranch work and we get them involved in as much as they're capable of."

Ian nodded. "Sounds cool." He looked at Gina. "That would make an interesting show, wouldn't it? A study of how the West is changing in order to survive?"

Gina frowned at him. "Don't start me on that one. I've tried for ages to get Liam to agree to it. He won't hear of it."

"Sorry." Ian looked uncomfortable.

Shane raised an eyebrow at her. "Wasn't that what you always wanted to do, G?"

She nodded. Her dearest professional dream had been to come back out here to do a study of the West. She knew the kinds of shots she wanted. The dilapidated old barns that dotted the landscape, the ghost towns in the eastern part of the state, the weathered faces of old cowboys. She would stand those in contrast to shots of places like Chico, the new organic farms that were springing up, and ventures like Shane's dude ranch. Setting the new and thriving against the old and disappearing ways of the West. Liam thought it was a sentimental indulgence on her part and refused to see the cultural value of documenting so much that would soon be lost.

She looked up as Liam and Kaitlyn came in. She couldn't help but compare him to Mason. Where Mason was tall and broad shouldered, Liam was shorter, five feet eight. He was a much slighter build, too. Where Mason's face was tanned and weathered, Liam's was smooth, unlined thanks to regular facials. While Mason was rugged, Liam was...pretty. She gave herself a mental shake. She didn't need to be thinking like that. The only difference that mattered between the two men was that Mason was her past, while Liam was her future.

When they reached the bar, he pulled out a seat for Kaitlyn and stood beside her. "Sorry, that took a while. Can you believe they don't have any hypoallergenic rooms? The staff are useless. I had to get the manager down before we could get anything sorted out. He wasn't much better."

Shane caught Gina's eye. Her heart sank. Liam was hardly making a great first impression. "Liam, this is Shane Remington, an old friend of mine."

Shane held out his hand and Liam shook it. "Nice to meet you."

"You too," said Shane. "I'm glad you could finally make it out here. What plans do you have for the weekend?"

Liam frowned at him. "If you'll excuse us, I need to talk to Gina about that."

Shane looked a little taken aback but took Liam's rudeness in stride. "Not a problem. I was just leaving." He pulled Gina into a hug and whispered in her ear. "You were right. I don't like him." He pecked her cheek and left.

Gina couldn't believe Liam had been so rude and told him as much. "Liam! Shane is a very dear friend of mine. I wanted you to meet him."

Liam shrugged. "Sorry, but Gina these people aren't exactly our kind of people, are they? I don't want to spend the evening talking about cows and bears."

Kaitlyn giggled, making Gina even angrier. Was he serious? Was he deliberately being a pig? It certainly felt like it. "These people, are my friends, Liam. I thought you were here to meet them. To let me show you around my life."

"I'm sorry, sweetie." He put a hand on her shoulder. "I think I'm just tired and grouchy from the trip. I didn't mean to be rude."

She smiled a tight smile. "That's okay." He got a little cranky when he was tired, and he had a habit of going for the laughs in front of his friends. It was just his strange sense of humor. That was all. They did much better when they were alone together. "I thought I could take you over to see my dad."

"Not tonight?" asked Kaitlyn. "We want to get some dinner and then soak for a while. After all that traveling I want to make the most of the hot springs."

Gina did her best to keep her temper. "That's okay, you go ahead. I was only asking Liam."

Liam squeezed her shoulder. "I'm looking forward to getting in the water, too. We can see your dad tomorrow."

Gina couldn't believe it. He'd rather soak in the hot springs with Kaitlyn than come to the ranch and see her dad? Why had he even bothered to come? And why the hell had he brought the others?

Ian smiled at her, always the one to try to keep the peace. "It does sound like fun, Gina. We can soak for a while and then hit up that wonderful wine cellar you were telling me about."

"I don't have a bathing suit." And besides she hated going in the water here. She loved the resort, but she preferred natural hot springs, the ones you had to hike to, where there was hardly ever anyone else there. She didn't enjoy sitting in the man-made pool with dozens of other people. It made her feel like one of the ingredients in a huge vat of people soup!

She turned to Liam, desperate to salvage what was looking like it would turn into a disastrous weekend. "Please come and see my dad with me?"

"Tomorrow, sweetie."

Well, screw him! "Okay. I'll see you tomorrow then." She stalked out of the bar and left them to it. As she climbed into the truck, her cell phone rang.

"Gina, what's wrong with you? We came all the way out here to see you and you're not even going to spend the evening with us?"

She was furious. "Liam, I asked you to come and see me. I don't know why you brought them. I didn't want to spend the weekend with your friends. I wanted to spend the weekend with you."

"Well, we still have work to do. We're pulling the Avery show together, but we changed our plans to come out here for you. You could be a little more gracious about it."

"You shouldn't have bothered coming at all if you couldn't spare the time for me, Liam!"

"I'm starting to wish I hadn't."

Damn him! This wasn't going anything like she'd hoped it would. "I'm sorry. I'm disappointed, that's all. I thought you understood how important this was to me." She had been a little hasty walking out like that. She should go back in. She had been planning on spending the night here with him.

Silence buzzed on the phone. "What time will we see you tomorrow?"

Wow! He was dismissing her. That was always his line when he didn't want to argue. And she'd thought he wanted her to stay. "How about you call me when you're ready?"

"Fine. Good night, Gina." He hung up.

Gina threw her phone so hard the battery came out when it hit the passenger door. "Screw you, Liam!"

The tires screeched as she pulled out of the parking lot.

Chapter Six

"Is there any point in my hanging around to meet the guy today?"

Gina made a face at her dad. "I told you. I'll bring him over around lunchtime."

"You said you'd bring him over last night, too. That didn't happen, did it?"

She scowled. "He was tired after traveling all day."

"And judging by the mood you were in when you came home—and the fact that you came home at all—everything is less than rosy in the garden."

Gina sighed. Things couldn't be less rosy. Liam was here, but instead of making things better it was making things worse. She was angry with him. Hurt by the way he was treating her. Hurt by the way he was treating Kaitlyn. She was starting to wonder if marrying him was the mistake her dad seemed to think it was. But if she didn't marry him, where would that leave her? Liam—and the gallery—was central to her life. If they split up what would she do? She shook her head. She couldn't think about that. She needed to get back over to the resort and make things right with him. She needed to feel happy with him, convinced that marrying him was the right decision before she saw Mason. His words kept echoing in her mind. I'm going to remind you how I make you feel. She'd need all her strength to resist his determination, and right now she wasn't even sure she wanted to.

"I'll call you when we're on the way, okay?"

"Whatever you say, love." Her dad came and wrapped her in a hug. "I want to see you happy. You know that, don't you?"

She nodded. She did, too. She just wasn't sure anymore that Liam was the one she could be happy with.

As she drove out to Chico, she wondered again whether she could ever be happy with anyone who wasn't Mason.

~ ~ ~

Mason stared at himself in the bathroom mirror and grinned. He looked good, if he did say so himself. The way Gina had looked at him had made it clear she was bowled over by the man he'd become, the same as he was bowled over by the woman she'd become. He had a good feeling about tonight. The fiancé couldn't have much of a hold on her. She wasn't even wearing a ring! What kind of man would ask a girl to marry him without giving her a ring? And no matter what kind of hold the guy had on her, Mason was convinced that the hold he had was stronger.

He hadn't thought of much other than Gina since he'd seen her coming out of the pharmacy the other day. She might say there was nothing left between them, but her body told him otherwise. He shifted in his pants as he remembered her arching up underneath him. He'd bet the fiancé had never made her come for him on the kitchen table without even unfastening his pants. He grinned. He was looking forward to the time when he would unfasten his pants. Maybe she'd do it for him. The thought of her little hands on his zipper had him aching for her. He pulled himself together. He shouldn't be thinking like this. He'd never gone after another guy's woman before. Didn't believe it was something a decent man would ever do. But this was different. This was Gina. She wasn't another guy's woman, she was his girl, his woman and all he needed to do was remind her of that. He knew it now. Whatever her reasons for pushing him away all those years ago, it didn't matter anymore. He'd been stupid for way too long. It was time to make things right.

"Are you coming out of there any time soon?" shouted Shane.

"Be right out." He took one last look in the mirror and nodded.

Shane wolf whistled when he stepped out into the hallway. "Damn, Mase! You're going for the kill, huh? If I wore panties, I think I'd throw them at you!"

Mason laughed. "I need to remind her what a real man looks like." He was wearing his best Wranglers and a black, long sleeved T-shirt that clung to his muscular chest and stretched over his biceps.

Shane laughed. "She might not be able to see you with all the girls that'll be flocking around you looking like that."

"I'm sure you can have fun fending them off for me."

Shane nodded. "Anything to help out." He sniffed the air. "You even smell good, too."

Mason grinned. He'd added a splash of the cologne that Gina used to love so much. Whenever he wore it, she used to bury her face in his neck to smell him. Then she'd wriggle her way underneath him, telling him that she could never resist it and he needed to just take her now. He'd always been happy to oblige. He'd give anything for her to do that tonight. He'd heard that smell was the sense most closely linked to memory, and he was hoping that this particular scent would evoke memories she'd want to re-create.

"Are we ready?" called Chance from the living room.

"Give me a couple," called Shane and pushed Mason out of the way so he could get into the bathroom.

Mason pulled his favorite boots out from the closet in the hallway.

Chance grinned at him. "You're going all out tonight, aren't you?"

Mason nodded grimly. "I am. I have to. I want her back. I intend to get her back, and I need to see off this fiancé in order to get her."

Chance nodded as he watched him pull on his jacket and cram his hat on his head. "The poor bastard doesn't have a hope."

Mason looked at him. "If it were just about two guys and her having to pick one, I'd agree with you. But she's held something against me for years, something that I don't even know about. I have to get past whatever that is, as much as I have to get past the fiancé."

"Yeah, but you seem pretty sure you can get past it."

Mason nodded. He had to believe he could. "There's only one way to find out," he said. "Come on, Shane. It's go time."

They all piled into Shane's truck.

"So you think things aren't good between them?" he asked Shane again once they were out on East River Road.

"For the hundredth time, Mase! No. I don't. She told me she didn't think I would like him. And she was right. He'd left her to go park the truck while he checked in, some gentleman, huh? And he seemed a little too close with the blonde chick that was with them. While Gina was playing valet for them, he was making sure blondie had the best room at the inn."

Mason frowned. "So what's she doing with a guy who'd treat her like that?"

Chance punched his arm. "That's what you're going to find out isn't it, Mase. But we need to get there so that you can—and quit playing twenty questions in the truck!"

Shane laughed. "See. Listen to your Uncle Chance, why don't you? And give my ears a rest."

Mason smiled through pursed lips. "Sorry, guys."

~ ~ ~

Gina sat on the end of the bed watching Liam get ready. She'd never known a man take so much care over his appearance. He was almost as engrossed in the mirror as he had been on his computer since they'd come back to his room.

"Your dad's going to have a hard time in New York, isn't he?"

She nodded sadly. That had become very clear this afternoon when she'd taken Liam out to the ranch. Her dad had made a big point of talking about everything he loved about his life here. He'd had his two old hounds by his side the whole time and kept making a fuss over them, saying he would never be able to leave them behind.

Liam had at least made an effort, telling him about things he might enjoy in New York. It had been a pretty awful afternoon though.

"So what are you going to do?" asked Liam.

That brought Gina back to the present. What was she going to do? For months, Liam had been talking as we. Making plans for how we would work things out to take care of her dad and get him settled into a new life. The only we she'd heard from him this weekend had included Kaitlyn and Ian, not her.

"I don't know, Liam. I don't know much of anything right now." She looked up at him sadly. "Do you still love me?"

He turned around to face her. "Of course I do. What kind of question is that, Gina?"

"It's a scared kind of question, Liam. I feel like everything is changing and I don't like it." Suddenly she felt as if it would all be okay if he would make love to her. She needed him to reassure her. She lay back on the bed and held her arms out to him. "Show me, Liam. Show me you still love me."

"Later. We don't have time right now. The others will be waiting."

"Let them wait. I need you to make love to me."

It worked. He started undoing the shirt buttons he'd just fastened and came to the bed. "You're a sensual woman, Gina. That's one of the many things I love about you." He took off his shirt and lowered himself onto the bed next to her, drawing her into his arms. She pressed herself against him and kissed his neck. "What else do you love, Liam?"

He closed his hands around her ass. Gina closed her eyes trying to close out the thought that his hands didn't feel like Mason's—didn't feel as good as Mason's. That as he pulled her against his erection, he didn't feel as good as Mason. She couldn't let her mind go there. She reached up around his neck and rubbed herself against him.

"I love the way..."

A knock at the door cut off the words he'd been about to say.

Gina pulled his head down to her. "Ignore it."

The knock came again. "Liam?" called Kaitlyn. "Are you ready?"

He sprang up from the bed. "We'll be out in a minute."

Gina heaved a big sigh. "Really?" she asked him.

He smiled. "We can get back to this later."

Gina pulled herself together and got up. "Maybe."

They found a table in the corner where they could see the band and the dance floor.

Ian grinned at her. "I thought places like this only existed in old movies. I had no idea that people still went out in cowboy boots and hats and did all this old-time dancing."

Gina laughed. "It's not old-time. It's country. You've spent your entire life in New York City, Ian. You need to broaden your horizons."

"Thanks, but I'd sooner get back to civilization."

"Me too," said Kaitlyn. "This is all very quaint to visit, but to think that people live their whole lives like this is kind of scary."

Gina turned to her. She'd considered Kaitlyn to be a friend these last few years, but that was wearing pretty thin this weekend. "What's scary about it?"

"The fact that they've never been anywhere else, never done anything else. They lead such small lives and don't know any better."

"What do you know about life outside New York?" asked Gina. "Where have you ever been? What have you ever done to make your own life so big?"

"I'm sorry. I didn't mean to offend you." Kaitlyn didn't look sorry at all.

"Calm down, Gina," Liam frowned at her.

Seriously? He was going to come down on Kaitlyn's side against her? Gina scowled at him. "I'm going to the ladies' room. Excuse me."

She pushed her way through the crowded bar and into the bathroom. She splashed cold water on her face and her wrists. She did need to calm down. She was wound up that things were going so badly with Liam, wound up at the thought that

Mason would be here tonight. Wound up that she didn't know what she was doing anymore.

Kaitlyn came in after her. "Sorry, Gina. I didn't mean to be rude about your home."

"That's okay. I'm a little tense. I shouldn't have snapped your head off. I'm sorry."

Kaitlyn smiled. "You probably have reason to be mad at me. I'm not being a very good friend, am I?"

"I thought it was just me. What's going on, Kaitlyn?"

"I hate to say it. But I don't want Liam to marry you."

Gina stared at her. "Why not?"

"Because I don't think you're right for each other."

Gina couldn't believe this! "And what gives you the right to be the judge of that?"

Kaitlyn smiled apologetically. "The fact that I've been in love with him for years. I've watched his girlfriends come and go and always known that they wouldn't stick around. I thought someday he'd realize that he and I are perfect for each other. I like you. I didn't think the two of you would last very long at all, you're so different. But once he started to get serious about marrying you I knew I had to let him know how I feel before it's too late."

Gina just stared. "So you're trying to come between us?"

Kaitlyn nodded. "Why do you think Ian and I came along this weekend? I need to make it clear to Liam that you're all wrong for him, and that I'm all right."

Gina didn't know what to say.

"I hope you don't hate me, but I want to be honest with you. If I thought you truly loved him I don't think I'd be able to do this, but you don't, do you?"

Gina swallowed. "Of course I do!"

"Really? You see, Gina, I love him. I want to see him happy. I know what makes him happy. I don't want him to be any different than he already is. You do. You want him to care about the things that are important to you. You want him to show you more affection. You want him to be interested in your opinions. And we both know he isn't. You don't love him, you love who you want him to be."

"So what are you saying?" Gina's head was spinning, trying to make sense of it. Trying to deny the truth of it.

"That I am making my move to get the man I love. I don't want you to hate me for it. And I'm saying you should take a long hard look at yourself and figure out what you want." She turned around and walked back out, leaving Gina staring after her.

She let herself into one of the stalls and sat there, dazed. It was true. She was always wishing that Liam was different. She didn't know what to think or what to do. Did she love him? Was Kaitlyn right, that she didn't love him at all? And how could she hate Kaitlyn if she loved Liam and always had? She sat there for a long time, confused by it all. She heard someone come in to the bathroom.

"Gina?"

"What, Kaitlyn?"

"I think you should come out. Liam is getting worried that you've been gone so long."

She opened the stall door.

"I'm sorry."

Gina shook her head. "Don't be. At least you're honest. But don't expect me to know what to say to you yet either."

Kaitlyn nodded and left.

Chapter Seven

Mason watched their table from his perch at the bar. He'd been surprised when Shane had pointed out the fiancé. He'd expected a big guy, someone like himself. Gina had always joked that she needed a big man, a real man. This guy was more of a weedy city type. Not Gina's type at all. He was sitting there sipping a glass of wine, chatting with his friend, looking way too clean and primped to belong out here. Gina was nowhere to be seen.

After a while, a blonde woman came and sat at the table. She put a hand on the fiancé's shoulder and from the way he smiled at her, it seemed Shane was right and those two were a little *too* friendly. Mason bristled with indignation on Gina's behalf. How could he even notice another woman when he had Gina? What kind of asshole would mess around on her? The kind of asshole who wouldn't have her for much longer if *he* had anything to do with it. But where was she?

Mason watched as the fiancé and his friends sat and chatted for a few minutes then fell silent. After sitting that way for a while, the guy started to look agitated. He said something to the blonde woman and she stood up again and headed for the ladies' room. She came out a few minutes later and Gina followed shortly afterward. She was so beautiful. But she looked pale and shaken. What was going on? He wasn't going to wait any longer to find out. He turned to Shane. "Are you coming?"

Shane grinned and nodded. "Let Operation Get Gina Back begin!"

Chance got down from his stool. "No way I'm missing out on this. Let's go."

Mason pushed his way through the crowded bar. He shoved Shane in the back when he stopped to let a pretty redhead pass in front of him then crowded against her. She smiled up at him. Mason did not have time for Shane's flirting. He looked at the girl. "I'll send him to find you later, okay sweetheart?"

She smiled at him and then Chance. "I hope you'll both be coming with him? I'm with my friends over in the corner."

Mason shook his head and pushed Shane forward.

Chance stopped to talk to the girl a minute and then caught up with them.

As they got closer to the table, Mason could sense the tension in the group sitting there. He had to wonder what was going on. Gina turned even paler when she saw them. The others looked up when Shane spoke.

"Good evening, folks. How's the visit going?" He looked around the table, but Ian was the only one to smile. He turned to Gina. "I thought you'd be pleased to see some more old friends." He gestured to Mason and Chance.

She didn't say anything for a moment, just stared at Mason. He didn't know what was going on with her, but she certainly didn't look like the visit was going well.

She visibly pulled herself together and then stood up with a smile. She surprised him by coming around the table to hug

Chance. "It's so good to see you. It's been too long." Then she turned to Mason and hugged him. It wasn't just a hug though, for a moment she clung to him. He closed his arms around her and struggled to let her go when she turned back to the others. "I'd like you to meet two of my oldest and dearest friends, Mason Remington and Chance Malone."

Mason tipped his hat at the blonde. He smiled at the other guy before turning a stony glare on the fiancé.

Gina continued with the introductions. "This is Kaitlyn Jones and Ian Rawlings. They both work with my fiancé, Liam Woodford."

Mason couldn't help crushing the guy's hand when he shook it, then stared him down, waiting for him to speak. He sure as hell wasn't going to say it was nice to meet him. The guy stared back, looking like a rabbit in the headlights. Pussy!

The silence lasted long enough to become awkward before Gina broke it. "It's great to see you guys. Maybe we'll catch up with you later, but Liam and I were about to dance."

She pulled the guy to his feet and they disappeared onto the crowded dance floor. The blonde chick and the other guy followed them. Mason shrugged and went to lean on the end of the bar to watch. He wasn't in a hurry.

Shane passed him a fresh beer. "She sure didn't act like she hates you."

Mason nodded. The way she'd hugged him so tight had surprised him—in a good way. He might not be in a hurry, but he didn't intend to waste too much time before he followed up on that hug. The way she was dancing with the guy told him that things weren't good between them. He held her stiffly and she stared out over his shoulder. Mason smiled to himself. *His* Gina didn't dance like that. It seemed he needed to remind her how to dance along with everything else. He handed the beer back to Shane, who grinned at him.

He made his way out onto the dance floor and enjoyed the way Gina's eyes widened when he tapped the guy on the shoulder. "May I?"

He didn't expect a no, and he didn't get one. The guy stepped away and Mason curled an arm around her waist and pulled her against him, much closer than her so-called fiancé had been holding her. He didn't enjoy the look on her face when she saw the blonde woman let go of her partner and catch Liam before he left the dance floor. She pressed herself up against him, making Mason scowl and hold Gina even tighter to his chest. She was shaking in his arms. He looked down at her.

"What the hell is going on, G?"

It hurt him to see tears well up in her eyes. He didn't want her to care enough about the guy to cry over him.

She rested her cheek against his chest. "I don't want to talk about it, Mase."

He couldn't force her to. Instead, he made the most of holding her close. It had been years since they'd danced together, but she felt as though she'd never left his arms. Their bodies moved together as if they were two parts of the same whole. He was hard as a rock being this close to her again. She must be able to feel him, but she didn't move away. She kept her face buried against him and clung to him as they moved. Whatever he'd thought might happen tonight, it certainly wasn't this.

He looked across to see Liam dancing with blondie. He didn't seem worried that his fiancée was holding onto another guy, crying into his chest. He was too busy laughing with his *friend*. Mason saw red.

He took hold of Gina's hand and led her off the dance floor. She must be in a state, she didn't even try to resist. He led her out of the saloon and into the little courtyard out the back. She stared up at him but said nothing.

He wrapped his arms around her again and rested his chin on the top of her head. "Tell me what's going on, babe. If he's hurting you, I will..."

"No!" Finally, she sounded like Gina again, an edge of fire tinged her voice.

"It's not his fault, Mason. It's all my fault."

"What's your fault?"

She looked up at him. "You are the last person I should be talking to about this."

He couldn't help smiling at her. "I was always the one you could talk to, G. Always the one you came to. I don't know what changed that, but I don't think it matters anymore. All I know is I want to change it back again."

Her eyes almost popped out of her head. "What...what are you saying, Mase?"

"I'm saying we need to put whatever happened in the past behind us. We need to start getting on with our forever. I want you back, Gina. And this time I'm not going to give up. That guy isn't right for you. You're mine babe, always have been, always will be. It's time you admit it. Don't you think?"

~ ~ ~

Gina stared at him. She could not believe this was happening. Mason still wanted her? Still wanted forever? Not ten minutes after Kaitlyn had told her that *she* didn't love Liam? She didn't know what to do with this. With any of it.

Mason was smiling at her, his eyes pleading with her. He couldn't mean it? She hadn't been his for years—because he hadn't wanted her to be.

"I don't understand."

"I don't know how I can make it any clearer. I want you back and I'm not giving up until I get you. You can't marry that guy. He's not good enough for you." Gina hated the pity she saw in his eyes as he added. "And I hate to say it, but if he's not messing around on you already, it won't be long before he is."

That stung. Even though she knew exactly what he meant. Instead of pulling away from him, she sagged against him. "What makes you say that?"

"I think you already know, don't you? It looks like that *friend* he brought with him is more than just a friend."

Gina heaved a big sigh and let out a sad little laugh. "She's certainly hoping to be. She just told me that she's making her play for him."

Mason's arms tightened around her. A tiny voice in the back of her mind was yelling that she shouldn't let him hold her like that. That she shouldn't even be out here with him, but she ignored it. He felt so good. He made *her* feel so good, nestled against him. She felt safe, protected, in a way she hadn't felt since...well, since Mason.

He didn't say anything. He'd always known when to stay quiet and let her think. He'd always known when he could push her towards finding her own answers.

"The thing is, she also told me that she's always loved him. She doesn't think he and I belong together either. And..." Her mind was racing, replaying the conversation. When Kaitlyn had told her she didn't really love Liam, Gina had been angry. Of course, she did! But sitting in that bathroom stall pondering it all, she had started to think that perhaps she didn't. When Mason had come marching over to their table, she had known for sure that what she felt for Liam had never come anywhere close to what she felt for this man. Dancing with him, coming out here with him, had only emphasized the fact that Mason was still the man she loved. Even though he was also the man who had destroyed her.

She looked up at him. "You're right, Mase. He's not right for me. I'm not right for him, and I need to get back in there and let him know that."

He searched her face. "And what about you and me?"

She couldn't go there. Not yet. "You broke my heart. How would we ever get past that?"

The lines around his eyes were etched with pain. "Tell me how, babe? I don't understand. I've never understood. What did I ever do to you?"

He really didn't seem to know. Maybe it was time to forget how much the boy he had been had hurt her? The man he was now seemed pretty genuine about wanting another chance. "That's not going to be a short conversation. Let me go and deal with Liam for now? We'll talk, Mase. I promise. But not tonight, okay?"

He nodded and held her close. "I'll wait, but I won't be patient. And I'm not giving up on us. Not ever again, do you hear me?" He tucked his fingers under her chin as he spoke and looked deep into her eyes.

She nodded. She wanted to believe him. Wanted more than anything in the world for him to mean it. His lips came down on hers. It was a gentle kiss, deep and tender, full of promises. Could she even dare to hope that he might mean them this time? When their lips finally parted she smiled up at him. "I'd better get back in there."

It felt as if they'd never been apart when he patted her ass with a grin. "Go get 'em, G. I'll be waiting for you when you're ready."

She frowned. "Not tonight."

He smiled. "I know, babe. I'll be waiting *whenever* you're ready."

It took everything she had to leave the circle of his arms and walk back inside. For a moment there, the last ten years had disappeared and she had felt as if they were back to the way they had been. Mason and Gina, the couple who were meant to be. As she opened the door to the saloon, she turned to look back at him. Her heart melted when she met his gaze. His smile offered the promise of future happiness while at the same time stripping away all the hurt of the past and making her remember all the love and laughter they'd shared.

He tipped his hat back and winked at her, making her smile and hurry inside. She'd once told him how much that particular little move turned her on—and he'd used it on her to great effect whenever he could after that. While part of her would love to turn around, go back to him, step into his arms and go wherever the night might take them, she couldn't. It seemed that her whole life had been turned on its head over the course of the last few days. She had to put the brakes on and sort through it all before she could let herself be swept along with it. The first thing she needed to do was talk to Liam. He was, after all, supposed to be her fiancé. Whether that was about to change or not, they needed to talk about it.

As she made her way through the bar, she had to second guess herself. Why had she forced herself to come back, to try to talk things out with Liam? He was still dancing with Kaitlyn, seemingly oblivious to the fact that she had left with Mason. Kaitlyn was laughing. She flicked her long blonde hair away from her face then rested her hand on Liam's shoulder. Gina wanted to hate her for it, but she could see the love shining in Kaitlyn's eyes as she smiled up at Liam. How could she hate her? No one could help how they felt—whom they loved. She of all people knew that. She'd tried for years to stop loving Mason, but her heart bluntly refused to let go.

As she approached the dance floor, she had no idea what she should do. She'd come back in thinking she needed to take Liam aside and talk to him. Watching him dance with Kaitlyn, she didn't want to intrude. It felt like *they* were the couple and *she* was the interloper, about to ruin their evening. She didn't need to decide what to do. Liam spotted her. He smiled and spoke a few words to Kaitlyn before letting go of her and making his way to Gina.

"Are you having a good time, Gina?" He smiled, seemingly unaware of anything amiss about the evening. He held his hand out to her. "Come dance with me? I think I'm getting the hang of it. All this country stuff is quite fun, isn't it?"

She took his hand and followed him back out onto the dance floor, even though she was struggling to believe that he was as oblivious as he seemed to be.

"Are you okay, Gina?" he asked after they'd danced in silence for a while. "You're being a bit of a stick-in-the-mud this weekend. Do you have your period or something? It'd be nice if you could make an effort to make it fun for Ian and Kaitlyn after they came all this way to see you."

Seriously? Gina couldn't believe her ears. Was he *that* clueless? And were Ian and Kaitlyn more of a concern to him than she was?

She stared at him. "Do you have any idea what's going on here, Liam?"

"No, Gina, sweetie. I don't. I got the idea there was some undercurrent with the big broody cowboy. I figured you probably used to date him, but you know I'm not the jealous type. I thought you may need to talk with him, so I left you to it."

"And you had Kaitlyn to keep you busy anyway, right?"

Liam frowned. "I'd rather not ignore our friends the whole weekend! You're being rather rude to them, the least I can do is try to make sure they have fun."

Wow! "I'm not being rude to them, Liam..."

"Oh, Gina, don't be ridiculous. You're hardly being the gracious hostess, are you?"

She couldn't believe this! "Well, considering I didn't even invite them, I'm not sure why you would expect me to be. I asked *you* to come, not them."

"For God's sake, Gina. Do you have to be so utterly self-absorbed? I told you. We still have work to do on the Avery show. We were trying to kill two birds with one stone. Why won't you appreciate that?"

"Because I thought I meant more to you than that. I thought you might make me a priority. But apparently I'm being ridiculous! Pardon me for thinking that the guy who wants to marry me might want to put me first!"

"Grow up, Gina!"

She shook her head. "If growing up means settling for a life where I'm never a priority, then I don't want to! If you'd ever made the time to get me an engagement ring, I'd give it back to you right now."

Liam shook his head. "Do you have your period? Is that what this is all about? You're always more unreasonable when you're hormonal."

Gina closed her eyes, determined not to drag this out any longer. She took a deep breath before she spoke again. "No, Liam. I don't have my period. I am not hormonal. I don't think I'm being unreasonable. I'm just being myself and whenever I'm myself you don't seem to like me too much."

She shook her head sadly and met his gaze. "And you know, it's a two-way street. Kaitlyn was right, I always want you to act differently than you do. When you are yourself, I don't like you too much either. So I think it's time we call it a day."

He looked thoroughly shocked for a moment. Then he smiled reassuringly. "You don't mean that, Gina. It's a stressful time, what with your dad and everything. I'm sorry I haven't been more understanding, but there's no need to overreact. Let's just forget this. When we get home and everything is back to normal, you'll see."

He wasn't even taking her seriously now! Gina suddenly understood how right Kaitlyn had been. She'd told Gina that she loved the man she wanted Liam to be. Now she realized that Liam loved the woman he wanted her to be. Whatever the practical realities of breaking up with him might be, she'd rather face them than face a marriage and a life with him that would only make them both miserable. She touched his cheek with a sad smile. "I am home, Liam. And when everything is back to normal, you'll see and probably be grateful to me, or at least relieved. I'm going back to my dad's. I'll drive you all to the airport tomorrow. But we're through."

As she pushed her way off the dance floor and out through the crowded bar, she could feel the relief flooding through her. She may not know what she was going to do about her career or her life, but she knew that she couldn't marry Liam. The fact that she'd done them both a big favor was enough to make her smile as she climbed into the truck and headed back down the valley. She might not be sure of too much of anything right now, but she did know one thing. She'd told Liam that she was home and as she headed south under the big starry sky, the moonlight reflecting off the river to her right, snow-capped peaks shining to her left, she knew that much was true.

Chapter Eight

Mason smiled at the girl sitting in the passenger seat of his truck. He was glad she and her friends were leaving. The guests staying at Shane's dude ranch didn't normally bother him too much. He didn't like having strangers on the property, but he mostly managed to stay out of their way. He admired the business his littlest brother was building and was glad that he'd chosen to come home. After his stint in the Navy, Shane had been determined to make a go of some kind of business on his own. For a while, it had seemed that he would head out in the world in order to make it. Then he'd had the idea of the dude ranch and he'd gone to work. He worked hard and was making it a big success. If a few city types wandering around the place was the price Mason had to pay to have Shane back, then it was worth it.

The girl handed him her business card. "We won't be able to make it back out here until the fall, but if you're ever in San Diego, call me. I'd love to show you how we do it in the city." Her smile clarified the innuendo in her words.

Mason tipped his hat. "Thanks, but I'm not into city living."

She wasn't going to give up so easily. "It's not the living I want to show you."

He shook his head and opened the truck door. He wanted to get her, her friends, and their luggage out of his truck, out of town and be on his way.

She reached over and put a hand on his arm. "I'll have to wait until we come back in the fall then. You can show me how cowboys do it."

Mason couldn't help but smirk at her as he climbed out. "You couldn't handle it, sweetheart."

He started pulling bags and suitcases down, regretting that he'd allowed himself to be roped into dropping the guests off at the airport. The other girls were collecting their bags and thanking him for the ride.

The persistent one stood before him as he straightened up. "Thanks for the ride, cowboy. My flight doesn't leave until an hour after the others, do you want to give me another ride before I go?"

Mason looked her over. Would he have done it if Gina hadn't come back? He might have, she was hot, willing, hell she was begging! Her pouty little smile as she moistened her lips, the way she leaned back so her breasts stuck out at him, everything about her was begging him to ride her hard. Whatever he might have done before, he had no interest now. Every woman he'd had sex with over the last ten years had been a way to try to forget Gina. But Gina was back, and the only place he wanted to be was back in her arms—well, that and between her legs.

"Sorry, sweetheart. No can do. You travel safely." He climbed back into his truck and turned the ignition, but he didn't pull away. He was supposed to go in with them, make sure they were checked in for their flights and that there were no delays that would leave them stranded here in Bozeman. He couldn't bring himself to do it. He wanted to get away from her. Whatever he might have been in the past, the thought of cheap sex with a stranger repulsed him now. He wanted meaningful sex with the woman who had been his best friend for years, and the best lover he'd ever had.

He watched in the rearview mirror as the woman pulled her suitcase along to catch up with her friends. She turned to look back at him before she went through the doors and gave him a shrug that clearly said *your loss*. He hadn't lost anything at all. More than that, he felt as though he was getting something back. He was getting back the guy who didn't want easy sex, the guy who knew how to love and cherish a woman. He only hoped that he was getting back the only woman who had ever made him feel that way.

He watched the automatic doors close behind Miss San Diego then checked the drop-off lanes before pulling out. He hit the brakes in a hurry when he saw a very familiar truck pulling in a few spaces back. He watched as Gina climbed down from the driver's side and Liam and his friends got out onto the curb. If there had been tension in the air around this group when he'd first seen them at Chico, it was positively crackling now. Even from this distance, he could see that Gina was pale. Liam was stiff and formal. The guy, Ian, looked uncomfortable and busied himself collecting a baggage cart. Liam took a step toward Gina. Mason gritted his teeth. He couldn't stand to see the guy kiss her! He needn't have worried though. Kaitlyn put her hand on Liam's shoulder and Gina turned away. Liam shrugged his *friend* off and started helping Ian load the bags onto the cart.

When Ian and Kaitlyn made their way inside, Mason wanted nothing more than to run over there, take Gina in his arms and send that asshole packing. He was talking to her, but Mason could tell that she was blocking him out. She was nodding and answering him, but Mason knew her too well. She was just going through the motions and waiting for him to be gone. It seemed that Liam understood that, too. He took hold of her arm and tried to draw her toward him. Gina pulled back and shook her head. There was none of her old fire to her. If anything, she looked tired and resigned. She smiled sadly and then leaned in to peck Liam's cheek. He put his arms around her to hug her and Mason couldn't hold in a little laugh when he saw the way she patted Liam's shoulder as she hugged him back. The pat was like the kiss of death on a guy's hopes with a girl. He knew that. He wondered if Liam did, too. Perhaps he did. He turned and followed the others inside without ever looking back.

Gina hurried around and climbed back into the cab of her dad's truck. *Oh, shit!* Mason realized he had to make a quick decision. Was he going to let her pull away or was he going to go talk to her before she left? He was out of his truck before his mind had caught up. His instincts decided for him that he could never again let her leave any place without making her talk to him first. She had her arms propped on the steering wheel with her head resting on them. He couldn't see her face, was she crying?

He tapped on the window and her head snapped up. In the instant before she recognized him, she looked tired, defensive almost. A smile transformed her face when she registered who he was. That had to be a good thing, right?

She rolled the window down. "Are you stalking me now?"

He had to grin. "Sure am, babe. What you going to do about it?"

She smiled back and shook her head. "It doesn't seem like there's much I can do, does it?"

"You could admit defeat and let me in?"

She looked at him for a moment and then unlocked the passenger door.

Mason climbed in and smiled at her. "Are you all right?"

She shook her head slowly. "I don't know. I think so. I don't know what the hell I'm going to do."

He frowned. "What do you mean?"

"What I said. I don't know what to do."

She looked so small and pale, almost fragile. Fragile was not a word he would normally associate with Gina, and it worried him. He wanted her to be happy that Liam was gone. He was hoping that her words meant it was over between the two of them, and if that was the case, he knew exactly what *he* wanted her to do. He smiled. "So how about you start by spending the afternoon with me?"

She shook her head. "I can't."

"Why not?"

"Because I need to be by myself. Think things through. Figure out what I'm going to do."

"What's to think about, G? You're done with *him,* aren't you?" Mason felt his heart pounding as he asked. He assumed that Gina had broken up with the guy, but he wasn't entirely sure. He needed to hear her say it.

She nodded slowly. "I told him it's over, but he doesn't think I mean it. He thinks I'm having a little freak out, and will come around and come home fine." She looked up and held Mason's gaze. "And you know, Mase. I'm not sure he's wrong. Maybe it's all the stress of being back here, of making dad sell the ranch..." She took a deep breath. "...of seeing you again, that has me all out of whack. Maybe once I get back to the city and back to my life I'll see it differently again, just like he said."

Mason pursed his lips. "Bullshit."

Her eyes widened. "Excuse me?"

"You heard me, G. That's bullshit and you know it. All those things are only stressful because he's trying to make you go against what you know is right. You belong here. This is your home, this is your life. You shouldn't be making your dad sell the ranch, and you know it. You should be finding a way to help him save the place." He glared at her. "And seeing me again is only stressful because you know we belong together, and you've been trying to hide from that."

She pulled herself up straight and glared back at him. "Get out, Mason. I don't know any such thing!"

He smiled, she was lying. He reached over and touched her cheek, sliding his fingers under her ear and into her hair. She closed her eyes as her cheeks flushed and she sighed. He had her. He leaned across and brushed his lips over hers. She didn't open her eyes, but her hands came up to his shoulders and pulled him closer. He smirked—no pat for him!

He slid his arm around her waist and drew her against him, then covered her mouth with his own. She tasted as good as he remembered. She kissed him as though she'd never forgotten how, as though the years in between them had never existed. He took possession of her mouth, crushing her to his chest as he explored with his tongue, nipped her lips, and then nibbled her neck. Damn, he wasn't going to be able to keep kissing her without getting her naked very soon. She seemed to feel the same way. She clung to his shoulders, her breath coming fast as she kissed him back hungrily.

~ ~ ~

Gina was drowning in his kiss. His arms closed around her, holding her to him, dragging her under. She'd spent so many years struggling, fighting against her feelings for him and now she was back in his arms. Part of her wanted to give up the fight, to surrender to the inevitable. She relaxed and kissed him back. Maybe she wasn't drowning, maybe what she was doing was flying? Flying high on the way he made her feel, letting him take her soaring away with him into the future that should have always been theirs.

The sound of her cell phone ringing brought her crashing back to reality. She tried to pull away from Mason, but he held her close.

"Let it ring."

"But, I..." His lips came back down on hers, but the magic of the moment was gone. She couldn't lose herself in his kiss while her phone kept ringing and her mind kept racing. "I need to answer it."

This time he let her pull away from him and she fished the phone from her purse. She was surprised to see the name flashing on the display.

"What is it, Kaitlyn?"

"I wanted to thank you. You've done the right thing, for all of us."

Gina didn't know what to say.

"The guy you're with obviously loves you, and I love Liam. This is all for the best."

"What do you mean, the guy I'm with?"

Kaitlyn laughed. "The guy in your truck. I'd be surprised if you make it out of the airport before he's the guy in your pants."

Gina looked around wildly. She spotted Kaitlyn standing outside the doors next to the baggage cart return.

Kaitlyn met her gaze and waggled her fingers in a wave. "I guess you'll be coming back to New York, at least to collect your things. You'll let me know if there's anything I can do, won't you? I have to go. Liam's waiting." She hung up.

Gina stared at her phone.

"What did she want?" Mason had followed her gaze and seen Kaitlyn. He watched as she disappeared back through the automatic doors.

Gina shook her head. "To say thank you. And to say that I'd done the right thing for all of us. Oh and she'll be happy to help me pack up and leave once I get back to the city!" Her heart was racing. She'd been wondering if she was making the wrong decision. Wondering if Liam was right and she'd feel differently once she got back to New York. Now it seemed that she wouldn't get the chance to find out. Events were taking on a life of their own and the decision was being taken out of her hands.

Mason smiled. "I didn't think I liked her, but I have to agree with her. You *have* done the right thing, G. You said she's always loved Liam. And I've always loved you. If you *have* to go back to New York, I don't want you to be gone for long. If she'll help you pack you can come home to me faster."

Gina was struggling to process this. "Mason..." She didn't know what to say, what to address first. He claimed he'd *always* loved her? He wanted her to come back home? To him? Both he and Kaitlyn were assuming that since she'd called it off with Liam she would leave New York—but how could she? That was her life, her livelihood. How could she just up and leave it all behind? And what would she do then?

Mason tucked his fingers under her chin and turned her to face him. "What, Gina?"

"I can't stay here." Even as she spoke the words, she looked deep into the blue eyes she knew so well and wondered how she could ever leave them again.

He seemed to read her thoughts. He didn't push her, just smiled and said, "You take your time, babe. You'll figure it out."

She let out an exasperated sigh. "Now we've come full circle back to when you climbed in here. I told you. I need to be by myself, take some time to do that—to figure it all out."

He wrapped her in a hug and she sagged against him. In the warmth of his embrace, she was no longer sure what she needed to think about. She was back where she belonged—end of story. He rested his chin on top of her head. "Okay. I'll leave you to it. Remember what I told you last night. I'll be waiting whenever you're ready."

She opened her mouth to reply but didn't get the chance. He closed one hand around the back of her neck and kissed her deeply, stealing her breath, as well as her words. His other hand found its way inside her jeans and stroked her through her panties. She moaned into his mouth as he teased. He eased the fabric to the side and traced her opening. His tongue thrust deep as he dipped his fingertip inside her. God that felt so good. She bucked her hips wanting more, pressing herself against him and drinking in his kiss.

He lifted his head and smiled. "Sorry, babe. You want to be by yourself, right?"

All she could do was stare after him when he broke away leaving her wanting. He got out of the truck and closed the door before tipping his hat up and winking at her as he walked away. She wriggled in her seat. The way he kissed her had always turned her on. Now she was all hot and achy with desire for him. He turned back to smile at her before climbing into his own truck and pulling away.

She was still sitting there, squirming in her seat a few minutes later when her phone rang. It was him. "You know, babe. I'll scratch that itch any time you want me to. But you have to be the one to say it."

"What itch?" She wasn't going to admit that she knew exactly what he meant.

He gave a low chuckle that made her breasts tingle just at the sound of it.

"Don't try to fool me, Gina. You're wishing I'd finished you off before I left. When I asked you to give me a reason to keep it in my pants, you told me you were getting married. Now you're not. I want you, I need you, but we're not going to go there until you want me and need me just as badly."

Gina swallowed. Apparently he didn't understand just how badly she wanted and needed him right now!

She could hear the smile in his voice as he added. "Actually, I mean until you *tell* me how much you want me."

Gina knew if she said it right now, his truck would be parked behind her again in a few minutes. As much as she wanted to, she wouldn't let herself do it. He chuckled again. "Like I said, whenever you're ready, babe."

Chapter Nine

"Did they get off all right?"

Mason stared at Shane. It took him a moment to remember the dude ranch guests he'd dropped off. He spent the whole hour of the drive back from Bozeman thinking about Gina. Thinking about what they could have been doing if he hadn't forced himself to get out of her truck.

"Huh? Yeah. I dropped them off."

Shane frowned. "Did you get them checked in?"

Mason shrugged. "They're fine." He turned to walk away. He needed to get out to the barn. He'd wasted too much time thinking about Gina lately. He needed to check on the mares and get caught up with his books.

"Mase?"

The concern in Shane's voice made him turn around. "What?"

"Is everything okay?"

He nodded and couldn't stop the corners of his mouth turning up in a smile. "I think it's going to be."

Shane came after him. "What does that mean? What's happened?"

Mason kept walking. He wasn't sure he wanted to talk to his brother about it yet, but he didn't think he could keep his mouth shut either.

"Talk to me, Mase. Is it Gina? I know she left alone last night and we couldn't find you after that. What's going on?"

"She broke up with the fiancé..."

"That's awesome! So are you two back together? Is she staying?"

"I hope so, but she needs a little time to get her head around it. I saw her at the airport, she was dropping them off. I was going to stick around and persuade her that we're back together, but she's got a lot to work through." He hated to admit it, but Gina *did* have a lot to think about. In his eyes, it was simple. She was here, she was single, and she should stay. They should forget the past and get on with their life— together. But that didn't take into account the life and career she'd spent the last ten years building. She needed to figure it out for herself that she wanted him and wanted to be here. He was concerned that if he rushed her or forced her somehow, it would come back to bite him in the ass. He wasn't about to lose her again. This time it *was* forever, and if he had to wait a while for Gina to reach that conclusion by herself, then so be it.

Shane nodded. As much as Mason hated to admit it, Shane probably knew more about Gina and her life than *he* did these days. The two of them had kept in touch while she had refused to speak to Mason. "She is going to have a lot to think about. Whenever we've talked over the years, she's said how much she would love to come home, but she couldn't make it out here. What would she do? There's not exactly a market for fine art photography, is there?"

"Bullshit! Look at all the California implants who are moving here. Bozeman is full of them. Big Sky is like Little California these days, and half the land in the valley has been bought up by out-of-staters looking to build their Montana McMansions! Those are the kind of people who'd buy up Gina's photographs like crazy, and they'd pay through the nose for them. There's a perfect market here for her if she works it right." He thought about it for a moment, it made all the sense in the world to him. "She'd probably be able to make more money here than she does in New York—and she'd be able to do the kind of work she loves. She could do all her wildlife photography and capture the Old West like she always used to talk about."

"I hadn't thought about it like that, but you're right."

Mason shrugged. "Don't sound so surprised, I usually am."

"Well, good luck convincing Gina of it."

"Why would I need luck?"

Shane laughed. "Because it's like saying all her reasons for staying gone all those years were wrong. That she stayed away when she didn't need to."

"Oh." Mason could see that. "But surely if she wants to be here, she'll be glad that there's a way to do it."

Shane laughed again. "Maybe, but how much do *you* like it when you're proved wrong?"

"Not much, but I accept it when it means that I'll be able to make things right." He looked at Shane. "I know she's stubborn, but don't you think she'll just be happy to be able to stay, to see that there is a way to make it here, after all?"

"Yeah, she should." He held Mason's gaze for a moment. "As long as you go about it the right way. I'm pretty sure that if you lead with your usual *that's bullshit* line, she'll be less open to hearing what you have to say.

Mason shrugged. Shane was right and he knew it. He'd already called her out on her bullshit this morning and her reaction then had been to tell him to get out of the truck. He'd have to find a more diplomatic approach to make sure that she didn't tell him to get out of her life. He wasn't entirely back in it yet, and he didn't want to screw up before he got the chance to be.

~ ~ ~

"So what are you going to do, love?"

Gina rested her elbows on the kitchen table and looked up at her dad who was leaning in the doorway. "I don't know. It's all happened so fast. A week ago I thought we were selling the ranch, thought I'd be marrying Liam, and bringing you to New York. Now it doesn't look as though the place is going to sell anytime soon. Liam and I are over, and I don't even know what *I'm* going to do in New York."

"Why the hell would you want to do anything there? You're going to stay here, aren't you?"

"How, Dad? How can I make enough for us to survive on here?"

He shrugged. "There are a couple of new galleries up in town. Couldn't you put your pictures in there?"

Gina let out an exasperated little laugh. "Dad, the galleries in town don't sell much and what they do sell is a couple of hundred dollars at most. In New York, my photographs sell for thousands. I need the exposure and the big money buyers."

"When was the last time you checked out the galleries in town, Gina girl? Do you think time stood still here, just because you left?"

"What do you mean?" Gina was surprised at the way he was scowling at her.

"Well, Miss Uppity-City-Girl, there are some mighty expensive galleries in town. Some big name artists and writers have moved to the valley since you left. You might want to check out some of them price tags they have on pictures of the wolves and the buffalo. All the Californian tree-huggers want a piece of the West as they understand it and apparently paying high-dollar for pictures of the critters is an important part of protecting 'em, or conserving 'em, or whatever it is they call it. The point is, you're basing your thinking on an idea of how this place works, and that idea is ten years out of date. If you want to stay, you should be working out a way to make it happen instead of bleating about all the things that make it impossible. You've never been a quitter, Gina, not when you want something. So am I right in thinking that you don't want to be here?"

Gina looked back at him, thinking hard about the answer to that. She'd told Liam last night that this was her home, so why was she making excuses about not being able to stay here? Were they really excuses, or was she just being realistic? She shook her head—she'd thought marrying Liam was being realistic! It seemed she had some thinking to do.

Her dad patted her arm. "Why don't you take yourself and your camera down to the park? That always used to help you get your head on straight."

She nodded. "I think I will. Thanks, Dad."

As she drove down the valley toward Gardiner, Gina wanted to call Ian. Wanted to talk to him about what she should do from here. He'd been supportive of her ideas about shooting in Montana, about the kind of shows she'd wanted to do. She valued his opinion and knowledge. She couldn't call him right now because he'd be sitting on a plane heading back to New York, with Liam and Kaitlyn. She wondered what the conversation between the three of them would be. Wondered if she would even be worth a mention, or whether they would all be focused on getting back to the gallery and pulling together the Avery show. She had a show of her own lined up for early next month. She had to wonder whether they would still go ahead with it. On the one hand, she hoped so. It was a showcase of the work she'd done in Brazil. A similar concept to what she'd wanted to do in Montana. Photos of bronzed bikinied bottoms drew sharp contrast with the huge brown eyes of street children. "Soccer on the Beach" was to be displayed next to "Laundry in the River." She'd been fascinated by the country and its many faces, by the huge divide between ostentatious consumerism and abject poverty. She had to hope the show would still run, just for its own sake. She wanted to be able to share her insight into the ultra-modern lifestyle in parts of cities that were ringed with *favelas* or ghettos. Wanted to share her shots of villages and villagers living their centuries old traditions... She shook her head to clear it. She needed to focus on the practical. Needed to bring herself into the present, stop daydreaming about work she'd already done and its meaning, and start figuring out what work she was going to do from here on out, and what it would mean for her future in practical terms. Would she be able to make a go of it in the valley, or would she need to be traveling and finding new big city galleries to work with? Perhaps she should start exploring any connections she had on the West Coast?

~ ~ ~

Shane stuck his head around the door to the office in the back of the gallery. "Hellooo. Anybody home?"

"I'll be right with you."

He grinned to himself. He liked the sounds of that voice. He'd heard that the owner of the new gallery on Main Street was something of a looker. After talking to Mason yesterday about Gina's options for staying in the valley, he'd decided to see what he could do to help things along. He figured Gina would be more open to his help than Mason's, and besides he'd been wanting to check out the new gallery—and its owner.

He turned to admire a series of paintings on the back wall. They were beautiful—oceanscapes and deserted beaches. Much as he liked them, he couldn't see that they would sell well. People here wanted mountains and bears. Visitors wanted a memento of their visit and locals wanted to decorate their homes Montana style. He was further convinced that these pictures wouldn't sell when he saw the prices listed underneath them. Damn! Most folks around here didn't make that much in a month—or two!

"Sorry to keep you waiting."

Damn! That was a sexy voice! Shane felt it flow over him like warm honey. When he turned to face her, he had to push back the thought that he'd love to cover her in warm honey and slowly lick it all off. Jesus! She was beautiful. Long, honey-blonde hair framed a gorgeous face, laughing, honey-colored eyes smiled at him. She was short, or maybe not so much. At six-four most people seemed short to Shane. His family joked that he was the *littlest* brother, when in fact although he was the youngest, he was the tallest. He took a step toward her, holding out his hand.

"Not a problem, you're worth waiting for." Damn! What was he saying?

Her eyes widened in surprise, but she smiled and shook his hand. "Thank you, I think. I'm Cassidy Lane."

He closed his hand around hers, it was warm and small and soft. He wanted to feel her running it over his chest, sliding it inside his pants. Jesus, Shane! He had to get it together but standing this close, her V-neck sweater was giving him an awesome view of her breasts that wasn't helping him any.

She followed his gaze down to her breasts then gave him a stern look. "What can I do for you?"

Oh, what could she do for him? He had to bite back a smile at the ungentlemanly suggestions that came to mind. She looked as though she was trying not to laugh herself. "I can think of several things you could do for me. If you're interested?"

She did laugh now. "Perhaps you should tell me your name first?"

"Oh, sorry." He grinned. "Shane Remington, it's a pleasure to meet you."

"Nice to meet you, Shane." She smiled and let go of his hand. "What did you have in mind when you came in?"

"I forget, but would you like to hear what I have in mind now?" He raised an eyebrow and gave her his best charming smile. Women loved him, and he loved women.

She laughed again. "From the look on your face I think I can guess, and no thank you."

Wow, he hadn't expected that. He was used to a resounding, *yes please!* when he turned on the charm. He certainly wasn't used to being turned down flat. He checked her left hand. No ring. Maybe there was a boyfriend?

She laughed again. "My God! If I'm not interested I must be married right?"

Oh, shit! She'd seen him check. He shrugged sheepishly. "What other reason could you have to turn me down? I mean, I'm adorable, right? And you do find me incredibly attractive."

"Adorable?" Her eyes shone with laughter, but she kept a straight face and a stern tone. "I was thinking more along the lines of deplorable."

That took him by surprise again. "Now you're hurting my feelings. Why the hell would you think I'm deplorable? You only just met me."

"Exactly. I've known you for less than three minutes and you're already making lewd suggestions and expecting me to jump at the chance. You're one of those guys who thinks he's so good looking that every woman he meets is going to throw herself at him."

He shrugged. "I never made a single suggestion. It was your mind that went there, all by itself." He took his time looking her over, letting his gaze linger on her breasts far longer than was polite. He was pleased to see her nipples harden, reassuring him that no matter how she was playing it, she was as attracted to him as he was to her. He looked up to meet her gaze and was pleased to see her cheeks flush. "And you're not going to throw yourself at me because you want to make me work for it."

She didn't have any reply for that. Her nipples were still standing at attention, though.

He smiled. He was pretty sure he had her hooked. "Don't worry, Cassidy. I'll make an exception for you. I *will* work for it. How about we start with dinner? I'll pick you up at seven."

She shook her head. "Thanks, but no thanks. I'm not interested."

Shane smirked and let his gaze travel to her breasts again. "The girls are betraying you, they're telling me otherwise. They're definitely interested."

She put her hands on her hips. "I said, no. Did you come in for something in particular? If not, then I'd like you to leave."

He smiled, hoping to win her over. "As a matter of fact, I came to ask how you work with local artists, whether you plan to put on shows, whether you'd be interested in working with a friend of mine. She's been working out of New York for a long time, but I'm hoping she's going to stay in the valley."

Cassidy shook her head in disgust. "You're coming on to me while trying to find work for your girlfriend? I feel sorry for her."

"No! I said my friend, not my girlfriend. I don't have one of those."

"I'm sure you have dozens of them. Sorry, but I'm not interested."

Shane realized he might be blowing an opportunity for Gina here. "Listen, I'm sorry, okay. I find you attractive, I'm the kind of guy who will give it a shot. You're not interested, you've made that clear, but please don't dismiss my friend because you think I'm an asshole."

That drew a laugh at least. "Okay, since you put it like that, here." She handed him a card. "Tell your *friend* to give me a call."

Shane grinned as he turned the card over and looked at the contact information, including cell phone number and email address.

Cassidy frowned at him. "That is not for your use. Do you understand me?"

"Sure." He met her gaze with a grin. "I'll pass it along. Thank you. It was good to meet you, Cassidy Lane. I'll be seeing you."

She shook her head at him. "Not if I see you first."

Shane laughed and let himself out. She was going to be a challenge, but then he hadn't had one of those for a while. He turned the card over in his hands again. He'd stop by the Delaney place and give it to Gina on his way home. Just as *he'd* made a mess of things with Cassidy back there, he was afraid that if *Mason* tried to help Gina get set up here, he'd mess up completely and she'd leave again. Gina had been his best friend when they were kids. When she and Mason had gotten together, it seemed the most natural thing in the world to Shane. Gina felt like family, she was part of the family. She and Mason were meant to be together, and Shane's world hadn't seemed right since they broke up. He was going to do everything he could to help get them back on track. He grinned as he made his way back to his truck—and if that meant having to deal with a hot gallery owner, then hell he'd do it—to help Mase and Gina, of course!

Chapter Ten

Gina stared out the window. She loved this view. How many times had she stared out of the window in her apartment in New York and looked at that brick wall she hated so much? How many times had she wished that she was sitting back here instead? Now that she was here and had the opportunity to stay here, she needed to pull herself together. The day she'd spent in the park with her camera had re-ignited her passion for the work she could do here. It was time to make a plan and get on with it.

She picked up her phone. It was time to talk to Ian and seek his input—both on what she should do about her upcoming show at the gallery and what she might be able to do here. She'd talked to a couple of old friends in California, two galleries in San Francisco were interested in helping her make a name out there. One was only interested in her previous work, but the other had loved the idea of putting on a Montana show.

She imagined Ian sitting in his office at the gallery as she listened to the phone ring. Would Liam be with him? She could picture the two of them, Ian pacing while Liam sat, feet on the desk, fingers steepled under his chin. She hoped Ian would be alone. She'd exchanged a few short texts with Liam, but he was holding to the idea that they would talk when she returned. He wasn't accepting that it was over between them, at all.

"Ian Rawlings."

"Hey." She had to smile at the sound of his voice.

"Gina! How are you? When are you coming back? You and Liam need to sort this out. Your show is coming up fast."

She sighed. "There's nothing to sort out. It's over, Ian. Why won't he accept that?"

Ian didn't speak for a few moments. Gina waited. He was deliberate and measured in everything he did. "I thought that might be the case. You really mean it, don't you?"

"Yes, I do. We're not right for each other. I finally get that. He's a good man. I hope he'll find someone he will be happy with, but that someone isn't me. We weren't very good at making each other happy and I think over time we would only make each other miserable. It's better that we face that now." She didn't like to say that she thought she already knew exactly who it was that would make Liam happy. She didn't know if Ian realized what was going on with Kaitlyn.

"I love you both, Gina. I hate to admit it, but I believe you're right. Unfortunately, Liam disagrees."

"I'm afraid it doesn't matter whether he agrees or not. It's over between us."

After another long silence, Ian spoke again. "So, what are your plans? What are you going to do? What about the show?"

"That's what I'm calling to ask you. I don't know if Liam will want to go ahead with the show once he finally gets it that we're done. I don't know if *you* will want to. As for my plans, I'm hoping to get your advice as to what I *should* do. I'd like to stay if I can find a way to make it out here, but I don't know if that's a pipe dream. I don't know if I can find a market, or if any of the galleries on either coast will touch me."

"Gina, you can make it wherever you want to be. Don't you doubt that for a moment. I will help you in any way I can, you know that."

Relief rushed through her. "Honestly, Ian, I didn't know that. I wasn't sure how you would feel, knowing that Liam and I are really done."

Ian laughed. "Gina, we've been friends for a long time. I won't lie, part of me is sad that the two of you aren't going to make it, but part of me knows it's for the best. I'm kind of relieved. I love you both, and much as I'd love to see you together, I think you're right. You would make each other miserable over time, and I'd hate that. I think we should go ahead with the show. It wouldn't make sense to cancel it. We've already built a lot of buzz about it. However clueless Liam may be about relationships, he's pretty astute about this business. He wouldn't want to cancel it either."

Gina could almost hear him thinking in the silence that followed. "But?" she asked.

He laughed. "But I think you need to be here for it. You're quite the celebrity these days and so many of those photographs have stories that need to be told. We both know that you're the one who needs to do the telling. So what do you say, will you come back for it?"

She nodded slowly. She'd known that if the show went ahead she would have to be there. "Of course I will."

"Don't worry, it'll be fine. Liam will be fine."

"I know." Gina did know. Once Liam finally got it in his head that it was over between them, he would be cold toward her, but polite. Excruciatingly polite, if she knew him.

She could hear Ian rifling through papers. Apparently he considered the topic of her show closed and was moving on to other business. "Okay, do you remember Alison Ford? She's in San Francisco these days and..."

Gina smiled. "Thanks, Ian. I already talked to her."

"Of course you did. And Jeannie Steele?"

"Her, too."

"See. You always come to me to help out, but you have everything covered yourself."

"I wish I did. Those two are about all I have, and Jeannie was only interested in the shows you and Liam already did. She was talking about simply recreating what we'd already done in New York."

"Don't worry about her. She's too conservative, only interested in emulating what already works. Oh..."

"What?"

"Sorry, I'm scrolling through my contacts. Did you ever meet Cassidy Lane?"

Gina racked her brain. "I don't think so. I feel as though I should know the name, but I can't place her."

"She's a painter, an absolute sweetheart, but a law unto herself. She took San Francisco by storm a couple of years back, then dropped off the face of the earth for a while. Next thing, she showed up down in Florida painting sunsets, oceans, and beaches. She licensed a lot of her work to one of those awful commercial operations that produce cheap canvasses for the masses. Everyone thought she'd sold out, but she was just bored. She made a shitload of money then disappeared again.

She's just reappeared on the radar and you'll never guess where she is."

"Where?"

"Right up the road from you, in Livingston."

"Oh wow!"

"That definitely could be a wow. I think the two of you will hit it off wonderfully. Both creatively and personally, you have a lot in common. You should call her. I'll email you all her contact info. Tell her I put you on to her and tell her when I come out there again to visit you, she owes me dinner."

Gina smiled. "You're going to come visit me?"

"Of course I am, you silly girl. For now though, I have to go. Let me know when you talk to Cassidy, I'll be very curious to hear what the two of you cook up together. I think you'll make a formidable team. Talk to you soon, okay?"

"Thanks, Ian. Bye."

As soon as she put her phone down it started to ring again. Mason!

"Hello?"

"Hey, G. How you doing?"

"I'm fine thanks." What did he want?

"I was, errr..."

She had to smile. He sounded hesitant, nervous even—very un-Mason-like.

"Well, I've been thinking. You're a single woman now. And you know I want you back. But it seems every time I see you, I grab you like a caveman."

She let out a little laugh. It was true, but she'd hardly tried to stop him whenever he'd done that.

"So, what do you think about going out to dinner with me? Like, a real date. Start out on the right foot, get back to where we were and go from there."

Gina's heart raced. Was she ready to start over with Mason? How could they go anywhere? Where they had gotten to was the place that broke her heart. But that was a long time ago. They were both different now, older—hopefully, wiser.

"What do you say, G?"

She smiled. "Okay. Where do you want to go?"

"How about the Valley Lodge?" She could hear the relief in his voice.

That made her smile. She knew it wasn't Mason's kind of place. It was an attempt to take her somewhere he considered *fancy*. She appreciated the thought, but if they were going to start over then she'd rather go back to their roots. "How about the Riverside instead?"

"You want to?"

She laughed. "I'd love to. When are we talking about?"

"Tonight? I'll come pick you up at six?"

"I could meet you there?" She'd prefer her dad didn't see Mason coming to pick her up. She didn't want him getting his hopes up before she knew if there was anything to even hope for.

"That wouldn't be a real date. I'll be by at six." He hung up before she could argue.

She sat there shaking her head. "Okay, Mason. See you at six," she said to herself.

~ ~ ~

Mason wrapped a towel around his waist and came out of the bathroom. It seemed he was a little overanxious. He was showered and shaved, and it was way too early. He almost bumped into Shane, who was stepping into the hallway at the same moment.

"Whoa. You smell good," Shane said with a grin. "Do I need to guess what you're doing tonight?"

"Nope. You already guessed. I called her up and I'm taking her out on a date."

"Awesome. Where are you guys going?"

"The Riverside." Mason's grin faded at Shane's response.

"Seriously, bro? You're taking her to that dive? Show a bit of class. She's been living in the big city for the last ten years. Why the hell would you want to take her there?"

"You love the Riverside."

"Sure I do, for a burger and a beer with the guys. Not for one of the most important dates of my life!"

"Don't worry. I was going to take her to the Valley Lodge. The Riverside was *her* suggestion, and I'm hoping that it means something. See, that was where we went on our very first real date."

Shane smiled. "Ah, sorry bro. I take it all back. Sentimentality and nostalgia trump class every time."

Mason punched his arm. "I have class, thank you very much."

"Yeah, right," said Shane with a laugh. "Cowboy class is what you have."

Mason nodded. It was true. He'd never had the need for any other kind. As he went into his room to get dressed, he couldn't help but wonder whether it would be enough for Gina now. As Shane had said, she'd been living in the big city for ten long years. What if all their fancy ways had come to be important to her? What if his cowboy ways weren't enough anymore?

He shrugged as he pulled on his jeans. If she'd changed *that* much, then she wasn't his Gina anymore and it wouldn't matter, would it?

It was a quarter till six when he pulled up out front. He wasn't surprised to see Al appear at the window and then come ambling out to greet him.

"Mason, good to see you, son. I think she's ready. Come on in and I'll give her a shout." The big grin on the old guy's face told Mason what he'd been hoping to hear. Al still wanted to see him end up with Gina, almost as much as *he* did.

He followed Al in through the back door to the kitchen and couldn't help smiling to himself at the memory of coming out here to see her last week. When he'd arrived, he'd only wanted to make her talk to him. When he'd seen her crouched down hiding it made him laugh. He'd worried that she might have become some fancy city girl over the last ten years, but seeing her squatting down in just a T-shirt, her bare ass sticking out, he'd known that she was still his Gina. He'd also known that she still turned him on as much as she ever had, more so, in fact. When she'd stood up to him, flushed and angry, her round breasts and curves that the T-shirt couldn't hide had made very clear to him that she was all woman, and still the only woman he wanted. He shifted in his pants, hoping to hide the evidence of what the memory of the kitchen table was doing to him.

When Al went out the door to shout for her, Mason shoved his hands in his pockets, regretting having thought that his tightest jeans were the way to go. Remembering the way she'd writhed underneath him, remembering how quickly *No, Mason, no!* had turned into *Yes, Mason, yes!* had him hard as a rock and wanting more, and these jeans left no room to hide that.

He smiled as Al came back in and spoke in a low voice. "I'm not going to say much, son. I don't think I need to, do I?"

Mason raised an eyebrow. He thought they were on the same page, but meeting Al's steely gaze, he had to wonder.

"I don't know what went wrong, but it's time the two of you made it right."

Mason let out the breath he didn't realize he'd been holding. "Yes, sir."

Al grinned. "That's all. I want my girl home, and I think you do, too."

"More than anything."

Al grinned. "Then don't fuck it up this time then, huh?"

Mason laughed. "No, sir." He wasn't about to say that he still had no idea how he'd fucked it up last time. He had the feeling Al already knew that and besides, anything he said would sound like an excuse. "I'm not letting her go again."

Al nodded as Gina appeared in the doorway. "Well, you kids have a good time. I'll see you tomorrow." He let himself out the back door without waiting for a reply.

Mason caught his breath. Damn, she was beautiful. She wasn't exactly dressed up, they were going to the Riverside after all, but she looked amazing. It seemed she'd decided that her tightest jeans were the way to go, too. The way they clung to her and emphasized her curves had him digging his hands deeper into his pockets. She wore a simple white top that clung to her breasts then flowed loose over her hips. All he could think about was sliding his hands underneath it, stroking their way up, and then filling them with her breasts. He swallowed, his throat was dry.

"Hi."

He met her gaze, her eyes were shining. She looked soft, maybe even a little scared? It seemed her time in the city had taken away some of her fire. *His* Gina had never been unsure of herself. It only made him love her more. "Hey, babe. Are you ready to go?"

She nodded.

He stepped toward her and held out his hand. She took hold of it and the smile she gave him melted his heart. She looked happy and nervous at the same time, but what made him smile the most was the love shining in her eyes. She hadn't been able to tell him that she didn't love him anymore and now, no matter what she might say, her eyes were telling him that she did. At that moment, he felt as though they were back on track. He loved her, she loved him. Nothing would be able to get in the way of that. Would it?

Chapter Eleven

Gina smiled when Mason came with her to the passenger side of his truck and opened the door for her. He was a gentleman in the true sense of the word, but he wasn't the kind to go in for gestures like this. At least, he hadn't been when she'd known him. She realized that there was so much of him she didn't know anymore. So much had happened in her own life in the last ten years, how could she think that nothing had happened in his? She didn't think he'd been in any long-term relationships, but why didn't she? Who would have told her if he had? Her dad certainly wouldn't, and come to think of it, neither would Shane. She climbed in and smiled through the window at him as he closed the door for her.

He came around and got in himself. "What's up, G? You're looking at me like you don't know me."

There he went, reading her thoughts again. "That's what I was thinking. I *don't* know you. I know who you were, but not who you have been these last ten years, not who you've become."

He tipped his hat back and winked at her, making her smile. "You know me. You know me better than anyone else ever has or ever will."

She shook her head. "The Mason I knew would never have suggested going to the Lodge for dinner, and he definitely wouldn't have opened the door for me."

He laughed. "I *am* the Mason you knew. You just never saw me nervous about taking you out before."

"You were nervous?"

"*I am* nervous."

She reached over and put a hand on his arm. It seemed the years had changed him a little. The Mason of old would never have admitted vulnerability of any kind. She liked it. It gave her hope that they could maybe share something very real now—now that they'd both done some growing up. She didn't want a tough as nails, ride-to-the-rescue infallible hero anymore. She wanted a real man, a man who could admit fear and pain and be a partner as much as a protector. She squeezed his arm. "Then I guess we're in this together."

He smiled at her, the creases around his eyes reminding her how much older he really was. "That's where I want to be, babe."

When he pulled up in the parking lot at the Riverside, she smiled to herself when he didn't come to open her door. He'd made his gesture, but it wasn't in his nature, and she wouldn't want it to be. She slid down and came around to join him.

"What do you think?" he asked. "Do you want to sit out on the deck?"

She smiled. "I do."

They'd come here on their very first real date. It was strange to call it that, strange because it hadn't happened until after the first time he'd made love to her. The night after he'd taken her virginity, he'd brought her here to make it official that they were dating. It might seem an odd way to go about things, but it was the way it had worked out for them. As far as Gina was concerned it was perfect, it was as it should be. It was their story, their history. That night had been busy, they hadn't been able to get a table inside and even though it was still chilly out on the deck, they'd sat outside and had dinner together as a couple for the first time.

It wasn't quite so cold tonight, but there were only a few hardy souls sitting out. She could see through the doors that most folks had opted to eat inside where it was warm.

Mason grinned at her. "I do, too. I'm going to run back to the truck. I put a couple of jackets in there, just in case."

Gina admired his long easy stride as he went back to the truck and returned moments later. She smiled as he held out a shearling-lined jean jacket and helped her into it. She snuggled inside it and breathed in the scent of him. He grinned at her and pulled on his own jacket, before wrapping his arms around her. "I'll keep you warm."

The feel of him standing so close, wrapped around her the way he used to, took her beyond warm—all the way to hot and yearning for him. She had no doubts that anything had changed between them there. Every time she was close to him, she wanted him. She knew he wanted her too, judging by the way he kept shifting around in those jeans!

He led her to a table over at the edge of the deck and sat down with a grin. She grinned back. He remembered which table they'd sat at all those years ago. She looked out at the river and its backdrop of snow-capped mountains then back at Mason. "It's so beautiful."

"Not as beautiful as you are."

"Do you still think so?" She wasn't fishing for compliments, she was genuinely curious.

He reached across the table and took her hand. "To me, you were always the most beautiful girl in the world. You know that. What I didn't expect is how much more beautiful you are now that you're older. I mean you're even more beautiful as a grown woman than you were as a girl." He hesitated. "I hope that came out right?"

She smiled and nodded. "Don't worry. It did. I understand exactly what you mean because that's how I feel about you, too. You were gorgeous back then." She had to smile at the way he grinned at that.

"Gorgeous?" he raised his eyebrows.

"Yes, gorgeous, but you were still a boy in some respects." She laughed. "A young buck, if you will. Now you're all grown up. Seasoned, weathered...I don't know. Just...a real man." She met his gaze. "And I find you even more attractive than I did back then, even though I wouldn't have believed that was possible."

He grinned. "Then you do know exactly what I meant, although you put it better than I did." He squeezed her hand. "You always said you needed a real man. Now you've got one, do you want to keep him?"

She drew in a sharp breath. Hell yeah, she wanted to keep him! But she was older and wiser. Much as she would love to step straight back into the fairytale, she was more cautious now. He'd broken her heart and shattered her world once. She wasn't in a hurry to jump straight into letting him do it again.

He frowned. "You don't want me?"

"I do want you, Mase. But I need to take it slowly. We're two very different people than we were back then, we need to get to know each other all over again. Get to know who we are now and whether we'll work as well as we used to." She didn't mention anything about how he'd hurt her before, but she didn't need to.

He was still frowning at her, but the server came out to take their order. She hoped that she could move the conversation on, but as soon as the girl had left, he said, "And you also need to tell me about what went wrong before, G. I need to understand what happened. I still don't know how I hurt you." He took a deep breath. "But, I do know how you hurt me."

That put a dagger through her heart. She would never, ever willingly hurt him. She was surprised that he admitted that she had. He'd moved on after she left, hadn't he? She hadn't come back because he hadn't really loved her or wanted her forever like he said. She'd just been one of a long line, the one after Marie, and the one before April. Even thinking of the name *April* sent a shudder through her.

His eyes filled with concern. "Can we talk about it?"

"Not tonight. I want to enjoy this evening. Laugh, have fun. Is that okay with you?" Her eyes pleaded with him. She wasn't ready yet to rake through all the old hurt. She wanted to spend some time with him. Have some fun with him and get to know the man he had become. She wasn't at all sure how long that would last once they went back and talked about what had happened. She wanted to feel a little stronger before they went there. After all, how could she hold against him what the boy he had been had done.

He nodded slowly. "Okay, but we do need to talk about it soon. I need to know what happened. I've never known and I've torn myself apart over the years, wondering what went wrong."

She squeezed his hand, why did she feel guilty? He hadn't wanted her, so she'd made it easy for him. The pain in his eyes made her wonder. "We will, Mase. Let's enjoy tonight though, please?"

Mason smiled. She could see he was making a conscious effort to let it go—for now. "How could I say no to that? I've waited all these years and you're asking me to enjoy a night with you." He winked and gave her the smile that made her heart race. "I hope you mean the whole night."

If her heart was already racing, it thundered in her chest at his words. Was she ready to go there? Who was she kidding? She'd been thinking about it since he'd called to ask her to dinner. When she'd suggested they come here, to the place where they'd had their first date, she'd also been thinking about what had happened afterward. He'd driven her down by the river and they'd climbed into the bed of his truck to watch the stars. He'd made love to her out there, in a pile of blankets under the big sky. They'd fallen asleep and spent the whole night in each other's arms.

His gaze told her he wanted to recreate that part of their first date, too. She smiled. "We'll see."

He grinned back at her.

She had to laugh. "What does that look mean?"

"It means you didn't say, *hell no!* And *that* means it's all down to me and my powers of persuasion. So, I'm a happy man."

"It seems you have a lot of faith in your powers of persuasion, cowboy."

He nodded and reached across to touch her cheek. "I sure do, babe. And your memory mustn't be too good if you doubt them."

The shudder that ran through her this time was one of desire. She remembered only too well how persuasive he could be—and how powerless she was to resist him when he wanted her.

If he kept looking into her eyes the way he was, she might have to drag him back to his truck right now!

The server came back with their food and shattered the moment. Once she'd left, Mason grinned at Gina again. "Don't worry. We can enjoy dinner first. I haven't had one of these burgers in years."

She nodded. She wasn't sure she could enjoy hers. Her whole body was humming with anticipation of what would come afterward.

~ ~ ~

Mason watched Gina closely as she took a sip of her beer and stared out at the river. It might be chilly, but it was a beautiful blue sky evening. He let his mind drift back to the first time he'd taken her. She'd been persistent in the years that followed her first declaration that she loved him. At fourteen, she'd been a cute kid to him, but nothing more than that. He'd gone off to college, but each summer when he came home, she was around. She and Shane did everything together in those days. Riding, roping, learning to drive and swimming down in the creek. The summer she was sixteen he'd been sorely tempted to give in to her when she came to him one afternoon. She had two horses saddled and ready to go. She was wearing the shortest shorts and a bikini top that barely contained her by then full breasts. She'd shown him another packet of condoms and said that it was time. That she understood why he wouldn't when she was younger, but now she was grown up and she still loved him, still wanted him to be her first. If Shane hadn't come barreling into the yard yelling about coyotes down in the bottom pasture, Mason probably would have gone with her.

She smiled at him, bringing him back to the present. "This has been wonderful, Mase. Thank you."

He nodded, it had been a wonderful dinner. They'd talked and laughed. They were still so comfortable with each other. He'd never felt anything close to this with another woman. Never wanted to.

"What are you thinking?" she asked.

His reminiscing about their past had him thinking that it was time to create some new memories. He shifted in his seat and told her the truth. "I'm thinking I'd like to get out of here, take a drive down by the river." He held her gaze. She knew what he meant.

Her cheeks flushed slightly and she nodded but didn't speak. Her eyes told him, she wanted him. That was all he needed to know. He called for the check.

He turned the truck off the main road and headed down to the old fishing access at The Rocks. He stole a glance at her, she looked nervous.

"Are you sure about this, G?"

She nodded rapidly. "I am. Don't you dare back out on me now."

He had to laugh. "I don't think I could if I tried."

"Good. Let's just hope there's no one down there."

"We'll be fine. No one ever comes down here anymore." He could feel her eyes boring into him. "What?"

"Do you come down here a lot, then?"

Ah. She must think he still brought women here. He shook his head. "Not in the way you think, no."

"It's none of my business. I'm sorry. I have no right to ask about what you do with your women. You brought me here, why wouldn't you bring all the others, too? It's a good spot for it."

That made him see red. "Damned straight you have no right to ask! If it were up to me, there would never have been another woman in my life after we got together. But *you* ended it. What did you think, that after you left I'd become a monk? Well, let me set you straight on one thing. I do still come down here, always have done over the years. I come to remember what we had. I come when I miss you so badly it hurts. I sit out in the bed of my truck and watch the stars like we did that night. So don't you go thinking this is just some place to bring a girl and get laid. This is a special place. It's *our* place."

He pulled the truck down on the riverbank and turned to glare at her. She looked shocked.

"I'm sorry, Mase. I didn't know. I thought after I left, you just moved on to the next one and never gave me another thought."

He slammed his fist on the dash. "How the fuck could you ever think that? I wanted to marry you, I thought we were forever!"

She shook her head. "I'm sorry." She leaned across and planted a kiss on his cheek.

He held her face between his hands and looked into her eyes. "I love you, Gina. I always have, I always will. Why won't you see that?"

Her face looked pained for a moment, then she smiled. "I'm starting to. But you were the one who taught me that it's not words that matter, it's actions." She smiled and slipped her hand inside his shirt to stroke his chest. His cock jumped to attention, throbbing as it pressed uncomfortably under his zipper. "What was that saying you taught me?" she asked.

He knew what she meant, it was something he believed and had told her before she went off to college. He'd thought then that she was too trusting and had hated the thought of some frat boy sweet talking his way into her panties while she was gone. "Don't pay too much attention to what people say. What they *say* tells you what they want you to believe. What they *do* tells you what you need to know."

She smiled and started to tug at his buckle. "I need to know that you still love me, Mase. But I need you to show me. Show me like you did the first time we came here."

He covered her hand with his own. He needed to pull himself together or it would all be over too soon. The way she was touching him through his jeans made him want to go hard and fast, what she was asking for was slow and tender.

"Wait here a minute. I'll get the back set up."

She nodded and watched him get out and go around to let the tailgate down. He pulled a bunch of blankets and pillows out of the box. She didn't need to know that he'd washed and dried them all this afternoon and stored them in the box, just in case. He pulled out a double foam sleeping pad and unrolled that. She didn't need to know how new that was either—he'd made sure to pull the tags off it before he went to pick her up. When he had a comfortable bed set up, he beckoned to her through the cab window. This was it. He was finally going to make love to her again. There was no denying the desire on her face when she came around back to join him. He closed his hands around her waist and lifted her up to sit on the tailgate. He stood between her legs and tipped her chin up so she was looking into his eyes. He didn't have any words left. She was right, it was actions that mattered. He closed his arms around her, lowering his lips to hers.

Chapter Twelve

Gina looped her arms up around Mason's neck and pulled his head down. She'd gotten all jealous back there for a moment. Jealous that he might have been bringing other women down here, down to their special place. His response had shocked her and made her feel bad. This place was still as special to him as it was to her. As his lips came down on hers they told her how special she was, too. She opened up to him as he tilted her head back, giving himself better access to plunder her mouth. His tongue explored, mating with her own. His free hand closed around her breast making her moan. He plucked at her nipple. The feel of his hard fingers pressing through her clothes made her wet for him. She tried to break away, wanting to crawl up into the bed of the truck and get under the blankets with him. He crushed her to his chest, not allowing her to move away. She writhed against him, suddenly fully aware of how much he liked to take charge of their lovemaking—and how much she enjoyed the way he did.

She made a half-hearted attempt to struggle away from him. She wasn't worried about lying down in the bed now, all she wanted was to provoke him into taking charge. It worked. He tangled his hand in a fistful of hair and squeezed her nipple hard, making her gasp. His other hand made short work of her button and zipper and found its way inside her jeans. He trailed his tongue down over her neck as he pushed the scrap of silk that was her panties to the side and his fingers found her heat. She put both hands out behind her and braced herself against the sensations he was filling her with. She moaned as he thrust his tongue deep while his roughened fingertips traced her opening. He was tormenting her, his fingers traveling slowly up and down. When they came back up, he squeezed her clit hard, making her yelp as she felt herself get wetter. He squeezed again, setting up a pulsing rhythm, squeezing then releasing, giving her a moment to recover before doing it again, sending currents of raw desire racing through her. She was panting, and he was taking her to the edge far too quickly. She brought her hands up and pushed against his chest in an attempt to get a reprieve.

He lifted his head and smiled down at her. "You're not trying to stop me are you?" He squeezed again as he spoke.

She gasped in a breath of air. "I want you, Mase." She cupped her hand over his erection. Even through his jeans, she could feel how hot and hard he was. "I want all of you. I want to be naked with you, underneath you. Feel you inside me."

His eyes glazed as she spoke. "I want you to come for me."

"I want you to come with me."

"Oh, I will, babe. But I've waited so long for this, I'm not sure how long I can last." He moved his hand down again, sliding a fingertip inside. "You want me inside you?" He thrust two fingers deep, making her clench around them.

She closed her fingers around his throbbing shaft. "I want this!"

"You'll get it, but first..." He was moving his fingers in and out, slowly at first. He widened his stance, spreading her legs as he pressed his palm against her clit. "First, you're going to come for me like this."

She couldn't argue. She was going to come and come hard. The pressure was building low in her belly as he thrust his fingers deeper and harder. He moved his palm, making her already swollen clit tingle under the pressure. He was taking her there, and there was nothing she could do to stop it. She no longer wanted to. She moved her hips in time with his thrusting fingers, pushing herself harder against his hand. When his thumb came up to circle her nub, she lost it. The pressure exploded and sent shock waves tearing through her whole body. He didn't let up, his fingers moved in and out of her frantically. She tightened around them over and over again as the pleasure crashed through her. "Mason!" She gasped his name, it had to be his name. No man had ever made her feel the way he did. Here she was panting and screaming her way through an amazing orgasm, and he was only using his hand. When she finally lay still, he pulled her boots off before pushing her jeans down over her hips and off. He threw them into the back.

"Weren't you saying something about getting naked and underneath me?" he asked with a satisfied smile.

She nodded and crawled up into the bed and under the blankets. She hadn't had an orgasm as good as that in years, and she knew he was only just getting warmed up. She hated to think about it now, but she realized that after her years with Liam, she'd forgotten what it was like to be with a man who took pleasure in her pleasure. Liam would roll off her and be snoring within seconds after sex, not knowing or caring whether she had gotten there. Mason, she knew, would stay awake all night to make sure he took her there—again and again and again!

He kicked his own boots off and hopped up on the tailgate to get rid of his jeans. With a wicked grin, he stuck his head under the bottom of the blankets and started to crawl up over her to join her. He led the way with his hands, massaging his way up her legs. His hot mouth followed, nibbling his way up her inner thigh, making her writhe in an attempt to get away while she recovered. She should have known better. His hands closed around her hips and pinned her down as he used his broad shoulders to spread her legs wider. Her hands came down to tangle in his hair when he blew into her heat. He used both hands to hold her wide open and flicked her clit with his tongue. She moaned as his lips closed around it and he began to suck. He was taking her straight back to the edge, but she didn't want to go over it again until he went with her. He seemed to understand that and nibbled his way up over her belly. His hands slid up inside her top and roughly pulled her bra down to give himself access to her nipples. Her hips bucked wildly underneath him as he kneaded and squeezed, then nipped and sucked.

He chuckled as she wrestled with his shirt, trying to get him out of it. He let her take it off him and soon got rid of her top and bra. When all that remained between them were his boxers and her panties, he knelt above her and stared down at her. His eyes filled with desire as he filled his hands with her plump breasts. "You have no idea how many times I've imagined this, G. How many nights I lay in bed wishing I could love you just one more time."

Her eyes filled with tears as she smiled up at him. "I may have some idea, Mase. I've done the same thing. I fall asleep aching for you. Wake up from dreaming about you."

He cocked his head to one side. "Really?"

She nodded as she pushed his boxers down. "Yes, really. And I don't want to wait another moment." She closed her hand around him and watched him close his eyes as he lowered his weight onto her. In a moment, his hand was between them, pushing her panties to the side, opening her up with his fingers as his hot, hard head pushed impatiently at her.

She couldn't wait any longer, she needed him to be inside her. She closed her hands around his ass and urged him on, lifting her hips to him. "Love me, Mason. Please!"

Her words were his command. He thrust his hips and buried himself to the hilt. She screamed as he filled her. He felt so good, so right. He was so damned hard. She'd thought she'd never forgotten the way he felt, but she hadn't remembered just how good it was. For a moment, they lay still, connected in the most intimate way, just as they had the very first time he'd made love to her. He was so big, she could feel herself stretching to accommodate him. She could feel him throb, pulsating inside her. It was like trying to ride a wild stallion she knew would break loose at any moment.

He lifted his head and looked down at her as he began to slowly move his hips. She clasped her arms and legs around his back, knowing that he was about to take her on the ride of her life. He slid one arm underneath her, curling it around her waist, lifting her hips to receive his thrusts, thrusts that were getting deeper, wilder each time. He braced his other hand above her head and smiled down at her. "I love you, Gina."

"I love you, Mason."

He was pounding into her, the slow and tender replaced by a desperate, almost animal need that possessed them both. She clawed at his back as his hips pistoned up and down, his cock stretching and filling her with every thrust. Gina clung to him, powerless to do anything but surrender as he claimed her body as his own. Each time he buried himself deeper inside her, he was taking her back, possessing her. Her body was his, *she* was his, he was owning her, leaving no doubt about where she belonged or who she belonged to. He was carrying her away. She was flying again, soaring on the sensations he was filling her with. Just when she was about to let go, she felt him tense. His release triggered and amplified her own orgasm, as he gasped her name and spilled his need deep inside her. Waves of pleasure crashed through her as she clenched around him, squeezing him, milking him as he pumped into her.

They lay there panting for a long time. He kept his arm wrapped around her, underneath her, holding her close to his chest. She kept her arms wrapped around his back, one hand stroking his hair as he recovered. He was still buried deep and she didn't want to let him go. He covered her face with little butterfly kisses, making her laugh. She used to do that to him—until he told her how annoying it was and then proved it by doing it to her. She swiped at him. "Quit it, would you!"

He laughed. "You once told me that you only did that as a way to show me how much you loved me. You said there weren't enough words to tell me, but maybe a million of those little kisses would do it."

"I was a dumb kid when I said that. You're a grown man and you should know better."

He nodded. "I do know better. I know there are no words, no gestures that will ever be able to tell you just how much I love you. I know that my love for you is as vast as the big sky. So maybe if we lie here a while and just look at it and watch the stars, you might get some idea of how much I love you."

Gina felt her eyes fill with tears. He was a romantic in his own way. And his way meant more to her than any more conventional gestures ever would. She hugged him tight and smiled at him. "I love you, Mason. All these years, I have always loved you, much more than you know."

He frowned as he rolled off her. "I hope someday you'll try to let me know just how much you loved me while you wouldn't even speak to me. It's difficult for me to believe."

She nodded. How could she explain to him all the pain he'd caused her? How much he'd put her through when he told Guy that night just how little she meant to him. She wasn't going to think about that tonight. The past and all its hurt was behind them. This was the present. She was back here, back in his arms. All she could do was make the most of it. Make a new start and hopefully build something stronger as adults than they'd been able to when they were kids.

~ ~ ~

Mason rolled up one of the blankets as a pillow and leaned back against it. He held his arm out and Gina came to snuggle against him, resting her head on his chest just as she always had. He felt as though they were caught in some kind of weird time warp. Part of him felt as if they'd never been apart, that they'd somehow erased the last ten years and jumped back to the first night they'd come and made love down here. Part of him felt uneasy. Making love to Gina had been as good as he'd hoped, better than he remembered. That made him aware of the fact that they were different people now than they had been back then. It made him realize that they couldn't just pick up where they'd left off. Especially since he still didn't know why it had ended. The woman lying in his arms was still his

Gina, but she was also a woman he didn't know, with a life and ten years of history that he knew nothing about. He hugged her to him as he lay his head back and stared up at the stars.

"What is it, Mase?"

"I guess I'm just realizing how different it is now."

She turned to look up at him, her eyes filled with concern. "It wasn't good for you?"

He had to smile. "It wasn't good, it was great! You were great, we are great together. But we're different. I think I'm just giving myself a reality check. I've been living with the hope and the dream that I'd get you back." He held her gaze. "I hope I am getting you back?"

She nodded.

"But we're not going to get the old us back, are we? We'll get each other and whatever we can create as the people we are now."

She nodded again. He waited for her to speak, knowing she was trying to find the right words. "I know what you mean, but don't you think that's a good thing?"

He was relieved. "I do, it's just a bit of a surprise because I never understood that before."

She nestled against him. "I didn't either. I think what we need to do is think of this as a new relationship. Instead of trying to recreate what we were, what we had, we need to just start fresh like any other couple would. We just have a bit of an advantage because we have more background knowledge than most people do when they meet someone."

Mason thought about that for a while. Then he laughed.

"What?" she asked.

He planted a kiss on her lips. "Well, if we're just starting out here, then I learned something about you tonight that I didn't expect."

"And what's that?"

"I wouldn't have guessed you'd be the kind of girl to sleep with a guy on a first date."

She laughed with him. "I am not! It takes a lot to get this girl into bed."

He rolled over and pinned her underneath him, trapping her hands above her head. "Unless it's the bed of my truck. It didn't take me much."

She struggled underneath him, turning him on with the way her warm, soft body felt moving against his own. Her eyes were shining as he put his knee between her thighs. Trapping both her wrists in one of his hands he slid the other down between her legs. "And I don't think it'll take me much to get some more of this either."

She moaned as he stroked her. The sound of it, so low and full of need had him hard again. He'd been playing at first, but he needed to be inside her again. He smiled as her hips started to move in time with his hand, she wanted him all right.

It seemed she still wanted to play, too. She managed to slip her wrists from his grasp and rolled over. He grinned as she tried to crawl away from him. He caught a fistful of her hair and slid his arm under her. "Where do you think you're going, babe?"

She gasped as he pulled her hair, he knew she loved it. She pulled herself up onto her hands and knees and kept trying to get away. The sight of her gorgeous round ass wiggling in front of him had him scrambling up to his own knees behind her.

He grasped her hip and pulled her back against him. "Are you going to lie down and let me love you again?"

He grinned when she shook her head. She loved it when he took her like this—and so did he. This had been one of his favorite fantasies for the last ten years and here it was coming true. He slid his hand between her legs and guided himself to her opening. She was hot and wet and panting for him, he pushed his way just inside then tormented them both as he rested there while he teased her clit between his fingers. He knew he wouldn't last long like this, he wanted her on the edge by the time he buried himself in her.

She was gasping and moaning as he worked her. He bent down and filled his hand with her breast. Nibbling her neck, he took his time to work her into a frenzy, squeezing first her nipple then her clit, harder and harder. She was soaking for him, wriggling around trying to thrust her hips back to take his cock deep. He was enjoying making her desperate. It was killing him too, but hearing her beg would be worth it.

"Please, Mason!"

"What do you want, babe?"

She pushed back against him. "I want you to take me. Take me now."

"Take you where?" He couldn't help grinning when he heard her desperate sob.

"I need you inside me. I need to feel you. I need you to..."

He couldn't make either of them wait any longer. He took a fistful of hair and a handful of ass and thrust deep. "Oh, God, Mason! Yes!"

He set up a pounding rhythm burying himself deep in her wetness. She felt so damned good! "Like this, baby?"

"Yes. Yes. Yes!"

She tightened around him, shuddering and gasping his name. He let himself go and came hard, thrusting and straining to give her all he had and all he was. Every nerve ending in his body felt like a firework exploding. He saw stars as she carried him away, her inner muscles milking him until he collapsed, his shaking legs unable to support him any longer.

He rolled onto his back and pulled her to him. "How the hell have I lived without you all this time?"

Her answer shocked him in the best possible way. "I don't know, but I don't want to survive without you anymore."

Chapter Thirteen

Gina shivered. Damn, she was cold. She reached out to pull the blankets closer around her. Her hand touched a hard, warm chest and it all came flooding back. She opened her eyes and saw Mason smiling back at her.

"Good morning. Looks like we recreated our first date to the letter." He put his arm around her and pecked her lips. "You fell asleep on me and I didn't want to wake you. I hope that was okay."

Gina's mind raced. Was it okay? What would her dad say?

Mason frowned. "You don't regret it?"

"No! It's not that, it's just that..."

"Just what?" She wasn't sure if he looked hurt or angry.

"Just nothing. I'm not even awake yet and I'm surprised that's all."

"Sorry, babe." He smiled, and it melted her heart. He'd never been one to stay angry for long. He reached for his hat and placed it on top of her head with a grin. "Want to go cowgirl before we get up?"

She was tempted, but she shook her head. She'd been planning to head up to town this morning, see if she could stop in and catch Cassidy Lane at her gallery.

Mason pouted and pulled her hips against his. He was hopeful,
but it seemed he wasn't fully awake yet either. "You don't want
me?"

"I do want you, just not right now. I have a full day I need to
get on with, and I'm pretty sure you do, too. I doubt the
horses have learned to take care of themselves, and it's not like
you to not be out there by eight-thirty."

His eyes widened. "Eight-thirty?"

She checked her watch and nodded. "Eight-thirty-five now."

"Shit! We'd better get going then."

She laughed. "Yes, we had." She sat up and started to pull her
clothes on.

When she was dressed, he lifted her down and wrapped his
arms around her. "Thank you for a wonderful first date, Miss
Gina. Can I see you again soon?"

She smiled up at him. "Why yes, you can, Mr. Remington. I'd
like that."

He turned around and sat back down on the tailgate, lifting her
with him so she sat straddling his lap. He was definitely more
awake now. The feel of his hard-on pressing between her legs
made her question her hurry to get started with the day.

He smiled a knowing smile. "So how long do you think you
can wait before I give my cowgirl a ride?"

She made a face at him, but couldn't resist gyrating her hips,
pressing herself down onto him. "Not too long."

He grasped her waist and thrust hard, then let her go. "Me
neither. Tonight?"

She nodded, disappointed now that he wasn't saying right now.
"Tonight then." As she said it, she realized he'd deliberately
taken her from being in a panic to leave to wishing they could
stay for more.

He smiled, pleased with himself and not worried that she'd seen through him. "Good, come on then. Let's get you home."

As they pulled into the long driveway back to the ranch, she had to wonder about her dad. "Did he say anything to you last night?" she asked Mason.

From the way he shrugged, she knew he had.

"What?"

"Sorry, G, but that was between him and me, man to man. You know?"

She nodded slowly. She did know and she didn't like it. That was one aspect of living out here that she hadn't missed. There was a gender gap here. The men folk were strong and protective of their women—even when their women didn't want or need protecting.

"He just loves you and wants to see you happy."

"Yeah, and he thinks staying here and being with you is what's going to make me happy."

Mason brought the truck to a stop in front of the house. "And you don't?"

"I don't know yet." She couldn't lie to him. She did want to be with him. She did still love him. But there were the lingering details of a past that needed addressing. There were also the details of a future that for her, in terms of career, was still very uncertain. She put her hand on his thigh. "I would love to be with you, Mase. But we have a lot to work through first, and I have to figure out how I'm going to make a living, no matter what else I do."

He nodded. "And are you making any progress with that? Shane said he talked to the owner of the new gallery up in town and she said you should give her a call."

"Apparently he stopped by to talk to me about that the other day, but I missed him. Did he tell you a name?" She was curious about another possible lead and curious what Shane's connection might be.

Mason frowned while he thought about it. "Hmm. Cassidy maybe?"

Gina grinned, pleased to have two introductions—Shane as well as Ian. She'd made a few calls after talking to Ian. Everyone she'd spoken to thought very highly of Cassidy and also thought that Gina would get along famously with her. She was looking forward to meeting the woman if nothing else. "Great, I'm headed up to see her today." She went to open the door.

"So, what time can I come pick you up?" asked Mason.

"Say six again? I've got a busy day lined up and I want to fix Dad some dinner before I go out. Where are we going anyway?"

He grinned. "Riding."

She laughed and jumped down from the cab. "See you later then."

~ ~ ~

Mason looked up when he heard footsteps in the barn. He wasn't expecting anyone out here this morning. His mom and dad had gone off to Bozeman to buy decorations for her birthday party this weekend. Chance was gone getting the cows moved up to summer pasture. Shane was busy with his guests. So who was wandering around in the barn? Mason kept an office out here in a stall he'd converted for the purpose. He didn't like to be bothered with people at the best of times. Whenever he had paperwork to do, he preferred to do it out here, surrounded by the familiar sounds and smells of his horses. He went to look out the window and cursed under his breath when he saw the man wandering around checking in the stalls, no doubt looking for him. He needed to keep his calm and run the asshole off.

He stepped out into the breezeway. "What do you want, Preston?"

The man swung around and sneered at him. "Thought I'd come by and let you know I'm planning on buying some property."

Mason scowled. What the fuck did it matter to him? He didn't want to give Guy Preston the satisfaction of showing any curiosity at all so he said nothing. Just stared and waited. He knew Guy wouldn't be able to resist bragging about whatever shit scheme he was up to now.

"Yeah. A nice little ranch, just off of East River. The house isn't much, but there's some good grazing and I can probably get the cattle thrown in."

He must mean the Delaney ranch.

Guy seemed a little frustrated that Mason wasn't showing any interest. "I hear old man Delaney doesn't want to leave, but Gina's moving him to New York. Did you know she's back in town? Maybe I'll give her a better price if she'll let me fuck her first. What do you think, Mase? Do you think little Gina will spread her legs for me to help daddy out?"

Mason took two steps toward him then stopped. He could not, would not, rise to this bastard's bait. All he wanted to do was beat the living crap out of him, but he'd already learned the hard way that was only a temporary solution that brought even worse consequences. The one thing he'd vowed he would never do was let Guy know just how much Gina meant to him. If Guy understood that, he would stop at nothing to destroy what they had. Over the years, he'd gone after everything he knew Mason cared about. All their lives, since a bust-up in grade school, Guy had made it his business to outdo Mason, to take away or damage anything that mattered to him. From bicycles and girlfriends in high school to cars, horses, and land later in life, Guy went after what Mason had or wanted. The only thing Mason had managed to keep safe was Gina. No way was he going to let that change now. He shrugged. "You'd have to ask her. She might. She's been away to the city a long time. I hear city girls aren't too picky. She might sleep with your ugly ass if she makes some money on the deal. Just don't screw Al over, or I *will* come after you, you hear me?"

Guy looked puzzled at his response. Which told Mason that he must have some inkling about him and Gina. He'd been hoping that his well-known friendship with Al was the target of this attack. Unfortunately, it seemed he was honing in on him and Gina, and that was something Mason was not going to allow him to fuck with. Guy had tried once before when Gina was still away at college. Guy had been accepted to two graduate schools. One in Portland where Gina was studying and one in Seattle where April Runyan went to school. Mason and April had dated in high school. When Mason found out Guy had been asking how serious things were between him and Gina, he'd known immediately that if he went to Portland he'd make a move on Gina and steal her away, or at least turn her against Mason somehow. That wasn't a risk Mason had been willing to take. He felt guilty about it, but he'd deflected Guy's attention away from Gina, by focusing it on April. He'd engineered a conversation with Guy where he *just let it slip out* that he was thinking about ending it with Gina. He'd said she'd been fun for a while, but that he wanted to get back with April. That he'd missed her since they broke up, and he was hoping that they might have a future together.

Guy had fallen for it. He'd gone to Seattle and made a move on April. What Mason felt bad about was that she'd fallen for it. She'd married him. Mason couldn't help but feel responsible for the miserable life that April had led since then. She had a nine-year-old son, and Mason was fairly sure that he was the reason she didn't pack up and run. Mason knew from experience that Guy was a vindictive bastard. He hated to think what kind of threats he used to make April stay.

Mason wasn't sure how to play this.

"You're not after a shot with her yourself?" Guy asked.

Mason laughed. "Me? I get all the ass I want at Chico on the weekends. Why would I complicate my life trying to do some girl I dated years ago?" He hoped he sounded convincing. What he really wanted to do was pound his fist into Guy's face and tell him exactly what he'd do to him if he went within a hundred yards of Gina. But that would give him all the ammunition he needed, and Mason had lost too much to the man over the years to dare risking the woman who meant more than anything in the world to him.

Guy shrugged and redirected his attention. "Maybe I'll see if she wants to get it on. Either way, I'm buying the place."

Mason had to hope that Gina could afford not to sell. He shook his head. "What about your *wife?*"

Guy grinned at that. The stupid bastard still believed that he'd stolen April away. Mason wasn't about to disabuse him of that illusion either. "She's exactly that, Remington. *My* wife. *You* can't go anywhere near her, and *I* can fuck whoever the hell I like."

Mason shook his head in disgust. "Yeah, you're a real winner, aren't you?"

"I am, and I guess that makes you a loser, huh?" Guy laughed and turned on his heel.

Mason wanted nothing more than to go after him and teach him what it felt like to be a loser. He made himself stand still. His fists were balled at his sides, the pulse in his temple was pounding, but he let Guy walk away.

He needed to talk to Gina and her dad and figure out what the deal was. He'd simply assumed that since Gina wasn't getting married and hopefully wasn't going back to New York, there'd be no need for them to sell the ranch. What he didn't know was whether they would be able to afford to keep it.

~ ~ ~

It was late afternoon by the time Gina pushed her way inside the Moonstone Gallery. She'd intended to get up here this morning, but she'd gotten busy with other errands and the day had gotten away from her. As soon as she was through the door, she stopped to look around. She immediately fell in love with several of the paintings hanging on the back wall. Oceanscapes, not something that would normally even catch her eye. But the way the artist captured light and movement was totally captivating. It drew you right into the canvas. As she made her way toward the office at the back, she admired the way the works were displayed. It seemed Cassidy had a similar feel for contrast to Gina's own. Perhaps more in color than in content, but the whole atmosphere of the place made Gina feel at home, at ease.

"Hi, can I help you?"

Gina smiled. As soon as she saw Cassidy, she understood Shane's involvement. With an incredibly pretty face, long, honey-blonde hair, and long tanned legs displayed between a short denim skirt and tall cowboy boots, Cassidy was the kind of woman Shane would be falling all over, trying to get her into bed. Gina decided to lead with Shane's introduction to see if Cassidy might give anything away about the two of them.

"Hi. I hope so. A friend of mine, Shane Remington, gave me your card and said he'd asked you about me stopping for a chat."

From the look on Cassidy's face, Gina gathered that Shane may not have made the best impression. "Are you the girlfriend?" she asked.

Gina laughed. "I most certainly am not. He's a dear, old friend of mine. We grew up together. And I know him well enough to know that whatever he did or said, probably needs an apology. So I'll apologize on his behalf. He's a bit full of himself, but he's a sweetheart when you get to know him."

Cassidy pursed her lips. "He's certainly full of himself, I'll give you that." She shook her head as if remembering something about Shane. Gina wanted to ask what it was, but she was here on important business of her own. She decided to change tack and leave Shane out of it.

She smiled at Cassidy. "Well, since Shane apparently isn't the best introduction I could have, how about I try again. You see, another friend of mine also gave me your contact information and told me to tell you he'd sent me."

Cassidy raised an eyebrow. "And who was that?"

"Ian Rawlings. And he said to tell you that the next time he comes out here to visit me, you owe him dinner."

Cassidy's face lit up. "Ian Rawlings! God, I love that man. And I definitely do owe him dinner. How do you know him? Have you seen him lately? How is he?"

Gina smiled. This was more like it. "I've been working with him and Liam Woodford in New York for the last few years." She didn't miss the look that crossed the other woman's face at the mention of Liam's name. "Believe it or not, they were both out here last weekend. Of course they didn't know you were here."

"How in the hell did you get those two to Montana? Ian thinks New Jersey is the boonies, and Liam?" She got that funny look on her face again. "Well, the least said about him, the better. How did you get them out here?"

Gina laughed. "Up until last weekend I was engaged to Liam."

"Oh. I'm sorry. I didn't mean to offend you. I mean, I can't take it back or anything, the guy is a prick. But no offense intended."

Gina laughed. She already liked Cassidy immensely and had a feeling they were going to get along just fine. "Hey, none taken. I said I *was* engaged to him. There's a reason I'm not anymore. It just took me a while to figure it out."

Cassidy nodded. "I'll give you that. Why is it that we women can't spot a neon-lit asshole at a hundred paces when our hearts are involved? We've all made mistakes. So I won't ask what in the hell you ever saw in that prick."

"Sounds fair to me," Gina replied. "And I won't ask you what kind of mistakes you've made that would make getting engaged to Liam seem excusable!"

This time Cassidy laughed and held out her hand. "As you already know, I'm Cassidy Lane. What might your name be, my new friend?"

"Gina Delaney, nice to meet you, friend." She grinned as they shook hands, feeling like something in her life had just turned a corner.

"Gina Delaney? Oh my God! I absolutely love your work. The way you use contrast, in light, in composition, in content. You tell stories, ask questions, and make statements, all through the use of contrast. I love it! What are you doing here? What are you working on? How can I be involved? We have to work together! You know this, right?"

Gina beamed. It still surprised her when someone recognized her name. She was thrilled that Cassidy knew—and liked, her work. "Thank you! I'd love to work with you. That's a lot of questions that will take me a while to answer."

Cassidy grinned and checked her watch. "Then let's close up shop and go get a glass of wine. You can tell me all about it, and we can begin concocting our plan to take the Mountain West by storm. What do you say?"

"I say let's go!" Gina loved the idea. She checked her watch. It was only four, Mason wasn't picking her up until six, and if she needed longer with Cassidy, she'd call and ask him to come up to town to meet her. This was important.

Chapter Fourteen

Mason crammed his hat on his head and grabbed his keys from the counter. He opened the front door to find Shane outside, keys in hand, about to unlock it.

"Hey, honey. I'm home," said Shane with a grin.

Mason laughed. "I hope you had a nice day at the office, dear, but I'm afraid there's no dinner on the table. I'm headed out."

"Are you seeing Gina?"

"Yep. I was supposed to pick her up at her place, but she just texted to say she's still with Cassidy up in town. So I'm going to meet her up there." He was hoping that wouldn't mean they'd be driving home separately later.

"She's with Cassidy?" Shane's eyes lit up. "Can I come?"

"Huh? You want to come on my date with Gina?"

"No, dumbass. I want to come with you and see if I can get my own date, with Cassidy. That is one hot little gallery owner."

Mason considered it. If Shane came, they could go in his truck and Gina would have to bring Mason back down the valley later. On the other hand, he wasn't sure he wanted Shane harassing the woman Gina was hoping to do business with.

Shane batted his eyelashes. "I'll be good, big brother. I promise."

Mason laughed. "I don't believe that for a minute. It'd help me out if we could go in your truck, but I don't want you screwing things up for Gina."

"I'd never do that! G's my best friend. I just want a chance to spend some time with the lovely Cassidy."

Mason pursed his lips. "As long as you wait until she and Gina are through talking business, okay?"

"Sure thing. Give me two minutes to make myself beautiful?"

"Nope. Gotta go. You're always beautiful anyway."

Shane ran a hand through his hair. "That's true." He turned around and headed back to his truck.

They rode in silence, each brother lost in his own thoughts. Once he pulled out onto the highway, Shane shot a quick glance at Mason. "I know why I'm quiet. I'm busy dreaming up fun ways to charm the lovely Cassidy into bed. What's eating you?"

"Guy Preston came out to the barn today."

Shane scowled. "What does that fucker want now?"

Shane hated Guy almost as much as Mason did. What had started as a falling-out between little kids in grade school had followed them over a lifetime. It had all started when Guy, who was Mason's age, had been bullying some of Shane's friends who were four years younger. Shane had always been big for his age and strong and mouthy. He'd stood up for his friends and Guy had flushed his head down the toilet for it. When Mason had heard about it, he'd waited for Guy to start picking on the little kids again and had called him out in front of them all. A few weeks later, Guy's *girlfriend*—hell they were eleven at the time! How serious could it have been? She had broken up with Guy and told him it was because she liked Mason. It didn't matter that Mason wasn't interested in her, it was enough to solidify Guy's hatred for him—and to set him on a path to destroy or take away anything Mason cared about. "He said he's going to buy Gina's dad's place."

"What? They're not going to sell it now, are they? I mean why would they? Gina's staying, isn't she? Oh crap, can she afford to keep the place going?"

Mason shook his head. "I hope so, but I don't know so. I feel like an asshole. I hadn't thought about her really needing to make her dad sell the ranch. I guess I was too tied up in being angry at her."

They drove on in silence for a while.

"Could *you* buy it?" Shane asked.

Wow! Mason hadn't even considered that as an option. He mulled it over for a while. "I could," he mused. "But how the hell would that work? What are you thinking? That I'd just buy it for them or move the stud operation out there or what?"

Shane shrugged. "I wasn't thinking anything, just throwing it out there. I mean if the two of you are back together then you could move out there," he laughed. "But then I can hardly see you and Al sharing a house—or Gina playing housewife to the pair of you. I don't know, Mase."

"Neither do I. I guess I need to talk to her, find out what her situation is. Find out what she wants."

"Yeah. I don't see Al selling to Guy Preston no matter what happens, do you?"

Mason couldn't believe Al would, but he couldn't rule it out either. "I hope not."

It was busy in town and Shane had to park a couple of blocks down from The Mint, where Gina was having a drink with

Cassidy. As they walked back down Fifth Street Shane grinned at Mason. "Do you plan on taking Gina straight off to dinner?"

"Why, what are you planning?"

"To get Cassidy to myself for the evening."

Mason laughed. "She must be quite something to have held your interest for this long. I mean, it's been days! Your attention span with women is usually measured in minutes. What's she like?"

"You'll see for yourself when we get in there, she's hot. I don't know, there's something about her. She's smart." He gave Mason a rueful grin. "And she wasn't taking any of my shit or falling for my moves either."

"And you're not used to that, right? So you're intrigued. And you need to prove to yourself that you're not losing your touch? Just do me a favor, and remember that Gina is hoping to build some kind of relationship with her? She and her gallery may be key in whether Gina can stay, and I don't want you messing things up."

Shane sighed. "You're probably right. Or at least I hope you are. I'm only intrigued by her because she poses a challenge to my ego. There couldn't be any other reason why I can't stop thinking about her, right? And I'd never do anything to mess up things for Gina, any more than you would. So don't give me that shit."

Mason gave his brother a puzzled look. "Did you just admit that you can't stop thinking about her?"

Shane stopped outside The Mint and nodded sheepishly. "I think I did. This is weird, Mase, but I've got butterflies about going in here."

Mason pushed the door open with a grin. "Maybe Gina and I will hang for a while. I have to see you around a woman who can give *you* butterflies."

Shane rolled his eyes and stepped inside. "Thanks, big brother. I wish you meant you wanted to stay to give me some moral support. Unfortunately, I think you just want to watch me make a fool of myself, right?"

Mason shrugged. "Either way. I just want to see."

He spotted Gina sitting at a table in the back. He immediately understood Shane's attraction to Cassidy. At least he assumed the pretty woman with long blonde hair that Gina was talking to was Cassidy.

Shane glanced back over his shoulder and waggled his eyebrows. "See what I mean?" he asked.

Mason only had eyes for Gina, but he nodded.

"Wish me luck," said Shane in a low voice as they approached the table.

Mason slapped his shoulder. "Since when have you needed luck?"

Gina turned and saw them. Her smile lit up her face as she waved. "Hey! I didn't know you were coming, Shane." Her smiled faded a little as she gave Cassidy a questioning look. "I believe you two have already met?"

Cassidy nodded grudgingly. Mason chuckled to himself at the look of exasperated amusement on her face when Shane caught her hand and brought it to his lips.

"I had the honor of meeting the beautiful Cassidy the other day," he said.

Cassidy looked at Gina. "Thank goodness, Ian put you in touch with me, too. It's down to him that we're going to be working together, you know. When I thought you were associated with *this guy*..." she jerked her chin toward Shane as she withdrew her hand from his grip. "...I wasn't sure I even wanted to give you the time of day."

Mason bit back at laugh at the crestfallen look on Shane's face. It seemed Gina was as loyal as ever to her childhood best friend. "I told you, he's a sweetheart. He's just a bit full of himself." She looked past Shane to Mason. "And this is his big brother, Mason Remington. Mason, I'd like you to meet my new friend and soon to be partner, Cassidy Lane."

Cassidy smiled and extended her hand. "Nice to meet you, Mason."

Mason tipped his hat and shook her hand. "You too. I'm happy to hear that you and Gina are going to partner up."

"Not as happy as I am," she replied. "We're going to make a great team."

Gina nodded happily. "We're making all kinds of plans, I'm so excited to get started."

"Me too," said Shane. "How can I help?"

Mason laughed as the girls exchanged a smile. "How would you like to help?" asked Cassidy. "Do you paint? Are you a photographer? Have any connections in the art world?"

Shane shook his head with a grin. "No, but there are a few things I'd love to do with you."

Mason groaned inwardly as Cassidy gave Shane a disgusted look. If he liked her, why was he being such an ass?

"No! Not like that," said Shane. "There you go again thinking dirty thoughts and blaming me for them! I meant I'd like to put you in touch with some of the guests at the dude ranch. We're getting a lot of repeat visitors. I'm guessing they'd be your ideal clients. Montana lovers with money to burn?"

Cassidy frowned at him, even as she nodded. "That does sound interesting. I didn't know you ran a dude ranch."

"I don't just run it, I own it. And you didn't know because you wouldn't give me a chance to get to know you when I came into the gallery. How about we change that tonight? We should probably let these two get on with their date, so why don't you have dinner with me and we can discuss all the ways we can help each other out."

Mason shook his head at the blatant innuendo. Jesus, Shane! Cassidy must have his head completely turned around. He was making a real mess of this, yet normally he couldn't miss with the ladies.

Cassidy didn't look impressed or interested in the least. "No thanks. I have to be going."

"But you have to have dinner, right? Why not have it with me?"

Gina gave Mason a puzzled look. It seemed she, too, was surprised at the way Shane was mishandling this one.

"Because I don't want to." With that, Cassidy stood and smiled at Gina. "This has been great. I can't wait to get started. I'll call you tomorrow, okay?" She turned to Mason. "Very nice to meet you. I hope you two have a great evening." She stepped past Shane with merely a "Goodbye."

When she'd gone, Shane sagged into the seat opposite Gina, and Mason sat down beside her.

"What the fuck?" asked Shane. "I don't get it. The woman turns me into a babbling idiot!"

Mason laughed. "You got *that* right. That was painful to watch."

Gina put a hand on Shane's arm and gave him a sympathetic look. "Sorry, but it was sort of cringe worthy, Shane. I remember you being a real charmer. Are you losing your touch?"

Shane shook his head ruefully. "It looks like I might be. I don't know. There's just something about her. She gets to me." He looked around and his gaze landed on a group of girls sitting at the bar. He grinned. "I think I'd better go put it to the test. See if I really am losing my touch."

Mason had to laugh. Apparently, Shane wasn't too devastated by Cassidy's rejection. "Good luck."

Shane scowled at him. "Don't say that. I asked you to wish me luck with Cassidy. That didn't pan out too well, did it? I don't need luck. I just need to be my charming self." He stood up and pushed his chair back. "I hope the two of you have a wonderful night." He grinned, his usual swagger returning. "I intend to."

Mason and Gina watched him make his way over to the girls at the bar. In just a few minutes he was sitting with them. They were laughing at his jokes and two of the four of them looked as though they would be more than happy to ensure that he did indeed have a wonderful night."

Mason grinned at Gina. "Doesn't look like he's losing his touch, huh?"

"Not at all." She pursed her lips. "And I don't think he should give up on Cassidy either."

"Seriously? What makes you say that? He was making a real pig's ear of it with her. She didn't seem interested in the least."

"Call it women's intuition, but I don't think Cassidy is as horrified by Shane as she makes out. I could be wrong, but I don't think he should give up hope."

Mason shrugged. He couldn't see it at all, but what did he know about how women felt? Hell, he'd thought Gina was in love with him. He'd been totally blindsided when she told him it was over and she wasn't coming back.

She was staring at him. "What is it? What's the matter?"

He pulled himself together. He didn't need to be dwelling on that. They had the evening ahead of them and he wanted to enjoy it, not waste it fretting over the past. "Nothing, just realizing yet again how little I understand about women and the way you think."

The look on her face told him she knew he was talking about her more than he was Cassidy. It seemed she didn't want to go there either. "We must seem strange creatures to you men, I'm sure."

He reached for her hand. "Strange yes, but beautiful, magical creatures that we just can't get enough of."

She smiled. "That's sweet."

"Not sweet, just true. So, my beautiful, magical creature, where would you like me to take you for dinner?"

She gave him a saucy grin and rested her hand on his thigh. "I thought you said we were going riding?"

He smiled down at her. "You want to?"

"I'd love to."

"Who do you want to ride?"

She laughed. "How about Annie first, then you?"

He grinned at that. It sounded perfect to him, but it would be dark by the time they ate and drove back down the valley. "How about me tonight and Annie tomorrow. We can take her and Storm out in the afternoon if you have time?"

She nodded. "I guess it is a little late now, isn't it? Sorry I made you come up here. The time just flew when Cassidy and I got talking."

"It's not a problem, babe. I'm glad the two of you got together. It seems like you really hit it off."

She grinned. "Totally! We have so much in common, both personally and professionally. I can't wait to get started."

"Do you think you'll be able to make enough to survive on?" He didn't want to pry into her situation, but he did want to know whether there was anything to be concerned about. The thought of her and her dad needing to sell the ranch bothered him. The thought that Guy Preston might buy their place bothered him, too. He'd find a way to buy it himself if they needed him to, but he wanted to figure out where she stood first.

She shrugged and looked away. "I never wanted to make Dad leave here, you know. I wasn't being insensitive, I was trying to be practical." She looked back at him. "It was a struggle to keep the place going, even when I was working with Liam and Ian. I don't know what kind of income I'll be able to generate. It scares me, Mase. I've been thinking that if we get an offer on the ranch maybe we should take it and find a little place up in town. It would be a compromise, he'd hate to lose the ranch—and so would I, but at least we wouldn't have to leave the valley."

Mason shook his head. They weren't going to lose the ranch. He wouldn't let it happen.

"What are you thinking?" she asked. "I know that look on your face."

He met her gaze. "I'm thinking I don't want you to leave. I don't want you to have to sell the ranch either. There's something I need to talk to you about, but let's head back down to Pine Creek, shall we? We can talk about it over dinner."

"Okay. I haven't eaten there in years. But before we go, at least give me a clue what you want to talk about."

Maybe it was better to give her time to mull it over on the drive back down the valley. "Guy Preston came out to the barn today..."

The color drained from her face.

"What is it, G?"

She shook her head rapidly. "Nothing. Nothing at all. What's he got to do with anything?"

Mason was puzzled. Her whole demeanor had changed at the mention of Guy's name. She seemed hurt, angry maybe? Definitely shaken. What was that about? He didn't know, but it seemed even more important to tell her about Guy's intention to make an offer on the ranch—and about his own intention to buy it himself if necessary. "He said he wants to buy your dad's place."

Gina sputtered. "Over my dead body! No way in hell do I want to sell to that man!"

Mason hadn't expected her to like the idea, but he'd had no clue that she would be so angry. No one liked Guy. Gina had known of the troubles Mason had with him, but her reaction seemed over the top. "What's your problem with him, G?"

The look she gave him stunned him. She was as hurt and angry as he'd ever seen her. She took a deep breath before she spoke. "Nothing. Nothing at all. Can we go now?" She stood up and grabbed her purse.

Mason hurried to catch up with her as she stalked out of the bar. Shane looked up from his flirting and gave Mason a puzzled look as he watched Gina exit. Mason shrugged. He had no idea what the problem was—but he intended to find out.

Chapter Fifteen

Gina tried to keep her hands steady as she pretended to study the menu. They'd driven down here in silence. Mason wanted to know what her problem with Guy was, but the only way to tell him that would be to tell him why she'd broken up with him. Perhaps it was time to do that? To go over what she'd heard Mason tell Guy that night. To finally tell him that she knew how little she'd meant to him back then. She knew she was overreacting about Guy, she shouldn't hate him for being the person Mason had confided in, but she couldn't help it. Mason didn't even like Guy, but he'd had no problem telling him that he was losing interest in her and wanted to get back with April. She tried to take deep calming breaths. All that was ancient history, wasn't it? Shouldn't she be mature enough to accept that what he'd done back then was what he needed to do for himself at the time? That now he wanted another chance with her? She couldn't ignore the nasty little voice in her head that kept asking how long it would be until he lost interest in her this time—and how would she survive if he did that once she fully gave him her heart again?

The server came and she ordered a salad. She didn't think she could eat much of anything, the way her stomach was churning.

"Are you going to talk to me?"

She nodded slowly. It had to be done. "Can we wait until the drinks come? I may need a little Dutch courage for this conversation."

"Sure. In fact, if you'll excuse me, I'm just going to step outside before they do."

She watched him head to the bathroom. She needed to get a grip. The poor man had no idea what her problem was. She just needed to calmly explain to him that she'd overheard his conversation with Guy. Surely he would understand how much it had hurt her.

She looked up as he made his way back to their table. He stopped when a woman at the bar called his name. Gina's heart began to race when she recognized who it was. Good God! It was all coming back at once tonight, it seemed. She watched as he turned away from her and made his way over to April. Just wonderful. That was all she needed when she was trying to put the past behind her—to watch him hug April and peck her on the cheek. He chatted with her for a few moments. It looked to Gina like much more than a *Hi, how are you?* type conversation. Mason was asking her questions, looking concerned. April seemed to be putting on a brave face. What the hell was going on between the two of them? April gave his arm a squeeze and he leaned in to give her another peck before coming back to the table.

She stared at him as he sat down.

"What is it?" he asked. He reached for her hand, but she snatched it away, realizing even as she did it how childish she must seem. She couldn't help it. Seeing him with April like that had brought back all the hurt she'd spent so many years trying to get over.

"What the hell, G? What's wrong?"

"I didn't realize you and April were still so close."

"Close?" He shrugged. "She's just a friend. What's the problem?"

"Just a friend?" Gina realized her voice sounded shrill, but she couldn't help it.

He shrugged. "Okay. I still feel kind of responsible for her. I didn't realize it would bother you. When did you turn into the jealous type, anyway?"

Gina was stunned. Why would he feel responsible for April? What had happened between them after she'd left? "You didn't realize it would bother me that you left me sitting here to go hang out with the woman you wanted to get rid of me for? Well, forgive me for being so jealous, Mason, but yeah, it does bother me. It bothers me so much that I think I'm going to go home. Perhaps she'll join you for dinner, and she can take my place again, just like she did when I was in college."

"What in the hell are you talking about, Gina?"

She wasn't going to stick around to explain it. She stood up and grabbed her purse. She didn't feel very grown up right now, but she didn't care either. She just wanted to get away from him, get away from April and get away from the memory of all the pain they'd caused her. She hurried across the parking lot back to her dad's truck.

Mason came running out after her. "For Christ's sake, Gina! Will you at least have the decency to tell me what the fuck's going on before you drive away and leave me stranded?"

"Why should I? You didn't have the decency to tell me what was going on, did you? Perhaps I should go find Guy and tell him all about it, just like you did."

She climbed into the truck, slammed it in gear and screeched out of there. She wasn't exactly proud of herself, but she just couldn't help it. She'd been on the verge of letting herself fall in love with him all over again. How could she ever trust in him now? How long would it be before he tired of her again and wanted April back? Maybe he'd wanted April all along and Guy had taken her away from him? Who knew? Gina didn't, and she didn't want to. All she knew was that she was not going to let Mason Remington destroy her life a second time.

~ ~ ~

Mason stood in the parking lot watching Gina's taillights disappear. What the fuck? His head was spinning. He'd never known Gina to behave like that before, never seen her so hurt or angry. Her parting shot, however, seemed to explain it. His heart sank at the realization that she must have somehow found out what he'd told Guy that night. He closed his eyes and shook his head. Had Guy told her? He doubted that, she would have come to him to ask him to explain, wouldn't she? She didn't trust Guy back then, no one did. But she had trusted Mason, and if she'd heard the words come out of his own mouth, that he was losing interest in her, that he wanted to get back with April, that would explain everything. He covered his face with his hands. He wasn't a liar, it wasn't in his nature, but it seemed that one lie that he'd told in an attempt to keep Gina had cost him ten years with her. In trying to make sure that Guy didn't try to steal her away, *he* had pushed her away. Guy fucking Preston had won again. Trying to outsmart that bastard had cost him ten years of his life with the woman he loved.

Mason started walking. He texted Kathy, who owned the restaurant and told her to put their drinks and untouched food on his tab. He didn't want to go back inside. He didn't want to call Shane to come give him a ride home either. He headed south back down the valley. It would be a five-mile walk home, but Mason needed the air, and the time.

~ ~ ~

Gina opened her eyes and stared at the ceiling. Her eyes felt puffy. She'd refused to cry last night, but the tears were there waiting to fall. She was a little ashamed of herself. She prided herself on being a low drama kind of girl, and yet last night she'd shrieked at Mason, gotten all jealous over him hugging an old girlfriend and walked—hmm, run—out on him without even explaining why. She'd left him stranded, too. April probably took him home chimed in the nasty little voice. She pursed her lips. She was bigger than that, and she was better than that. She needed to call him and apologize for her behavior. He'd been right, she did owe him an explanation. As she lay there thinking about it, it started to seem ridiculous to her that she'd let ten years go by without ever telling him, or anyone else, why she'd ended it with him. She should have told him what she'd heard him say. Should have let him know how he'd destroyed her. She was supposed to be a grown-up. Well, she was going to handle this like a grown-up. She'd call him, arrange to go see him and talk it all through. Clear the air between them, once and for all. Then she'd make a start trying to build a life for herself and her dad here. She hoped to God they wouldn't have to sell the ranch, but if they did, they did. And if Guy's was the only offer, then so be it. She'd have to be realistic and he'd never really done her any harm anyway. He'd simply been the person Mason had chosen to talk to about his true feelings. That was hardly Guy's fault, was it?

"Gina love, are you planning on getting up anytime today?" called her dad.

"I'll be down in a minute." She knew he'd be worried about her having come home alone and early last night. Well, she wasn't going to hide. She was going to get up, go down there and tell him what she'd refused to tell him for years. It was strange that something that seemed so life shattering when you kept it to yourself, started to seem a lot less so when you brought it out in the open. She wondered what her dad would think. She hadn't wanted to tell him because she hadn't wanted him to think any less of Mason. Now that she was getting ready to tell all, she was wondering whether he would think any less of her. Had she been stupid to keep it secret all this time? One thing was for certain—if she had been, her dad wouldn't hesitate to tell her so.

She pulled on some clothes and unplugged her phone from the charger. She had two new texts. One from Mason:

> *Still want to come for that ride?*
> *Be at the barn at 3 if you do.*
> *We need to talk.*

One from Shane:

> *WTF G girl? Call me!*

She had to smile at that. It was so typically Shane. She would call him after she talked to her dad. And she would go to the barn at three and talk to Mason, too. It was time to clear the air and finally put the past to bed. She had no idea what the future would hold. She knew she loved Mason, but she couldn't even think about a future with him in it until she came to terms with their past. Last night had taught her that much. She couldn't move forward with him at all while there were still secrets undermining her trust. He thought he'd kept a secret from her, and she knew that she'd kept secret that she knew what it was. What a mess.

Her dad gave her a worried look when she came into the kitchen. He poured her a mug of coffee and carried it out onto the front porch with his own. She followed with a rueful smile on her face. He wasn't giving her any choice about sitting down and talking to him. He knew she'd follow her coffee wherever he took it. He sat in one of the rockers and placed the mugs on the table between them while she settled herself into the other.

"It's a bit chilly to be sitting out here, don't you think?" she asked.

He gave her a sad look. "It is love, but we've had all our important conversations here, haven't we? It just seems fitting to sit out here this morning."

She'd been sitting in this very rocker when her mom had told her about the cancer. She and her dad had held each other and cried right here when they came home from the hospital for the last time. Gina heaved a big sigh. She didn't need to be thinking about that this morning.

"So, what happened last night?"

She sipped her coffee and stared out at the mountains for a few moments before she answered. "I got upset with Mason and came home."

Her dad nodded and waited for her to continue.

"I got upset because we saw April Runyan. Mason went to talk to her, and I got jealous and left."

"Why would you get jealous, love?"

"Because..." Gina took a deep breath. Finally, she was going to tell him. "She was the reason I never came back, the reason I broke up with him."

"Why? What did she do?"

"She didn't do anything, but Mason was bored with me and wanted to get back with her. It broke my heart because I thought we were forever." She felt a single tear escape and roll down her cheek.

"If Mason was done with you and wanted April back, why's he never gotten over you? Why did he never get back with her? And why's he always said he doesn't know what went wrong between the two of you?" Her dad looked thoroughly confused. "It don't make no sense to me."

"He didn't know I knew."

Her dad looked even more confused. "He didn't tell you that himself? Then what makes you think it? How do you know? Who *did* tell you?"

"I heard him tell Guy Preston. We were all out at Stacey's one night. Guy kept trying to get me to dance with him and Mason was pissed. I couldn't find him for a while and I couldn't see Guy anywhere either. I went to look for them out back because I was afraid of what Mason might do. Those two were always fighting when they were kids. They were out in the parking lot, but they weren't fighting, they were talking. Mason was telling Guy that I'd been fun, but he was getting ready to break up with me because he still loved April and wanted to get back with her." There, she'd said it out loud for the first time.

Her dad stared at her. "And that's been your big secret all these years? That's your reason for not coming home after college? For not talking to Mason for almost a decade?"

She nodded.

He shook his head. "And you never even asked him about it?"

She shook her head.

Her dad ran his hand over his face, then sipped his coffee for a while. "Gina, girl. Didn't you say Mason was the only one you could talk to about anything at all? The only one who always understood you?"

She nodded again. She was starting to feel as though she had made a horrible mistake. Why *hadn't* she gone to Mason and asked him about it? Because it had hurt her so much, that's why. She'd been reeling from the shock of it. From hearing that what they shared, while it meant the whole world to her, meant so little to Mason. When she'd heard him talking to Guy that night, his words had taken him from being her best friend who was going to love and protect her forever, to being a stranger who didn't even care enough about her to tell her that he didn't love her anymore. "I always felt that way, but listening to what he told Guy that night made me realize how wrong I was, Dad. I was stupid. Just a stupid girl who was so deeply in love that I had no clue anything was wrong between us. It broke my heart. I just had to get away. I left for college a couple of days later and I couldn't face the thought of coming back here and not being with him. Let alone coming back and having to see him with someone else, knowing that he'd broken my heart and destroyed my world so that he could be with her."

"And what did he say about it last night?"

"I didn't give him a chance to say anything. Seeing him with April brought back all the hurt and I had to get away. I left and came home."

"So you still haven't talked it through with him?"

She shook her head.

Her dad shrugged. "Seems to me that you need to. It still don't make sense to me, love. And you know, when things don't make sense there's usually a reason. You're missing something. I can't believe he would say all that, but you heard him. It just don't make sense. He was devastated when you didn't come home. As far as I know he never went out with April." He met her gaze. "But I'm just guessing. I don't have all the facts. But neither do you. You need to talk to him."

"I know. I'm going out to the barn this afternoon."

"Good. I can't believe the two of you won't be able to figure it out. You're meant to be with him, Gina. No two ways about it. I've known it for years, just been waiting for you to get your act together."

Gina gave him a sad smile. "I don't know what to think, Dad. I love him..."

He grinned. "You're finally admitting it, so that's progress!"

"Maybe, but I'm not sure it will be enough."

"It will be. If you both want it enough and you're prepared to work together instead of keeping secrets."

She nodded. "I figured that out already."

"Good. So what are your plans for the day? What time are you going out there? That realtor fella called and wanted to bring someone out to look at the place. I told him I'd get you to call him back." He gave her a pleading look. "I was hoping you might tell him we don't need him anymore? That we're not selling after all?"

Gina closed her eyes and took a deep breath. "I'd love to be able to do that, but I'm not sure that we can. I don't know how much I'm going to be able to bring in to support us. Let's put them off for a while until I figure it out, okay? I'll tell them we can't have any showings this week." No way did she want Guy coming out here. "And I'm going to see what I can put together with Cassidy to bring some money in. Maybe we won't have to sell, but just give me a little time?"

He nodded. "Whatever you think is best, love."

She smiled at him if only she *knew* what was best.

Chapter Sixteen

Mason had spent most of the day working the new mares in. It was calming to him, to be out here putting them through their paces. He enjoyed bringing on the green youngsters. This latest group he'd bought at auction down in Sheridan. Shane had his eye on a couple of them for the dude ranch and Mason wanted to make sure they were bomb-proof before he'd allow them to take novices up into the back country.

He watched a green Chevy pickup turn into the long driveway, kicking up a dust trail as it came out to the barn. What was Carter doing out here? Mason turned out the mare he'd been working with and headed over to meet his brother. They didn't get to visit much these days, but Mason wasn't in the mood today—he had too much else on his mind right now.

Carter jumped down from his truck and slapped Mason on the back.

"How's it going?"

Mason shrugged. "I've had better days. How about you? What brings you out here in the middle of the week?"

"Can't I stop by to see my brother without needing a reason?"

"You can, but you don't normally. Is everything okay?"

"Everything's okay with me. I'm more worried about you. Talk got around that Gina walked out on you at Pine Creek last night. I wanted to see how you're doing, that's all."

Mason smiled. "Thanks. I don't know how I'm doing. I found out last night that something I did to make sure she was okay, turned out to be the thing that broke us up. She's coming over to talk about it later, but I don't know what she's thinking. I'm not sure if she wants to get past it or if she's going to tell me that she can't."

Carter nodded. "Want to talk about it?"

"Nope."

"I didn't think so." He shrugged. "I don't know why I came really, just wanted you to know I've got your back if you want it."

Mason punched his arm. "Thanks, bud." Carter was the quietest of the four of them. He didn't tend to say much of anything, but he was always there whenever any of his brothers was having a hard time. He owned a nursery and landscaping business on the edge of town and had built himself a little house up there a couple of years ago. He usually came down the valley on the weekends for a family dinner or barbecue, but it was unusual to see him out here in the week. "Are you doing okay yourself?" asked Mason, wondering if there was more to this visit than brotherly concern.

Carter shrugged again, looking uncomfortable. "I guess. Guy Preston was over at the nursery the other day, pricing out landscaping for a new place. He said he's buying Gina's dad's place and..." he hesitated.

Mason thought he had a pretty good idea of what was coming. He waited.

"Well. He was talking as though a night with Gina was going to be part of the deal." He studied Mason's face. "I thought you should know."

"Don't worry. I do know." Mason felt sick to his stomach at the thought that Guy had cost him ten years with Gina. He knew Gina would never do it, but the thought of her sleeping with him had the pulse in his temple throbbing again.

"She wouldn't, Mase. You know that. Even if the two of you weren't back together. Gina's not like that."

"I'm not sure we are back together, but you're right. She'd never go anywhere near him."

"You think they'd sell to him?"

"I don't." He didn't add that they wouldn't because he'd buy the place himself before he'd let that happen.

"Okay, well I guess I'll get my dumb ass outta here then," said Carter.

"Want to come back over to the cabin for lunch since you're here?" Mason hated for him to drive all the way down here for a two-minute conversation. He wasn't prepared to talk about it all because he didn't know what to think, let alone what to say, but he didn't want Carter to leave either.

Carter grinned. "You know I'll always stick around if you feed me."

Mason laughed. "True. What time are you coming down here on Sunday? Are you going to help get the party set up?"

"Sure am," said Carter as he followed Mason back up to the house. "There are going to be a lot of people out here and I don't want Mom overdoing it, trying to get too much done by herself."

Mason nodded. "Yeah. I figure if we all get together we can take on most of it and she can do the light stuff. I've noticed lately that she gets tired fast."

"They're getting old, Mase. Has Dad talked anymore about taking her to Arizona for the winter?"

"He has. He keeps handing more off to me and Shane and Chance. I think they're about ready to step back."

"I do, too. I'll move back down here and help out with anything you need me to anytime, you know. Just say the word."

That surprised Mason. Carter was all about family, but he had enough on his own plate. "You've got your hands full with your business, haven't you?"

"I sure have, but if you need me, all you have to do is say so. Family comes first for me. You know that."

Mason had to wonder if everything was okay with Carter. He didn't get to ask. As they approached the cabin, the front door swung open and Chance grinned at them. "Why is it that anytime I fix something to eat, at least one of you always shows up?"

Mason laughed. "Hey. I didn't know you were back. How did it go?"

"Yeah, we got the whole herd up to summer pasture. Looks like it should be a good year. I'm beat though. I just got back in and I plan to eat and then sleep. Lucky for you two, I made enough to feed everyone for a couple of days so come on in. Eat up."

Mason watched Carter and Chance as they ate. Chance felt like a fifth brother, he'd been around for so long and they were so close.

He looked up and grinned. "Are you and Gina back on track then?"

Mason pursed his lips. "Not quite, no."

Chance frowned. "You'll figure it out." He wasn't one to talk about women or anything to do with relationships. Mason had never known him to have one—not a relationship, he'd certainly had his fair share of women. When he thought about it, they were all held prisoner by their past in some way. He'd never been able to get over Gina. Chance had come here from California—via a stint in prison. He'd been escaping a tragic past, but it seemed he'd never escaped it, just moved away from it. He hadn't moved on any more than Mason had. Carter was in the same boat. As so many guys around here seemed to, he'd married his childhood sweetheart straight out of high school. They'd lived in one of the cabins that Shane now used to accommodate his guests. Carter had come home one night and found her in their bed with one of the ranch hands. She'd left with the guy the next day. Mason had never known Carter to even date another woman since then. Perhaps that was why he was so concerned about him and Gina?

He grinned at Mason. "I think I need to come back down here more often if I'm going to get fed like this when I do."

Chance laughed. "Well, don't expect me to be the one cooking when you do. This is me done. Now I'm going to catch up on some sleep. It was good to see you, Carter."

"Yeah, you too, and thanks for lunch. I'll return the favor sometime. I'd better get going myself."

Mason followed him out to his truck. "Thanks for coming down."

"Sure thing. Sometimes I feel like I'm too far out of everything, being up there in town and all. I just wanted to remind you that whenever you want me, I'm around."

Mason nodded. "I appreciate it." He watched Carter drive away before heading back to the barn. He wanted to get more of his paperwork taken care of before he needed to get Annie and Storm saddled up and ready. He wasn't even sure if Gina was coming. She hadn't replied to his text, but he was pretty sure she'd be here.

~ ~ ~

Gina's stomach was tying itself in knots by the time she pulled up at the barn. Since she'd talked to her dad this morning, she'd been driving herself nuts. Why hadn't she talked to Mason about what she'd heard him say? Why had she thrown away everything they'd shared? She knew why. Because she'd heard from his own mouth that he didn't want her anymore. What woman would stick around after that? Whatever he might have to say about what had happened ten years ago, she wondered what else he would say about what might happen now. Did he really want a shot at forever? Was she prepared to take the risk? She cut the engine when she saw him appear in the open doorway to the barn. She'd tormented herself with those questions all day. She wasn't going to be able to find the answers by herself. She needed to talk to him. And there he was.

He was leaning in the doorway, watching her get out of the truck. Damn him, why did he have to be so handsome? Broad shoulders, narrow hips, such a handsome face—even without its usual smile.

He didn't come to her when she got out. He just stood there waiting for her to make her way across the parking lot to him.

It felt strange. He'd always been one to come to meet her as soon as he saw her, wherever they were. There seemed to be some meaning in the way he stood there waiting for her to come to him. It was up to her to close the distance between them. That thought stuck in her head. Was she the one who had caused the distance? No. He had.

She stopped before she got to him and held his gaze. She'd come most of the way to him, but it was important to her that he do the same. She needed to know that it wasn't going to all be up to her. If they were going to be able to come back together they both needed to put forth the effort.

He seemed to understand that. He gave a slight nod and pushed himself off the doorframe where he'd been leaning. His long stride closed the final gap between them in a few steps. He stood before her, his eyes boring into hers. She felt an almost overwhelming urge to throw herself into his arms, but she resisted.

He reached out and put his hand on her shoulder. The warmth of it spread through her, untying the knots in her stomach and making her relax a little. "We've got some talking to do, huh?"

She nodded.

"Annie and Storm are all ready to go. What do you say we head up to Overlook Point? It won't take long, and we can let them graze up there while we talk."

"Okay."

When Mason brought Annie out, Gina buried her face in the mare's neck. "Hello, beautiful. I've missed you." Annie had been such a huge part of her and Mason's time together. Gina loved her and had missed her. From the way she nuzzled into Gina's neck, it seemed the feeling was mutual.

Mason brought Storm out and Gina had to say hi to him, too. Just like his rider he was handsome and strong, but older than Gina remembered. He'd been a headstrong youngster back then, now he was a seasoned old pro. As soon as she swung herself up into the saddle Gina felt as though she truly was home.

The horses knew their way up to the point well enough. Annie fell in behind Storm and the two of them picked their way up the path through the trees. It was still early in the season, recent rainfall had filled the air with the scent of juniper—the scent of home, Gina couldn't help but think. She watched Mason's back as he rode ahead of her. The set of his broad shoulders made her feel uneasy. She kept re-running last night's conversation in her mind. From what she'd said, he must know that she'd heard him talking to Guy that night. He must know that she'd heard what he'd said about her, and about April. After not wanting to talk to him about it for all these years, now she was impatient to do just that. She wanted to hear what he had to say. Mason didn't seem in the same kind of hurry as she was. He led the way on Storm and made no attempt at conversation. It was strange not to ride beside him, but the trees would open up soon, the trail would widen, and she'd be able to bring Annie alongside. In the meantime, all this riding in silence was causing the knots in her stomach to retie themselves.

Once they emerged from the pines, Gina urged Annie into a trot to catch up. Mason met her gaze. She couldn't figure out what his eyes were trying to tell her, but it seemed as though there was an awful lot that needed to be said. Gina bit back all the questions she'd been about to launch into, deciding instead to wait and hear what he had to say.

"From what you said last night, I'm guessing that you heard me talk to Guy Preston?"

She nodded.

"And you believed what I told him?"

She nodded again. Why wouldn't she?

Mason shook his head sadly and rode on in silence.

When they reached Overlook, Gina reined Annie in and stared out across the valley. It was so beautiful up here. Even under these circumstances the view took her breath away. The valley lay before them, yellow fields turned to green around the edges as the land rose, all ringed with snow-capped peaks. She and Mason had come up here so many times, she'd always remembered it as one of their special places. As she watched him dismount from Storm, she wondered if today would make it an even more special place or whether it—and they—would be nothing more than a memory once they got done talking.

Mason took care of the horses before showing any sign that they'd come up here to talk. Gina didn't know where to begin, so she waited. Once Storm and Annie were tethered and grazing happily, Mason came back to the point where she was standing, taking in the view. He held his hand out to her. She looked at it before meeting his gaze, then nodded. She let him lead her out onto the rocky promontory, the 'Point' that gave this place its name. It was windy, but then it always was up here.

Mason sat down on a rocky outcropping that looked for all the world as if someone had carved a bench ready for weary travelers to rest a while. Gina sat down beside him and stared out. Maybe this was the perfect place for them to talk. Sitting side by side would be easier than holding each other's gaze the whole time. She didn't want him to see all the pain on her face.

Nor did she want to see the pain on his, and she had the feeling there was going to be a whole lot more there than she had ever dreamed in all the years she'd been gone.

They sat in silence for a while, listening to the wind.

"I'm so sorry, babe." He spoke so softly that for a moment she wasn't sure whether he really had. He still stared out at the valley, but his hand sought hers. She let him take it and gave him a squeeze. She didn't want to speak, to interrupt him, but she wanted him to know she was with him.

"Tell me what you heard?"

She took a deep breath and nodded. It was only fair. "I don't remember the exact words, Mase. It was a long time ago. But you told him that you weren't so sure about me, about us, anymore. You were losing interest." She stopped and swallowed down the lump that was forming in her throat. Even now, it was hard to say it out loud. "That...that you wanted to get back with April. I just wish you'd told me before you told him." She doubted it would have been any easier to hear. It still would have broken her heart, but at least she wouldn't have that deep feeling of betrayal that had plagued her all these years. The feeling that she had been just a stupid young girl, that she'd been blind because she'd loved him so much. She'd hated feeling that all the love she'd thought they shared only existed inside her head, that Mason hadn't felt it at all.

He wrapped his arm around her shoulders and looked down at her. There was no avoiding the pain she saw in his eyes. "I'm not going to deny I said it, Gina, but I need you to know I didn't mean it. Not a word of it."

She sucked in a deep breath. She didn't want him to make excuses. "Don't try to make it easier for me. After all this time, please just tell me the truth."

He gritted his teeth in frustration then took a deep breath of his own. "I was afraid you'd think that. Please hear me out. I fucked up. I see that now, but I did it because I was trying to protect you, protect us. You know how Guy has always been with me. He's tried to take away or destroy anything I've ever cared about." He scowled out into the distance for a moment. "He's succeeded, too. I swore to myself that I would never allow him to mess with you or what we had. The irony of it is that in trying to stop *him* from destroying us, I went ahead and did it all by myself. I knew he was looking at grad schools in Portland and Seattle. I didn't want him going to Portland, living in the same city as you. I didn't trust him to not go messing with your head, trying to turn you against me. I was trying to steer him away from you. That's why I told him I wasn't into you anymore."

It was hard for Gina to watch the regret play on his face. She knew he was speaking the truth.

"Last night I told you I feel kind of responsible for April. I do. I knew when I told Guy that I wanted to get back with her, that he would probably make a move on her. I got what I hoped for when he went to Seattle. He left you alone. What I didn't realize at the time was that in trying to stop him from destroying what we had, I was going ahead and destroying your life...and mine." He shook his head. "And April's, too."

Gina stared out at the big, blue sky. It all made sense now as he explained it to her. If only he'd explained it to her then. If he'd trusted her to include her, to talk to her about it. She shook her head. If only she'd explained to him then, trusted him enough to talk to him about what she'd heard. She couldn't blame him when she was just as guilty.

"Can you forgive me?"

She studied his face. Of course, she could. "Can you forgive me?"

He looked puzzled. "What for?"

"For believing your words without ever asking you about them. For refusing to talk to you about it for so long afterward. What you said, it made me call everything off. But if I'd talked to you just once, out of all those times you tried. If I'd answered you when you asked me over and over what went wrong, we could have gotten past it, together."

"It's all on me, Gina. None of it's your fault."

She shook her head. "I'd say if we want to start blaming then we share it equally."

"No, babe. I..."

She put a finger up to his lips. "Don't, Mase. Whichever way you cut it, we both screwed up and it cost us ten years of our lives. Ten years that we'll never get back." Her heart was heavy with the realization that all the time she'd lived without him, all the time she'd spent missing him, wanting and wishing she could have back what they'd lost, had been needless. She felt a tear roll down her cheek.

Mason brushed it away with his thumb. "Can you forgive me?"

She nodded as more tears escaped to follow the first. "I'll forgive you on one condition."

"What's that?"

She wrapped her arms around his neck and looked deep into his eyes. "That you forgive me too, and promise me we can spend the rest of our lives making up for the time we lost."

The ghost of a smile formed on his lips as he searched her face. "There's nothing to forgive..."

She shook her head. "That's my condition. I need you to forgive me."

"I forgive you."

"And I need that promise, too, cowboy."

His smile spread. "I promise you, G. I want to spend the rest of my life making it up to you."

"And I want to spend the rest of mine making it up to you."

He closed his arms around her, pulling her close to his chest. "Shall we get started right now?"

She nodded in the moment before his lips came down on hers.

Chapter Seventeen

Mason leaned on the stall door, watching Gina brush Annie down. He was still struggling to reconcile everything that he'd learned in the last twenty-four hours. He'd screwed up big time. It was hard to wrap his head around the fact that his mistake had cost him ten years. He shook his head to clear it. He couldn't help wishing that Gina had come to him, that she'd told him what she'd heard. There was no point dwelling on it. All he could do was be grateful for the fact that they'd finally gotten everything out in the open. That they could move forward together into whatever future they decided to build. His smile returned with the realization that everything he'd thought was lost forever was now possible. However bad he might feel about his mistakes in the past, he couldn't contain his happiness about the future. He'd believed that he would spend the rest of his life loving Gina from afar. Now he would get to love her up close, every day.

She tugged the comb through Annie's mane one last time then turned to smile at him.

"What do you want to do now?" he asked.

"I need to talk to Cassidy and get things rolling there." Her smile faded. "And I need to talk to the realtor and put him off for a while."

Mason raised an eyebrow. He didn't like the sound of that *for a while* part.

Gina shrugged. "I don't want to sell, you know that. Especially not to Guy, but I have to be practical."

Mason wasn't sure if he should bring it up yet. They hadn't exactly made any decisions about what their future would hold. She'd talked about spending the rest of their lives making it up to each other. Surely that meant they were back on the track that they had been? He hedged, just in case. "Do you think there's a possibility you'll have to give the place up?" Didn't she realize that he wouldn't let that happen?

"I hope not, but I need to get things in place first. I need to talk to Cassidy. I have a show coming up in New York I need to go back for. Right now I'm in a precarious situation and until I know where and how I'm going to be able to make enough money to pay the bills every month, I daren't tell Dad we won't have to sell."

Mason nodded. He knew how Al felt about losing the place. "I could help."

Gina stared at him for a long moment. "Thanks, but I need to figure it out for myself."

That stung. What did that mean? That she didn't want his help?

"Don't look like that, Mase. You need to understand that I'm used to making things happen by myself. I appreciate you offering to help, but this is my problem."

Mason didn't understand. If they were back together and going to spend the rest of their lives together, shouldn't it be his problem, too? "Aren't we in this together?" he asked.

"Yes. That's exactly the point. Together. I don't want you riding to the rescue and solving my problems for me. I want us to be equal partners. We have to be if we're going to make this work, don't you see that? Back then, you were the big strong hero striding in to save the day whenever something went wrong. I was just the little girl waiting to be saved. When you..." She stopped herself, apparently deciding to change tack. "With everything that happened, I learned that I had to take care of myself. I'd believed in *us* so completely that I never bothered to become *me*. After we broke up, I had to learn to fend for myself and I've gotten pretty good at it. I'm not just going to throw my hands up in the air now, give up my independence and say, please rescue me."

"But..."

"But nothing. Let me do this my way. Please?"

Mason nodded reluctantly.

"Thank you. If we're going to make it work, I need to know that you respect me and will respect my decisions."

"I do respect you, G. Is it so wrong of me to want to be part of it, to help?"

She came and planted a peck on his lips. "It's not wrong of you at all. I love you for it. I just want you to love me for me. I want us to be equals. I don't want to feel like the little damsel in distress who needs you to rescue her."

Mason shrugged. He could see that, but he was a man after all. Part of being a man was taking care of the people he loved. Especially taking care of his woman. "I'll go along with whatever you say."

~ ~ ~

Gina sat back and smiled at Cassidy. "So should we go ahead and book our tickets, then?"

Cassidy grinned. "Definitely. It's only a couple of weeks away." This was looking as though it might work. Gina had been dreading going back to New York for her show, but now she couldn't wait to do it. Cassidy was going with her and they were going to use the opportunity to establish a name for themselves, to get the word out that they were working together, and, hopefully, to garner interest in the Moonstone Gallery and their upcoming Montana collection.

"Will you be bringing the sexy Mr. Remington with you?" Cassidy asked.

"I don't think so. It's hard for him to get away from everything at the stud ranch." If she was honest, Gina hadn't even considered asking Mason to come. She was going back to New York, back to the life she'd built without him. She smiled. "What's your problem with the other sexy Mr. Remington anyway?"

Cassidy pursed her lips. "Shane? He is hot. I'll give you that. But guys like him are nothing but trouble. I've been there, done that, got the scars and the T-shirt to prove it. I have no intentions of letting another good looking rat-bastard into my life."

Gina leapt to defend her old friend. "Shane's not like that! He is a big flirt. In fact, scratch that. He's a total man-whore, but he's not a rat-bastard. Honestly Cassidy, if you just get to know him, you'll see. He really is a sweetheart. He's just never found the right woman." She hesitated but decided to say it anyway. "Maybe you could be the right woman."

Cassidy laughed. "No thank you. I'm done with men. You asked me what mistakes I've made that would make getting engaged to Liam seem excusable. Someday, when we've got a whole evening and a couple of decent bottles of wine, maybe I'll tell you some of my horror stories. For now, I'll just leave it at a flat no. I will admit that I'm attracted to Shane." She rolled her eyes and grinned. "Far too attracted to him, okay? But I came out here to get away from all the messes I've made with men. Not to make another one. So do me a favor and drop that one?"

Gina nodded reluctantly. "I'll drop it for now, but I think the two of you might hit it off. He's such a good guy, and he's really taken with you. I've never seen him like that before. He's usually such a charmer, but he gets all tongue tied and goofy around you."

"Whatever. I've told you, I'm not going there. So how about we shut up shop and you come over to the studio with me? I want to show you what I've been working on. I hope that once you see what I'm doing, it'll give you some ideas and you'll go scuttling down to the park with your camera and we can get things rolling."

Gina couldn't wait to get started. The plan was to produce a whole new line of Montana-based images. Cassidy had been painting landscapes since she'd moved to Livingston. Until she met Gina, she hadn't made any plans as to how she would market them. Gina was going to shoot a whole series of wildlife photographs and they would produce a mixed media collection. Their styles were similar enough that they would be able to produce a consistent theme, and between the photography, oils, and watercolors, they should appeal to a wide range of buyers.

When they arrived at Cassidy's home, Gina looked around in wonder. "This place is gorgeous!" It was a beautiful two story log-built home. It stood on what Gina guessed must be at least a hundred acres, judging from the length of the driveway and the winding path that led out from the deck down to the river's edge.

"Thanks." Cassidy laughed. "I just couldn't believe how low property prices are here, so I went a little overboard."

Gina hadn't liked to mention that the place was huge. It was more like a ski lodge than a home, in terms of its size at least. Once they were inside, it certainly felt like a home. And there was no mistaking whose home it was. The whole place had a feel of Cassidy to it. It wasn't just the paintings that covered so much of the wall space. Everything about the place was touched with Cassidy's personality—bold and bright.

It made Gina feel a little inadequate that she was worried about being able to make enough money to keep her dad's ranch going while Cassidy must have made millions. Judging by the house and its furnishings, many millions.

Cassidy seemed to pick up on her thoughts. "I never thought money mattered much. It's never been important to me. Whether I had it or I didn't, it couldn't ever help me with what really mattered." She looked around as if the place surprised her, then went to stand before the peaked windows that soared up to meet a cathedral ceiling. She shrugged. "When I was ready to leave Florida, I finally caved in to the Home Decor people. They'd wanted to buy the rights to most of my beach-themed works. I didn't like the idea of being mass-produced—until I saw the numbers they were talking about. I was done with my 'beach period' anyway so I took the money and ran."

She sounded almost defensive about having made what, to Gina, sounded like a very smart business decision.

"Hey, I'm certainly not judging you. I don't believe commercial and beautiful are mutually exclusive at all. If I ever had the chance to do what you did, I'd be all over it. I could use the money."

Cassidy turned a shrewd gaze on her. "I figured as much. Do you need any help until we get this up and running? I forecast we'll be making serious money within six months, but if you need a loan to tide you over, I'd be happy to help."

Gina sighed. "I think I can hang it all together until we start making it."

"You don't have to though. I want you stress free and happy, wandering around the mountains without a care in the world as you shoot. You know as well as I do that your mood always comes through in your work. This line has to speak of the freedom and happiness that can be found out here. We don't want it tainted by stress and financial worries."

Gina had to laugh. "We *do* think alike, don't we? If I said that to anyone else, they'd think I was nuts."

Cassidy grinned. "They probably would, but we know the truth, don't we? People think that our pictures—your photographs, my paintings—show *what* we saw. We know that they only show *how* we saw it. How we see anything is affected by how we feel at the time. So, I'm not talking charity here. We can call it a bona fide, up-front business expense. If you need money to take the pressure off until we're fully swinging, then you say so, okay?"

"Thanks." Gina wondered why she felt genuinely grateful to Cassidy and was seriously considering taking her up on the offer. When Mason had suggested she let him help, she'd felt much more defensive than grateful. Even though she knew he had the best of intentions.

~ ~ ~

Mason looked up when Chance emerged from his bedroom.

"You look like crap, bro. Do you realize you slept for twenty-four hours?"

Chance nodded and rubbed his face. "So would you if you'd driven the herd up with me. It's been years since you came along, and we were a hell of a lot younger in those days. I tell you, it's tougher now I'm an old man. I could still sleep for another week."

"Yeah. I guess we're not getting any younger, are we?"

Chance stopped on his way to the kitchen. "You feeling philosophical? What's going on with Gina?"

Mason explained everything that had happened while Chance had been gone. "I'm struggling with the fact that we lost ten years that we could have been together. You're right, we're not getting any younger. I want the time back that Gina and I lost, but I know we can never get it back. So, I want to live the hell out of every moment that we can. It'll never make up for it, but I don't want to waste any more time."

"And Gina doesn't feel the same way?"

"I don't know." Mason shrugged at the steely glare Chance gave him. "I want to help her out with her dad's place. She doesn't know if she can afford to keep it going, but she won't let me help. Wants to figure it out by herself."

"And you have a problem with that?"

"I just don't see why she would let her pride get in the way of us just getting on with it. We've lost enough time already. I think we should do whatever it takes to make things right and to be together straight away. I don't see why she wants to go running back to New York to try to make money when she could just stay here and let me take care of it."

Chance laughed and shook his head. "Seriously? You want her to give up everything she's built, not to mention her own pride, just because you're back on the scene? Asshole!"

Mason glared at him. "What do you mean?"

"Exactly what I said. You're being an asshole. The girl's had...what? Less than a day, to digest that everything she's believed for the last ten years was wrong? And you want her to step back into the roles that the two of you had back then? Don't hold your breath, Mase. She's got to find her own way. Even if she let you help her, she'd end up resenting it. She needs to do this for herself."

Mason thought about it. He could see how Chance was right, but he just wanted to help. And he wanted them to get on with their life. Why was that so wrong of him?

"I'm saying she hasn't had time to catch up, but you need to do the same. You need to catch up with who she's become. You need to make sure that you still love who she is now. You've always wanted her back. Wanted to get back what the two of you had. I've got news for you—that's just not possible. And if you try to recreate what you had and treat her like the girl she was, you're setting yourself up for a whole world of hurt."

"But...I'm not...I..."

Chance shrugged. "Just think on it." With that he made his way to the bathroom and soon Mason heard the shower running.

He sat there staring at the wall. Chance was right, of course. He couldn't just pick up where they'd left off and expect everything to be the same. They were both different people now. He knew one thing that hadn't changed. He was still an impatient man. He didn't like waiting around in any situation, and he liked it even less when he saw a solution that he could be getting on with.

He started when his phone rang in his pocket. He was surprised to see Al's name displayed on the screen.

"Al! Is everything okay?"

"No worries here, son. I was calling to ask you the same thing."

Mason smiled. "I think so. We finally cleared the air between us."

"I'm glad. So have you got any good news coming for me?"

"Not yet, but I'm working on it."

"Well, can you hurry it up? She won't promise me that I don't have to move out of here yet!"

"I'm working on it. I can only hurry it so much, Al. It's up to Gina more than me."

"Jesus! She got you whipped already, has she?"

Mason scowled at that. Gina wasn't dictating how things went. He was just giving her time. That was all. Wasn't it?

Al's laugh sounded raspy. "I'm just giving you shit, Mason. You'd better get used to it, seeing as we're going to be family soon. Aren't we?"

That made Mason smile again. "I hope so."

"That's all I wanted to know. I'll leave you in peace then." Al hung up.

Mason got a cold beer from the fridge and took it to sit out on the back porch. He and Al *would* soon be family, wouldn't they? In his mind, it was a given that he and Gina would get married. He started to worry whether she thought so, too. But if she did, why wouldn't she let him help with the money for the ranch?

Chapter Eighteen

Mason was edgy on Sunday morning. Gina still wouldn't hear of him helping her out financially, and it was starting to get to him. It seemed she spent most of her time with Cassidy, figuring out whatever it was they were going to do together. To Mason, it seemed as though they were most focused on going on their little jaunt to New York. He didn't understand why she even felt the need to go anymore.

As he made his way up to the main house, he saw Beau's SUV coming up the driveway. At least that made him smile. Beau came out to the ranch even less than Carter did these days. He wouldn't miss their mom's birthday for the world though. None of them would. Mason gave himself a mental shake. That was what he needed to focus on today, his mom's party. Now that Beau was here, the five of them would be able to pitch in on all the work that needed to be done to get the place ready. Guests were supposed to arrive at three, but some would be early, they always were. Mason wanted to have everything set up by two at the latest. He made his way out front to greet his brother.

"How's it going?" asked Beau.

"Pretty good. Shane's started setting up the tables out back and Carter's in the kitchen."

Beau laughed. "Carter's always in the kitchen."

"Yeah, but this time he's prepping food instead of eating it." Carter's appetite was a standing joke amongst the brothers.

"I'd put my money on him eating at least half as much as he prepares."

"Probably, but from the amount he brought in, there should still be more than enough to feed the whole valley, and I think only half the valley is coming."

Beau nodded. "Want me to get the bar set up?"

"You can give me a hand stringing the lights on the back deck. Chance is already working on the bar." He didn't miss his brother's scowl at that piece of information. "Let it go, bro. I don't know why you still have a problem with him. He's one of us."

Beau glared at him. "He isn't one of us though, is he? You, me, Carter, Shane, we're brothers. Chance isn't. I know the two of you are close. I know Dad sees him as one of his own, but I don't know why. He's not family."

Mason sighed. He didn't want to get into this one today. Beau had had a problem with Chance since he first came to the ranch. Mason had to admit he had been a little wary of Chance back then as well. Their dad had met him through a youth rehabilitation project. He'd been a volunteer, working with kids who'd been in prison. He'd seen something in Chance and wanted to give him the opportunity to get his life back on track. He'd brought Chance home with him and given him a job working the cattle, even though he knew nothing at all about ranching. He'd given him a place to live in the cabin that Mason and Shane now shared with him. Mason admired his

dad's kindness and generosity. He and Chance had soon come
to be the best of friends. Shane had accepted Chance as
another big brother fairly quickly. As far as Mason and Shane
were concerned, he was a fifth brother. Carter liked Chance,
but wasn't as close to him. He'd been caught up in his own life
and was more of a loner. Beau was the only one who had a
problem. As the second eldest, he'd been competitive as a kid.
He'd always pushed himself to try to prove his worth and,
Mason guessed, to win their dad's approval. He'd resented
Chance from the day he arrived and didn't seem prepared to
let it go. "Let's not go there, huh? Not today. Today's about
Mom and making sure she enjoys her birthday, right?"

Beau nodded. "Right." He smiled. "So let's go get these lights
strung. And while we're doing it, you can catch me up on
what's been going on with you and Gina. Why's her dad's place
still showing on the listings? I thought she'd have taken it off
the market by now. She is staying, right?"

Mason rolled his eyes. "She is, and if it were up to me, it would
be off the market by now."

Beau gave him an inquiring look. "But?"

"But she wants to take care of it herself." He shrugged. "I
guess it's just a matter of time while she figures things out, but
I'm not a patient man."

Beau laughed at that. "Sounds like you're going to have to be
on this one. You can't force her hand."

"I know, but we already lost ten years. I don't want to lose
anymore. I just want to get on with making up for it. I want to
hurry up and start living the life we've missed out on."

"You will, but don't let your impatience screw things up,
okay?"

Mason nodded reluctantly. "I'm trying. Anyway, enough about me. What's going on with you?"

Beau shrugged. "Same old, same old. The market's picking up and with spring around the corner I'm expecting we'll get busy with new listings and out-of-staters starting to look for vacation homes." Beau had sat for his realtor's license as soon as he came back from college. He'd done very well for himself and owned his own real estate brokerage. Unlike most of the realtors in the area, he worked the whole market. He sold multi-million dollar estates on the river, and he sold condos and tiny cottages in town. Everyone had thought he'd made a big mistake a few years back when he'd bought an entire section of land just outside the city limits. His plan was to build a new subdivision, but market conditions had never been right. Mason didn't know much about real estate, but he did know that Beau would make a huge profit on that investment someday. Where he was impatient and occasionally impetuous, Beau was patient and shrewd.

"Well do me a favor and don't go showing the Delaney place to anyone, would you? If Gina *does* have to sell, I plan on buying it myself."

"You do?"

He nodded. He did. No matter what Gina had to say about it.

~ ~ ~

Gina let herself back into Cassidy's kitchen. They'd had a great morning baking together. She was glad she'd persuaded Cassidy to come to Monique's birthday party. She didn't seem to know many people yet and, although she insisted that she liked it that way, Gina wanted her to show her face in the community. She knew her dad would love Cassidy, and she also had the ulterior motive of getting her in the same room as

Shane again. She wanted the two of them to talk about ways
they could market to Shane's dude ranch guests. More than
that, she wanted to see how long Cassidy would be able to
resist Shane's charms—or whether Shane would be able to
summon said charms or would go all tongue-tied around
Cassidy again. Gina was fairly sure sparks would fly between
the two of them at some point, she just wanted to hurry the
process along.

Cassidy was pulling two huge pies from the fridge. "I'll take
these in my car, shall I?"

"Oh, aren't you riding with me?"

"No, thank you very much. I'm not stupid, Gina. I know what
you're up to, and I want my trusty car at the ready so I can
make a quick getaway whenever I want to."

Gina feigned innocence. "What do you think I'm up to? I'm
just trying to introduce you to your neighbors and maybe make
some connections that will be useful to us. Why would you
need a getaway?"

Cassidy scowled at her. "You're hoping that if you leave me
alone with Shane, I'll start to see why you love him so much.
Sorry, but it's not happening. I already told you. I came here to
get away from man messes, not to make another one."

Gina shrugged. "Okay, I'll admit I'm hopeful, but you don't
need to bring your car. I promise I'll bring you back whenever
you're ready to leave."

"Thanks, but I'd sooner drive myself."

"Okay, do you want to follow me over to pick my dad up,
then?"

"Yep, just let me load these up and I'll be right behind you."

The party was in full swing by the time they got there. Crowds
of people milled around in front of the main house. Carter was

working the grill out on the porch and waved when he saw Gina. She waved back and turned to look for her dad and Cassidy. To her amusement, her dad had announced he was going to ride with Cassidy and get to know her on the way over. She saw them, arm in arm, making their way down the long line of parked cars. Cassidy said something that made him laugh and Gina had to laugh herself as she watched them. It was so good to see her dad looking happy and sprightlier than he had in years. She was hoping that her working with Cassidy would give him a new lease on life, too.

He grinned at her. "I'm going to say happy birthday to Monique and leave you girls to it. Cassidy here doesn't trust me to carry nothing." He squeezed Cassidy's arm before he let go of it. "She's a smart one, this new partner of yours."

"It's not that I don't trust you, Al. I just think you should get to the party as quickly as you can. It looks like your friends are up on the porch and I can only see two empty seats. I thought you might want to go claim one."

Al squinted up at the front porch, then turned back to Cassidy with a scowl on his face. "All I see up on that porch is a bunch of old farts. What are you trying to say?"

Cassidy didn't miss a beat, she pointed out past the garage to where a group of youngsters was standing around. "That I don't think you'd have too much fun with them, even if your hip could take it, so you'll probably want to go grab a seat with the old farts, while you can."

Gina loved the way her dad laughed at that. Cassidy wasn't going to take any of his crap, and it seemed the two of them were already forming a bond of their own. It looked as though everything was coming together. She had found a new friend in Cassidy and was getting her old friends back. Her dad was happier than she'd seen him in years. She and Mason were back together even though they had yet to figure out what their future would hold. She didn't want him trying to solve her financial problems for her. It was important that she do that herself, both for the sake of her own pride and for the sake of the kind of relationship she wanted to build with him. She'd almost reconciled herself to accepting Cassidy's offer to help her out until they started making good money. As she had said, that wasn't charity, it was simply business sense.

"He's an absolute sweetheart!" said Cassidy as they watched Al make his way up onto the porch.

Gina laughed "He's an old grouch, but I think he's taken a shine to you."

"I've taken a shine to him, too."

"And here comes another one who's taken a shine to you." Gina saw Shane's face light up when he spotted her and Cassidy.

"Uh oh. Hadn't we better get these pies and cakes to whoever is in charge of the kitchen?"

Before Gina could reply, Cassidy was heading back to her car to collect the goodies they'd brought. She was tickled that Cassidy's usual confidence and composure seemed to evaporate as she stuck her head in the trunk at Shane's approach.

He hugged Gina and then addressed himself to Cassidy's butt. "Hey, it's good to see you again."

Gina had to stifle a giggle as Cassidy straightened up and bumped her head. She whirled around. "I wish I could say the same."

"Then why don't you?"

She scowled. "Because I'm not a liar."

Gina was surprised to see the disappointment that flashed in
Shane's eyes for a moment. Normally everything was a joke to
him. If he got the brush-off, he didn't care. He moved on. He
certainly didn't stick around for more. It seemed he was a
glutton for punishment where Cassidy was concerned.

Cassidy straightened up and glared at Shane. "I don't know
how many times or how many ways I need to tell you before it
sinks in. I'm not interested, Shane."

Shane recovered quickly and grinned. "That's only because you
don't know me yet. I'm trying to rectify that situation. So, how
about we let Gina take that stuff inside and you come let me
get you a drink?"

"No, thank you." She looked at Gina. "Shall we?"

Gina gave Shane a sympathetic shrug. "I guess we'll see you
later."

Shane shot Cassidy a rueful smile. "Not if you see me first,
right?"

There was the tiniest hint of a smile on her face when she
replied. "You got *that* right."

Gina led the way up to the kitchen. "You're not even going to
give him a chance?" She had a feeling Cassidy's resolve might
be fading a little.

"I doubt it. I figure if I brush him off a few more times he'll
get bored and target someone else."

Gina would normally have agreed, but she hadn't seen Shane
like this before. "And if he doesn't?"

Cassidy almost smiled as she replied. "If he doesn't, then we'll
see about that, won't we?"

"Hey, babe."

Gina didn't have time to consider Cassidy's answer before
Mason was taking the cake tins from her and planting a kiss on

her lips. She wrapped her arms around his neck and kissed him back. It felt right and familiar, yet new and exciting all at the same time. Mason wrapped an arm around her waist and pulled her against him. "Hey. It looks like a good turnout. Is everything going okay?"

Mason nodded. "Everything's great. Most importantly, Mom's having a wonderful time. She's holding court in the kitchen right now. You should probably go say hi, she's been asking about you."

"We were on our way there."

Mason looked up. "Oh, hi Cassidy. Sorry."

Cassidy laughed. "That's okay. Why would you notice me when you've got Gina?"

Mason shrugged sheepishly. "Sorry. I'll let you both go and do the women's stuff." He landed another kiss on Gina's lips. "I'll be with Carter on the grill when you get done."

Gina watched him walk away, hoping that she'd be able to get him to herself for a while later. He was looking absolutely breathtaking, and they had a lot of making up to do.

"Do all the Remington boys look like sex on a stick?" Cassidy asked as she, too, watched Mason's muscular frame make his way through the crowd.

Gina laughed as she turned to her friend. "Let's go say hi to Monique and then we'll find Carter and Beau so you can judge for yourself. I have a feeling you'll still like Shane the best."

"Who said I like Shane?"

Gina shrugged. "I don't know. Maybe it's that little smile you get on your face every time you talk to him, no matter how mean you're being to him."

"I am not mean! I'm just honest, that's all."

"Whatever you say. Come on. Let's go see Monique."

When they finally escaped the ladies in the kitchen, Gina dipped them each a glass of punch and led Cassidy out back to a quiet spot behind the garage.

"Phew! I think I'm ready to escape," said Cassidy. "That was a lot of ladies with a lot of questions."

"Yes, but they all loved you. Hopefully now that they've met you, you've dispelled some of the mystery."

"I hope so."

"Don't be surprised if they start coming in the gallery now. And don't be surprised if they start buying. Newcomers are an object of mystery for a while and then they're either accepted or rejected. I think you've just been accepted."

Cassidy nodded. "I thought I'd been rejected from the outset. It seemed that none of the locals ever came in."

"That's because they didn't know you and what you were about. Now they do."

Cassidy laughed. "Now they know everything about me, and more. That was an inquisition, for sure."

"Ha. You got off lightly. You're good at deflecting, plus they were more focused on me and Mason. We've been a source of gossip and conjecture for years. You should think yourself lucky."

Cassidy shuddered. "Ugh. If this is lucky, I'd hate to be unlucky. Can we go find that hot cowboy of yours and get a burger? I didn't eat this morning and this punch is going to go right to my head."

Gina was only too happy to go find Mason. He was right where he'd said he'd be, with Carter.

When Mason introduced them, Cassidy shook Carter's hand warmly. Gina noticed that Carter wouldn't meet her eye. She still wished that he could meet a good woman. He hadn't been the same since Trisha. Gina had never liked her. She hated the way Carter had changed. He'd always been the quietest of the

Remington brothers, but he used to be so warm and funny, too. These days he was much more reserved. From what she'd seen and heard of him since she'd been back, he didn't have much of a social life unless you counted the gym.

"So you're the Remington Nurseries brother?" Cassidy asked him.

Carter nodded. "That'd be me."

"Oh good. I've been meaning to give you a call. I want to get some work done at my place, but I have no clue what I'm doing in this climate."

"What kind of work?"

"Planting…landscaping. The way the wind blows all the time at my place, I was wondering about planting trees."

"Where are you?"

"Down by the river at the bottom of Mill Lane."

Carter's eyes widened. "You bought the Allen house?"

Cassidy nodded. "You know it?"

"Know it? I used to work with old Mr. Allen before he passed on. There was so much he wanted to do, but after he got sick, his kids didn't want him spending money out there. They wanted to move him down to Colorado to be closer to them. I have so many ideas for that place. There's so much you could do down there." He stopped himself. "Sorry. As you can tell, I love what I do. Give me a call when you're ready and we can talk about what *you* want to do."

Gina smiled at Cassidy's reply. "Please don't apologize. I only work with people who love what they do. I drive normal people nuts. I'd love to hear your ideas. Give me a call tomorrow?" She handed Carter her card, just as Shane came to join them.

He shot a look at Carter. "I've been trying to get her number for weeks."

Cassidy pursed her lips and turned back to Carter. "So call me? I have to be leaving now, but I can't wait to see you again."

Gina exchanged a grin with Mason at the expression on Shane's face as he watched Cassidy leave.

"What the...?"

Carter grinned at Shane and lifted a shoulder. He saw what was going on and was happy to play along. "What can I say, bro? You win some, you lose some. I guess she prefers the strong silent type."

They were all surprised at Shane's angry response. "Thanks, Carter. Thanks a bunch." He turned on his heel and left them staring after him.

"Oops," said Carter. "I didn't realize it was a big deal to him. I guess I fucked up again, huh?"

Mason put a hand on his shoulder. "No, you didn't. I think the problem is that Shane didn't realize it was a big deal to him either, and now he's realizing he doesn't know what to do with it."

Gina nodded at his assessment. "Don't worry about it, Carter." She gave him a hug. "Shane will be fine."

Carter nodded. "I know. She likes him. I can tell."

Mason laughed. "Jesus! Are Shane and I the only ones who don't pick up on what women mean?"

Gina slapped his arm. "You're certainly not the only ones, but you might want to take some lessons from Carter. He could probably help you both out." She loved building Carter up and had done so instinctively since they were all kids. The other three brothers could and would toot their own horns at any opportunity. Carter was less confident and more caring.

"I don't think my track record qualifies me to be giving anyone lessons." He gave them a sad smile. "But you know I'm here if anyone needs me."

Gina hugged him again.

"Okay, enough with the mushy stuff." Even as he said it, Mason slapped Carter's back. They all knew the subject was better changed, but it seemed none of them knew how.

"Sorry," said Gina. "I'm going to leave you to it and go see how Shane's doing."

She pecked Mason's lips then made her way through the crowd in the direction Shane had gone.

Chapter Nineteen

Gina smiled at people and waved as she made her way through the crowd. She figured Shane had probably gone out to his office. It wasn't like him to be snappy or to walk away. She wanted to talk to him.

"Hello, Gina."

The voice stopped her in her tracks. She'd heard it so many times in her dreams over the years. Heard him asking Mason about getting back with April. She felt the shiver run down her spine as she turned to face him.

"Guy."

He let his eyes wander over her, making her shiver again. She wanted nothing more than to walk away from him and not look back. However, she did at least want to tell him that he would not be coming out to view the ranch. Hearing his voice had confirmed that she would never sell to him, and it made her decision. She couldn't sell at all. She'd accept Cassidy's offer of a loan to keep her going.

"You're looking good, Gina. Good enough to...I bet you're quite something between the sheets."

God, he was disgusting. "Well, you'll never know, will you?"

He grinned at that. "Actually, I thought we should find out. I hear you've been seeing Mason since you came back, but we both know how that ended for you last time."

How dare he. She wasn't going to let him come between them again. "Mason and I are just fine thank you very much, and it's really none of your business."

The sneer on his face made her stomach turn. "I'd say it is kind of my business since I've been raising his kid all this time."

She sucked in a sharp breath and felt her heart stop. What the hell was he talking about?

"I thought you came to your senses back then, figured out what he was like and got away from him. Poor April wasn't as smart as you. She let him knock her up and I picked up the pieces. I've raised the boy as my own, but..." His grin was sickening. "Don't tell me he hasn't told you? I thought that was why you walked out on him at Pine Creek the other night."

Gina's mind was racing. When she'd watched Mason talking to April, it had looked like a lot more than a *Hello, how are you.* Mason had even said he still felt responsible for her. Was that why? She shook her head. No, it couldn't be. After everything they'd talked through these last few days, everything they'd promised each other about being open and keeping no more secrets, there was no way he would have omitted to tell her that he had a child—with April no less.

Guy put a hand on her shoulder. "Sorry, I didn't mean to shock you. I thought you knew. He's an asshole. Always has been. I'd hate to see you get involved with him again after you had such a lucky escape. He makes me out to be the bad guy, but it's always been him, Gina. I'm the one trying to buy your dad's ranch to help you out. What's he doing for you? Nothing." He squeezed her shoulder. "Why don't you get out of here with me and I'll tell you everything I know. We could get some dinner and..." He ran his gaze over her, letting it linger on her breasts, making her skin crawl.

"No." She turned and walked away. She couldn't bring herself to say another word to him.

She didn't want to find Shane anymore. She just wanted a moment to herself. She kept walking until she came to the barn. She made her way to Annie's stall and buried her face in the mare's neck. As she breathed in the warm reassuring scent of horse, she felt the trembling start to subside.

Guy Preston was a bastard. An evil, meddling bastard. That was all. She wasn't going to let him come between her and Mason this time. She knew what she had to do. She wasn't going to make the same mistake again. She needed to find Mason and talk to him. Ask him whether it was true. She didn't believe it was, but the nasty little voice in her head kept doing the math and telling her that it could be. She wanted to stay here for a little while, get over the shock. She ran her fingers through Annie's mane. "It isn't true, old girl, is it?" She hated the break in her voice. It shouldn't be there, she should sound—and feel—strong, convinced that this was just another of Guy's attempts to hurt Mason. She wished she didn't feel the gnawing doubt. But it was there. She knew from experience that it wouldn't go away until she talked to Mason about it, and this time she wasn't going to wait ten years before she did. She patted Annie one last time and made her way back out of the barn.

~ ~ ~

Mason knew something was wrong as soon as he saw Gina's face. Whatever it was, it couldn't be good. He started making his way over to where she was standing out by the barn. She was scanning the crowd, but she hadn't spotted him yet.

He tried to be as polite as he could in brushing people off on his way to her. He didn't want to talk about the weather or the party or even his horses. He just needed to get to Gina and ask her what the hell was wrong. He saw April sitting alone at one of the tables. She looked terrible, but he didn't have time to check on her at the moment... She looked up and saw him and called him over. Gina was still searching the crowd, he was pretty sure she was looking for him. April raised a hand to wave him over and he noticed the bruises on her arm. Damn. He had a pretty good idea how she'd gotten those. He had to make sure she was all right.

"Is everything okay?" he asked when he got to her.

She nodded but looked as though everything was far from okay.

"What is it?"

"I'm sorry, Mason."

"What for, April. What is it?"

"He's really got it in for you this time. I can't stop him. I'm sorry, but I have to put my son first."

The pulse in Mason's temple started to pound. "What are you talking about? What's he doing?"

As she looked up at him, he thought he could make out bruises under her makeup. What was that bastard doing to her? Mason had tried to get her to leave Guy many times over the years. She said she'd made her bed so she had to lie in it, that she believed marriage was forever and it would get better. He was pretty sure that Guy had some hold on her that she wasn't talking about. If he was hitting her, there was no way Mason would be able to stand back and do nothing. "I can't tell you, Mason. I just wanted you to know how sorry I am. You know I wouldn't do it if I had any other choice."

"April, what are you talking about? You wouldn't do what? And why don't you have a choice? You're worrying me. I think it's time we get you away from him."

She stood up suddenly. "I have to go. He's looking for me."

Mason followed her gaze to where Guy was standing. How he hated that asshole. "Let me help you, April. You don't need to go with him."

Her eyes were wide with fear. "I do, Mason. I just had to tell you how sorry I am." She turned and fled before he could ask her again what it was she was sorry for.

He turned to see Gina staring at him. What was it with the women around here today? She looked as though the world was about to end, too! Oh shit, she had just seen him talking to April, but they were over that, right? Gina knew that all April had ever been to him was a decoy—didn't she? He crammed his hat further down on his head and made his way to her.

"What is it, G?" he asked when he reached her.

She took a deep breath and met his gaze. "I hate asking you this, but I have to. We promised each other we wouldn't keep any more secrets, that we'd be completely honest with each other, right?"

Mason nodded. "Whatever it is, just ask." He had nothing to hide.

"Is April's son yours?"

He stared at her for a moment, the words didn't make sense. "Is April's son...what!?" As he spoke the words himself, he understood their meaning. "Jesus, Gina! Why in the hell would you think that? I told you. I never wanted back with her. I never got back with her. What the..."

She put a hand up. "Don't be mad at me. I had to ask. Guy told me the boy was yours. I knew it had to be a lie, but once the doubt takes hold there's nothing you can do. I had to ask you, Mason."

He took a deep breath to calm himself then drew her to him and wrapped her in his arms. "Sorry, babe. I get it, you did have to ask. We promised no more secrets. That is not a secret I am keeping, nor would I ever keep. You know me. If I had a kid, I'd be taking care of him myself. I'm glad you asked me." He held her a little closer. "If anything, we can thank Guy for making us stronger. You came straight to me. That means a lot." He tipped her chin so she was looking up at him. What he saw in her eyes killed him, because what he saw was doubt. His heart raced. "You don't believe me?"

She shook her head rapidly and tightened her arms around him. "It's not that. I do believe you. I'm just still in shock from hearing him say it. And...and I just saw you with her. What's going on between the two of you, Mase?"

"Nothing. There's nothing between me and her, not like that. I told you, I do feel responsible for her. Not responsible for her kid or anything, but as I said, she has a horrible life, and I feel as though it's my fault. I put him on her. You know?"

Gina nodded, but she didn't look convinced. "Do you still care for her?"

Mason gritted his teeth and let out an exasperated sigh. "Not in that way...no. I never did. We dated in high school, before you and I ever got together. She was a friend, Gina. I think he's hurting her, so yes, I do care. But then I'd care for anyone in that situation, especially since I feel like I was the one who put her there. I think you would, too?"

She met his gaze and he saw all the compassion in her eyes that made her who she was. "He's hurting her? Why doesn't she leave him? We have to help her, Mase."

"I don't know how. I've offered to help her get away from him over the years. I knew she was miserable, but I never thought he'd hit her. He has some hold over her. Honestly, I think he threatens her about the boy, but I don't know that."

"What did she say just now? Is she all right?"

Mason shrugged. "She kept telling me she's sorry. She wouldn't tell me what for. Just that Guy's really got it in for me this time."

Gina nodded. "Well, if we hadn't already cleared things up between us, I hate to admit it, but I probably would have believed him."

Mason nodded. Much as he hated to hear it, he could see why Gina would think that way. He dropped a kiss onto her upturned nose. "It's a good thing we already talked everything out then, isn't it?"

She nodded. "He can't come between us anymore, Mase. I love you. I'm not going to let anything destroy what we have this time. Especially not him."

"I love you, too, babe. You did the most important thing, and you trusted me enough to come to me and ask. You trusted me to tell you the truth."

She nodded.

"Babe, I want to put the past behind us. Please let me help you with keeping the ranch. I'll buy it if you need me to or I'll help you keep up with the cost of running it if you prefer. Just please say that we're back in it together?" He held her gaze.

"You said we can make it up to each other every day for the rest of our lives. I want us back on track, and to me the rest of our lives mean we share them, as man and wife. Do you agree?" He'd been thinking for days about how and when he would ask her to marry him. He didn't want to ask her like this, now, motivated by Guy's meddling, but at the same time he needed to know that it was still what she wanted.

She nodded, but her eyes were troubled. "I told you I need to take care of this by myself. I need you to understand that. I love that you want to help, but I have to do it by myself."

He stared at her. He could understand the pride side of it. What he didn't understand was how she felt about marrying him. He waited for more, but no more came.

"Do you understand?"

He nodded. He didn't want to, but her lack of an answer made it pretty clear.

"Thank you. We'll figure it out."

Together, but not married? Was that what she meant? He had to be as strong as she'd just been and ask. "What do you mean? What are we going to figure out?"

She stared at him for a moment. "I mean about the ranch. I need to do that myself, what we need to figure out is how that fits in with us being us."

"And how does it fit in with us being married?" He had to know. In his mind, a married couple shared finances, just as they shared everything else.

She searched his face. "We're not married though, are we?"

"Do you want to be?" He didn't want to ask her here and now. He wanted to ask her at the right moment, in the right way. But he did want—no, he needed—to know that it was what she wanted.

She nodded.

That was enough. For now. He'd hoped for a little more enthusiasm, but then she'd probably hoped for a proposal, too. "Okay. Do you want to get back to Mom's party then?"

She blew out a big sigh. "Yeah."

He took her hand and led her back into the crowd of people. It was late afternoon, but the party was still going strong. He knew more folks would show up into the evening and most would hang out until it got dark. His mom loved to have her firework display. She was fortunate that her birthday fell in mud season. This time of year, there was so much rain that there were no concerns about wildfires. The Fourth of July saw them head up into town to watch fireworks since most of the valley was under no-burn restrictions by then.

~ ~ ~

Gina spotted Shane sitting on the fence with Chance. She'd been going to find him and make sure he was okay when she'd been waylaid by Guy. She tugged on Mason's hand. "Can we go check on Shane?"

Mason nodded. "He's not right lately, and I think that new friend of yours has a lot to do with it."

"It looks that way, doesn't it? I wasn't sure whether it was just an ego thing. You know what he's like. He wants what he wants and he expects to be able to make it happen with a snap of his fingers."

Mason smiled. "Especially when it comes to women. I don't know. This seems different. It's not like him to get snappy. Especially at Carter. Those two are close."

Gina nodded. "Well, he looks okay now." He did, too. He and Chance were perched on top of the five bar looking out at the crowd. They each had a beer in hand and were chatting and laughing as though neither had a care in the world.

Chance saw them coming first and waved his bottle at them. "How's it going, guys?"

"It's going," said Mason. "Guy was out here trying to mess things up for us again." His smile, as he hugged Gina to his side, made her so happy. It also filled her with relief that she'd gone straight to ask him about what Guy had said. He was right, she should be grateful to Guy for presenting them with a test that had only made them stronger.

Shane rolled his eyes. "I hate that asshole."

Chance nodded his agreement, then smiled at Gina. "He's not going to come between the two of you this time though, is he?"

She shook her head. "No matter how hard he tries." She smiled up at Mason. "I'm back for good and we're back together. Nothing is going to get in the way of that."

"Have you figured out what you're going to do with the ranch then?"

She squeezed Mason's hand. "We're not going to sell. Cassidy and I are going into business together. Hopefully, we'll be making good money soon and it won't be an issue anymore."

"And I'm ready to help, in the meantime." There was an edge to Mason's voice that she didn't like. She knew he was ready to help. Why wouldn't he see that she couldn't let him?

Shane picked up on the uneasiness between them and changed the subject. "I thought you and Cassidy wanted to talk to me about what marketing we could do through the dude ranch?"

Gina nodded. "We did. She got a little overwhelmed though. You know what it's like when you're the subject of an inquisition by the local ladies. It's exhausting. She headed home. We'll have to get together and talk about it during the week."

Shane brightened a little at that.

Chance grinned at him. "I thought you'd have given up on her by now."

"I would if I had any sense, but it seems I don't when it comes to her. I'm starting to understand how moths feel."

Mason gave him a puzzled look. "What have moths got to do with anything?"

Shane rolled his eyes. "Dumb little creatures are attracted to the light, aren't they? They must know they're going to crash and burn, but they keep flying back to the light. They just can't stay away. That's how I feel about Cassidy. Every time I get around her, I know nothing good's going to come of it, but I have to fly back in for another try." He hung his head and swung his legs. "Just a dumb moth! I should learn from experience and go fly somewhere else."

Mason and Chance exchanged a grin. Gina laughed. "You're not a quitter, Shane. You never have been, and I don't think you should start now."

He lifted his head. "You think there's a chance?" he asked hopefully.

She nodded. "But you may have to wait a while."

"I can do that." He was grinning again.

Mason shook his head. "Since when have you known how to be patient?"

Shane hopped down from the fence and pointed to a group of girls sitting at one of the tables. One of them looked up and waved at him. "I don't," he said with a grin. "But I do know how to distract myself to make the time pass quicker while I wait."

They watched him make his way over to the girls and slide onto the bench to sit in between them. Soon he had an arm around the girl on either side of him and the whole group was laughing.

Watching Shane's hand slide down one girl's back to rest on her backside, Chance shook his head. "I don't think we need to worry about him and Cassidy too much."

"Me neither," agreed Mason.

Gina wasn't so sure.

Chapter Twenty

The party had been a huge success. Mason was pleased to see his mom so happy. The fireworks had been the perfect end to a wonderful day. He was ready to get some time alone with Gina. It seemed they spent too much of their time dealing with other people's issues. Whether it was Guy or Shane or Gina's business with Cassidy, there was always something preventing them from just being alone together and enjoying each other. They'd dropped Gina's dad back home and now Mason pointed the truck up toward Six Mile.

Gina smiled over at him. "Where are we going?"

He put his hand on her knee and smiled. "I thought we could go watch the stars for a while like we used to. The fireworks were pretty, but they've got nothing on the shooting stars. Do you want to?"

She covered his hand with her own. "I'd love to."

They drove on in silence for a while, the headlights illuminating the road ahead. Mason had to bring up something that was bothering him. "It's not like we have a place of our own we could go to anyway."

"What do you mean?"

"Even if we just wanted to go home." He slid his hand a little higher and squeezed her thigh. "To bed. Where would we go? I wouldn't feel right going to your dad's place or to the cabin with Chance and Shane on the other side of the bedroom walls."

He waited while she thought it over, wondering what she might say. "What do you want to do about that?"

He shrugged. "I don't know. Do you have any ideas?"

"Honestly, I hadn't even thought about it yet, I've been so busy with everything else."

Mason nodded. Maybe it just wasn't that important to her. He was starting to feel as though he wasn't such a priority for her as she was for him. "When do you think you might find time to think about it?"

She sighed. "I don't know. Cassidy and I are leaving in a couple of days for New York. I'm scrambling to get everything ready. Can we talk about it when I come back?"

Wow, it seemed he really *was* slipping down the priority list.

She squeezed his hand and slid it further up her thigh. "I'm kind of glad we have an excuse to come up here. I mean we're a bit old to be sneaking off in your truck, aren't we?"

"Are we?" Mason didn't think they were. Making love under the stars wasn't solely reserved for kids with nowhere else to go. At least not in his mind. In his mind, it was something special.

Gina's smile faded. "I guess we're not, no. I think I've gotten a little confused lately about the difference between being responsible and simply enjoying myself. Everything's changed for me in the last couple of weeks, and I'm playing catch up." Her smile returned as she met his gaze. "Can we make the rest of tonight about enjoying ourselves and each other?" She reached across to put her hand on his thigh.

Mason wasn't going to argue. Even if he wanted to, his cock was firmly on Gina's side. She wanted to enjoy each other? Hell yeah, he was in. Talk of where they might live could wait—for a while.

~ ~ ~

Gina leaned against Mason and looked up at the stars. She felt at peace. Sitting here under the big, velvety-dark sky, with Mason's arm around her, she knew that everything would work out. She didn't know how or when, but, right now, that didn't matter. She just knew it would.

She turned to look up at his handsome face. She loved to look at him. She could still see the boy he'd been, but she loved the man he'd become. His face was weathered, the lines around his eyes made him even sexier. His full lips still had a ready smile, but when his face was resting he looked distant, lost in thought.

"I love you, Mason."

"And I love you."

She slid her arm around his waist. "Want to show me how much?"

His smile was all the reply she needed as he lowered his lips to hers. His kisses still stole her senses—that hadn't changed. She had wondered whether it was just because she was a girl back then how the way he kissed her made the rest of the world— every thought in her head—disappear. She knew it was just the effect he had on her. Even with everything that was going on, her head emptied as he claimed her mouth. She kissed him back hungrily, sliding her hand into his lap to cup his hard-on. It was chilly out here now. She could see her breath, but it was warm under the blankets. She was eager to shrug out of her clothes as he peeled them off her.

When they were both naked, he rolled her onto her back, sliding his hand between her legs to torment her. For all the ways she wanted them to be equals, this wasn't one of them. He was in charge, and she was happily at his mercy. She moved her hips in time with his fingers as he stroked her. She wanted him badly, wanted him to take her hard and fast. She was surprised when he lifted his head, his gaze intense.

"Ride me, Gina."

She wasn't about to say no. She pushed him onto his back and straddled him, wrapping the blanket around her shoulders as she went. Taking hold of him, she guided him towards her, her breath coming slow and shallow in anticipation of the moment he would thrust his hips and fill her. He filled his hands with her breasts as she positioned him. His eyes were soft as he looked into hers. This used to be her favorite position with him. He would pull her on top of him and then grasp her hips while he gave her the ride of her life. This time it was different. His words confirmed it. "Take me."

She'd never taken him. He had always taken her—and she'd loved it. But just like when he'd made her come to him at the barn, she felt the balance was shifting between them. It felt right. She held herself above him, stroking herself with the very tip of him. Seeing him sigh, watching him close his eyes, she felt powerful. Now he was at *her* mercy. She took her time, rubbing him against her clit, teasing herself until she was soaking for him. His hands rested on her hips, occasionally tightening when she stroked his head, but never grasping and pulling her down onto him. Never taking control or taking over.

He met her gaze, his eyes pleading, his breath coming hard. "Please?"

Wow! Mason didn't beg, he took. She *had* to take him. She thrust her hips hard, taking him deep inside her. They both moaned as she impaled herself on him. He felt so damned good. She leaned forward, taking her weight onto her hands so she could kiss him while she rode him desperately. There was nothing slow or tender about it. *She* was fucking *him*! And it felt wonderful. She could feel him tense up, so she slowed down, pushing herself back to sit upright. She rocked her hips back and forth, sliding herself up and down the length of his cock. Tormenting him felt so good, but she was close to the edge and ready to go over. She caught his hands and brought them up to cover her breasts. She gasped when he fingered her nipples and squeezed, sending her back into her desperate rhythm. He grew harder with each thrust and she could feel herself tightening around him.

"Gina!" his release triggered her own, making her moan as she rode the waves of pleasure that crashed through her. His hips bucked wildly underneath her and she hung on for the ride. When she finally collapsed back down onto his chest, he closed his arms around her and buried his face in her neck, just as he'd always done. It was so familiar and yet now completely new. He wasn't resting on her after doing what he'd wanted with her. He was nestling into her after giving himself up to her.

When their breathing had returned to normal, she propped herself up to look down at him.

"Ride 'em, cowgirl," he said with a smile.

She smiled back. "I'll have to wait a while before the next round. I've got jelly legs right now."

He closed his hands around her ass. "That's okay, you won't have to work so hard for it next time."

"I'm surprised you let me this time."

He shrugged. "You're different. We're different. It only makes sense that what we do will be different. His grin was back, letting her know the balance between them would never shift completely. "And besides I wanted to see what you had for me."

"And you approve?"

He winked. "I dunno yet, we may need a few repeat performances before I can give you a final verdict."

She laughed and rolled off him. "Why does that not surprise me?"

He curled an arm around her and hugged her to his chest. "Because you know me, babe. Better than anyone ever has or ever will."

~ ~ ~

As they rode down the long driveway back to Gina's dad's, Mason shot a look over at her.

"I don't like this. I really have to drop you home in the middle of the night and go back to a cold bed in the bunkhouse?"

She laughed. "You hardly live in a bunkhouse, Mase."

"I know, but it's the same principle. You're going home to your father's house and I'm going back to the place I share with a bunch of guys."

She stared at him for a long moment. "You could come in, stay with me? I hardly think Dad would be surprised to see you in the morning."

Mason thought about it. He didn't like the idea of staying in Al's house, in his daughter's bed. It just didn't seem right. But the alternative was going back to the cabin and sleeping another night without her. "I don't know, G. I want us to work something out. Have a place that's ours."

Her smile felt as though she was trying to appease him. "I do, too. Let's both think about it while I'm gone and we'll figure out what to do when I get back."

Mason scowled. He didn't like that idea. She was putting him and their future on the back burner while she focused on her career. Was that really more important to her?

"Don't look like that. I swear I just saw thunderclouds roll across your face."

"Well," he shrugged, "whatever you say, babe. I just don't want to wait too long. We've got ten years to make up for."

She nodded as he pulled up in front of the house. "I know that. I feel the same way. But after waiting ten years to get here, I think it's worth taking a couple of weeks to make sure we get it right, don't you?"

He couldn't argue with that, no matter how much he wanted to. Instead, he leaned across and slid his fingers into her hair. "I suppose. But you know I'm not a patient man." He pulled her head back and took advantage of her open mouth to kiss her thoroughly.

When they came up for air, she smiled at him. "Are you sure you don't want to stay?"

He nodded reluctantly. He did want to stay, but he wouldn't feel right doing what he wanted to do to her under her father's roof. No matter how old they were. "Call me in the morning? I'll be out at the barn early. You could come ride Annie if you like?"

"I wish I could. I'm going over to Cassidy's and then I'm hoping to get down to the park in the afternoon. I want to have some shots that I can show people in New York, to give them an idea of what we're planning."

There she went again. Cassidy and New York were all she seemed to think about. "Okay. G'night then." He pecked her lips and put the truck back in gear. She gave him a puzzled look, but opened the door and slid down. "Good night."

He waited until she was inside the house and he saw her bedroom light go on before he pulled away. He wanted to speed things up, yet Gina seemed content to take it slowly. He didn't get that. Why wasn't she in as much of a hurry as he was? He shook his head, he knew he had a tendency to be impatient. What if he just took things into his own hands? He did understand that she felt the need to get busy with her career. Maybe he should take the pressure off her and get things in place for their future by himself. If she didn't want his help with her dad's place, then he was free to find them a place of their own. He didn't want to bring her to live on the ranch and he knew that the two of them living with her dad wouldn't work. He decided he would talk to Beau in the morning, see what property was available. He didn't want to move too far, he needed to be near the barn and his horses. Despite her having said she'd do it if she had to, Gina didn't want to move up to town either. Maybe there would be something for sale down here. He didn't exactly keep an eye on the property market, so maybe there was.

He pulled up outside the cabin and decided to go check on the horses before he went to bed. The sense of peace in the barn always calmed him. The smell of straw and the small sounds of the mares in their stalls was so familiar and comforting. Storm stuck his head out and nickered.

"Hey, old fella." Mason rubbed his nose. "What do you think I should do, old boy?"

Storm butted him gently and nibbled on his collar making Mason chuckle.

"I wish you could tell me what you think. You've always been the smart one, huh?"

Storm nodded his head as if he understood and agreed. Mason scratched his forehead and then moved on down the line, checking on the mares. He made a special fuss over Annie and then went to check on his office. Sitting at his desk looking out of the window, he laughed out loud at the sight of the moonlight glinting off a metal roof in the distance. Why hadn't he thought of it before? A couple of years ago Beau had bought a strip of land down on the creek with the intention of building vacation homes down there. He'd only had one finished when the economy had dried up and he'd shelved the idea. The place had mostly stood empty since then. Shane used it to accommodate overflow ranch guests occasionally, but that was all. Most of the time, the cabins were enough to cater to as many guests as he could handle.

Mason decided to call Beau first thing in the morning. He might want to sell it. It would be ideal if he did. Even just renting it for a while would work. It would be a place he and Gina could call their own while they figured out what to do long-term. He smiled as he let himself into the cabin. He'd had some great times sharing this place with Shane and Chance, but it was time to move on. Time for him to start the next chapter of his life, the chapter where he and Gina finally got their happily ever after.

Chapter Twenty-One

Gina smiled at Cassidy. "So, what do you think?"

Cassidy grinned. "I love them! I can't believe how you managed to capture the light and color. Look." She held the photograph Gina had showed her up next to one of her paintings. She was right. The watercolor almost shimmered with the light greens and pale yellows of a cut hayfield under a bright blue sky. Gina's photograph echoed and reflected the colors. The bright hues of a bluebird perched in sunlight that shone through early yellow and green leaves.

Gina nodded happily. "We seem to look at things in the same way, even if we capture them differently, we reflect each other perfectly."

"I can't wait for people to see these," said Cassidy. "Are you all packed and ready to go tomorrow?"

"Ha. You don't know me very well yet, do you? I'll be packed and ready about ten minutes before we need to head to the airport."

Cassidy laughed. "I see. Good to know." The bell sounded out front, alerting them to the fact that someone had just entered the gallery. "Oops. Give me a minute?"

"Of course." Gina looked around the back office where they'd been sitting. She loved this place. She'd never felt this at home in Liam's gallery. To be fair, she wasn't comparing apples to apples. While the Moonstone sat on Main Street and was open to the public, who often wandered in out of curiosity or simply hoping to buy postcard prints, Liam's gallery was very different. It was one of those places you'd never find unless you knew where to look. It made Gina feel inadequate. Even the doorman looked down his nose at her—or so it felt.

She started when Cassidy popped her head back around the office door. "Sorry, this may take a while."

"No worries. Do you want me to run over to the coffee shop and get us some lunch?"

"That'd be great. Thanks. I'll take a Turkey Rueben and an apple juice."

"Okay, see you in a little while."

Gina gathered her purse and made her way out through the gallery. She was pleased to see that the customer Cassidy was dealing with was Mrs. Dunbar. She was a good friend of Monique Remington and had been one of the ladies interrogating Cassidy in the kitchen at the party. The fact that she was here confirmed that Gina had been right. The locals were accepting Cassidy and the Moonstone as their own. With Mrs. Dunbar's stamp of approval, many of the other well-to-do ladies would soon become clients, too.

She enjoyed the feel of the warm sunshine on her back as she wandered down Main Street. She waved through the window of the hardware store as she passed, glad that Iris had a long line waiting at the cash register and she wouldn't be able to come out to talk—or dig for gossip.

She pushed open the door to the coffee shop and hesitated a moment. Guy and April were sitting at a table in the corner. Guy looked angry while April looked terrible. She looked scared and pale. Gina would love to be able to help, but she didn't know how she could without making things worse for April. She averted her gaze and hurried to the counter to wait in line.

She knew Guy was coming over to her, even with her back turned to him. Her creeper alert was finely tuned after living in New York for so long.

"Good to see you again, Gina. Have you considered my offer?"

She didn't turn around to face him, simply shook her head. "I told you. I'm not interested. Not interested in selling to you and certainly not interested in anything else."

He placed a hand on her shoulder. "I hate to see him make a fool of you again, Gina. Don't forget that I'm here for you when you see the light."

She shrugged his hand off, hating the feel of it, but decided not to waste any more words on him. She waited until he walked away before she shuddered. The girl behind the counter gave her a sympathetic smile, but said nothing. It seemed Guy had the same effect on most people. Gina watched him leave and was surprised to not see April with him. She turned and saw her still sitting at the corner table. The poor thing looked even more miserable. Gina would have thought she'd be happy just to be away from Guy!

When she finally reached the head of the line, Gina ordered the sandwiches and went to get the two apple juices from the fridge. April caught her eye and beckoned her over.

"Are you okay?" Gina asked.

April nodded slowly. Gina could see she was shaking. "I'm fine, thank you. I need to talk to you."

What on earth might she have to say? "Give me a minute?" She went back to collect and pay for the sandwiches, then pulled out a chair to join April. The two of them had never really known each other. April was a couple of years older than her. Their only real connection over the years had been Mason. "What is it?"

April fiddled with her coffee cup with trembling hands and refused to meet her eye.

"Are you okay?" Gina was starting to worry about her. Was this going to be a cry for help? Was Guy hitting her?

April nodded. Her reply couldn't have been further from what Gina was expecting. "I'm fine, but there's something I have to tell you."

Gina waited.

"I think you should know."

She was starting to get impatient, wishing April would just spit it out—whatever it was.

"Guy told me you didn't believe him."

Gina drew in a sharp breath. Was April saying what she thought she was? "That I didn't believe him about what?"

"That Marcus is Mason's son." April's face turned even paler as she said it.

Gina felt her heart starting to race. It couldn't be true. Mason had told her. For a moment her mind began to spin wildly. What if he'd lied? She held April's gaze and saw the truth in her eyes. She took a deep breath. "I don't know what's going on with you. I don't know why you would tell me something like that, but it's not true, is it?" She slammed her fist down on the table, causing heads around them to turn in their direction. "Is it, April?"

April looked panic-stricken, her eyes wide with fear. She shook her head mutely and her eyes filled with tears.

"What the hell are you playing at, then? Why would you say that?"

"I'm sorry, Gina. I'm so sorry, but I have to. He's threatening me. He told me if I don't make you believe Marcus is Mason's then he'll take Marcus away from me. Claim I'm an unfit mother. He'll do it, too. You don't know what he's like."

Gina stared at her. "He'd try to take your own son away from you?"

"He won't just try. He'll do it."

Gina shook her head. "So, what are you going to do?"

"I don't know. Once he finds out that you don't believe me, he might do it anyway. I just want to take Marcus and run, but even that would be no use. I've got nowhere to run to. He'll take my boy and ruin me." April was shaking as she spoke, the tears starting to run down her face. "I don't know what I can do, Gina."

Gina covered her hand with her own. "We'll come up with something. You're not alone, you know. You have friends here." She squeezed her hand. "Including me and Mason. And you have family, too. What about them? Can't they help you get away from him?"

April shook her head sadly. "I haven't told them. They told me I was a fool to ever marry him. I knew it even then. He's not a nice man. But it was already too late. I was pregnant, and you know how that goes around here."

Gina did know how that went. A single mom here was destined to a life of poverty. There was very little work to be had for anyone, and few of the businesses were willing to hire women who needed to make their kids a priority.

"Well, for now, I guess all you can do is tell him I believed you. It's hardly your fault if I choose to stay with Mason anyway, is it?"

"I guess not. You mean you're not going to tell Mason about this? I know he wouldn't just let it lie. He'd be straight onto Guy and then I'll get it."

"Don't you worry about that." Gina knew what Mason's reaction would be, too. But they had promised one another no more secrets and this was a big secret to keep. "For now, you just tell Guy that you did what he wanted you to and that I was shocked. That's all he needs to know."

April looked around wildly. "But he'll ask me what you said. He'll know we sat here and talked."

Gina shrugged. "Tell him I was asking you questions. That's not a lie."

April nodded. "Thanks, Gina. I'm sorry. I never wanted to hurt you, or Mason. But I had to do what I must, for my boy."

Gina nodded. "I can see that. I should go, but you call me if you need to, okay? I hate the thought of you going home to him."

"So do I, but it's all I can do. If I leave him, I have to leave my boy, too. I'll never do that, so I live with it."

"I have to go." She needed to get back to the gallery, but she also wanted to talk to Mason.

"Please don't tell Mason." April seemed to read her thoughts.

"I have to, but don't worry. I won't let him do anything that will cause more trouble for you."

April looked terrified again. "I know you love him, Gina, but do you think you can stop him from doing what he sees fit?

He's not the kind of man who will bow to what a woman wants, is he?"

"Don't worry. It'll be all right."

As she hurried back down the street, she saw Guy standing on the corner. She did her best to look worried so he would think she'd taken April's news to heart. It wasn't too difficult to look worried, either. April's last words had struck a chord with her. Mason wasn't the kind of man to be told what to do or to show any patience or restraint when it came to Guy. She couldn't help but wonder what he would do when she told him. She hated that she doubted him, but she did. For all she wanted the two of them to be equal partners in a relationship, she was concerned that he didn't know how to do that. He would want to step in and take charge, do as he saw fit, no matter what she might say. She had a heavy feeling in her stomach at the thought that that was just the way he was. Could she live with that?

She arrived back at the gallery and went in. Cassidy was still talking with Mrs. Dunbar, so Gina went through to the back to call Mason. She didn't want to live with doubts or secrets anymore. She needed to talk to him as soon as she could.

~ ~ ~

Mason slid down from the mare he'd been working and led her over to the fence where Shane was sitting watching.

"See, I told you. She's bomb-proof. You can send your city slickers out on her without a worry now."

Shane grinned. "Thanks, Mase. She's turned into a real sweetheart. I never would have believed it when she first came in, she was so spooky."

"She just needed some time and understanding. Most of them are that way. When you show them they can trust you, they start to trust themselves, too."

He'd just ridden the mare around an obstacle course where she'd had to pass a burning oil drum, waving flags, a parked car with its headlights flashing and horn blaring, and she hadn't batted an eyelid. She'd stepped over a fallen tree trunk and waded through water, coolly and calmly. It had taken him several weeks to get her to this stage, but he truly believed that horses were just like humans. Once you showed them there was nothing to be afraid of, they started to gain confidence in themselves and ended up believing that they could handle anything, and take care of their rider, too.

Shane gave him an odd look. "Are you doing any better about giving Gina time and understanding?"

"What do you mean?"

"Yesterday it seemed like you were trying to push her faster than she's ready to go."

Mason scowled. "We lost ten years already. How much longer do we have to wait?"

Shane laughed. "Patience is a virtue, you know that."

Mason shook his head. "Why can't hurry the fuck up be a virtue, huh? Why waste more time?"

Shane pursed his lips. "It's not wasting time. It's giving her the time she needs to be comfortable with it all. Nothing much is changing for you in all of this. You still have your life, your work, everything the same as it's always been. You get to add the woman you've always wanted into what you already have. It's not the same for G. She's giving up the life she's known, the city she lived in, her work, everything. She needs to find her feet with who she is *here*, now."

Mason nodded grudgingly. "I suppose."

Shane hopped down from the fence. "All I'm saying is don't screw it up, okay. You know how to do it for the horses. You've got all the time in the world to do the groundwork with them, make them feel comfortable and gain their trust. I don't understand why you can't do the same with Gina. Anyway, I need to get back up there. We've got a new group checking in this afternoon and I want to make sure everything's ready. I'll catch you later."

Mason thought about it as he watched his brother walk away. Everything Shane had said was true, but he didn't understand how much Mason wanted to make up for lost time. He just didn't get it. He led the mare back to her stall and brushed her down. When he got done here, he was going to call Beau again. He'd left him a message this morning, but hadn't heard back yet.

When he got back to his office, he did have a message, but it was from Gina, not Beau. She sounded agitated about something. He called her straight back.

"Hey, Mason."

"Hey, babe. What's up?"

"I need to talk to you. What are you doing later?"

"I was hoping to see you."

"Good, do you want to meet me at Pine Creek at six? Cassidy and I need to get everything packed up and ready for tomorrow, but I should be done by then."

"Pine Creek? You're not going to walk out on me this time?"

She sounded exasperated. "No. I'm not."

"Want to tell me what it's about?"

"I'd love to, but I think it should wait until I see you."

"Okay. I'll see you there then."

"Bye."

As he hung up, he couldn't help but wish she sounded more excited to see him. That he wasn't just something she had to fit in before she headed off to New York. He shrugged and tipped his hat back. Maybe Shane was right and he needed to learn to be a little more patient. He picked his phone back up to call Beau. A guy could still get the ball rolling on a place to live while he was being patient, couldn't he?

~ ~ ~

Gina hung up and put her phone down on the table. She was apprehensive about what Mason would say—or do, once he heard what Guy was up to. Surely he wouldn't fly off the handle, knowing what that would mean for April? She frowned at that, she wasn't sure that he would stay calm about it for *her* sake, but he probably would for April's. That didn't do too much to make her feel better.

"Sorry that took so long." Cassidy came into the office. "It looks like you were right about me being accepted by the locals now."

"I'm glad," said Gina absently.

"Hey, what's up with you?"

"Nothing really. Just Mason stuff."

Cassidy came and sat opposite her. "I don't get the two of you."

"What do you mean?"

"Well, from what I understand, he's your long lost love. You've been apart for years because of a horrible misunderstanding and now you're back together. If I were you I wouldn't be able to think about another thing until I knew we were back on track."

Gina shook her head. "You sound just like him!"

"But you're not so sure?"

"I am! But it's not that simple. When we were together before we were kids, he's four years older than me and at that age it was a big difference. He was the big strong hero, riding in to save the day, protecting me from anything and everything."

Cassidy grinned. "Just like every girl wants."

"Yeah, *girls* want that. I'm a woman now. In the last ten years, I've grown up, I became strong and independent and I don't know how to give that up. I don't *want* to give that up."

"Why would he want you to? You're a pretty awesome lady."

Gina shrugged. "I guess I'm not sure that he's changed that much. He's a man—a Montana man at that. It's part of his identity to protect and provide. I love that about him, don't get me wrong, and I love him with all of my heart. I'm just not sure that he can accept me, truly love me, the way I am now."

Cassidy frowned. "I don't see that. I'd say he's totally in love with you. He's got some adjusting to do, but if you ask me, he's doing it."

"I hope so. Anyway, enough of all that. Here, have your sandwich and then we need to get busy."

Chapter Twenty-Two

Mason felt his heart fill up when he saw Gina pull in. He'd arrived at Pine Creek a little early and was sitting at a table by the window waiting. She smiled and waved when she spotted him. Man, she was beautiful, and she was all his—as long as he didn't blow it. He was a little apprehensive about what he'd talked to Beau about earlier, but he didn't have to worry about it yet. She'd said she needed to talk to him about something. They'd deal with whatever that was first.

Once she was seated and had a glass of wine, he took her hand. "You sounded stressed today, G. What's up?" He didn't like the way she looked at him. She looked nervous, almost as though she didn't trust him. "What is it?"

"I need you to make me a promise before I tell you."

"Promise what?"

"That you won't fly off the handle and that you won't take matters into your own hands. I don't want you to do anything about what I tell you, unless I agree that you should."

Whatever she was talking about, he didn't like the sound of it. Why would she want to control his reaction to anything? He scowled at her.

"Don't look at me like that. Do you promise?"

It seemed he'd have to. She wouldn't tell him otherwise, he knew that much. It must be something pretty important if she thought she wasn't going to like his reaction. "Okay. I promise."

"I ran into April in town today." She took a sip of her wine before she continued. "She told me that Marcus is your son."

"Why in the hell would she say that? I already told you..."

She put a hand out to stop him. "I know. Just listen, will you?"

Mason gritted his teeth. He couldn't believe that April would do that.

"I *know* it's not true. I trust you. I believe you. I told her that much, too. You can imagine how mad I was."

"And what did she say?"

"She fell apart. Admitted that it was a lie. Guy put her up to it. He's threatening to take her son away from her. I'm sure he's hitting her."

Mason was fuming. That bastard was screwing up lives—hurting people—all in an attempt to get at him. He felt guilty as hell about April. She wouldn't even be in that situation if it weren't for him. He wanted to go wring Guy's neck right this minute.

Gina was watching him. "We need to help her, Mase."

"How? If I could have figured out a way to help her, I would have done it by now."

"I have an idea."

He liked the smile on her face. She looked confident, sure of herself. This Gina was so much more than the girl he'd known and loved before. She was smart, self-assured, and by the looks of it, about to come up with a solution that he'd never been able to find. "What?"

"He wants her to convince me that Marcus is your son, not his. What if I ask for proof? I've been thinking about this all afternoon and I'll bet if I asked him to swear an affidavit that Marcus is not his son, he would."

Mason raised an eyebrow. "And what good would that do?"

"Once I had that, I could give it to April. She'd love to take the boy and get out of here. An affidavit like that would give her some security. Even if he went looking for them and found them, it would be hard for him to prove that she was an unfit mother and that he should have custody, when he has officially denied that the boy is even his."

"I'm not sure that would stand up legally."

"Neither am I, but if she reports the domestic abuse on her way out of town, I think she'd have enough backup to make her feel safe. It's just an idea of course, we'd have to see what she thinks, but she needs to get away from him."

He nodded. "I'll talk to her. I'll take care of it."

Gina frowned. "How about *we* take care of it, Mase? Aren't we in this together?"

"Sorry, babe. Yeah, we are. Except you're not going to be here, you're going to be in New York, aren't you. Do you want April left hanging until you come back?"

"Oh." She obviously hadn't thought of that.

The server came to take their order and when he left, Mason decided to try to lighten the mood. This was the last time they'd see each other until she got back from New York. He didn't want it to be all about solving other people's problems again. He winked at her and smiled. "So…will you miss me while you're gone?"

She smiled back and nodded. "I will. I wish I could just slow everything down for a while and take the time to just enjoy ourselves."

"I do, too. It seems like you don't have much time for me."

"Oh, Mase. I'm sorry. You know I do. If it weren't for you, for wanting to be with you, I wouldn't be so desperate to find a way to make it possible to stay here."

He frowned at that. "You have a way to stay here. I'm sitting right in front of you. I've told you. I can buy your dad's place. We can live there or find a place of our own. You don't need to do all this running around. Just let me take care of it."

She took a deep breath, apparently needing to calm herself before she spoke. "Thank you. I appreciate what you want to do, Mase. Truly. But please, can you try to understand me? I need to do this for myself. It's not about not wanting your help. It's about me needing to do it for myself. I'm proud of who I am. Proud of what I've achieved. I'm capable of handling it myself, and, for the sake of my own self-respect, I need to. I love that you want to help, but if I let you, I wouldn't be me. I'd be the little girl I used to be. Can you see that?"

He could see that and he respected her for it too, but that didn't make him any less impatient. He nodded. "I'm sorry. I guess I'm just being a butthead. As much as your self-respect is on the line here, so is mine. In my mind, a man takes care of his woman. I *do* understand you, but it's frustrating for me. Can you see that?"

She nodded and squeezed his hand. "So what do we do?"

"I guess I step back and let you handle it your way, and you try to understand me when I get antsy about it?"

She laughed. "That sounds about right. Apart from anything else, it's important for me to continue to prove that I can make it in the big world outside the valley. You know?"

Mason didn't know. He'd never understood why people needed to leave and go off to find themselves or prove themselves. Why couldn't they do that right here? He nodded, knowing that she wanted to explain to him how she felt.

"You remember what I was like even in high school. I knew my photography was good. I wanted to share it, show the world. It was a huge boost when the galleries in town started selling my work, but I knew there was more. I love this place, but I wanted to do something bigger, better than I could ever do here."

Mason sucked in a deep breath. She thought that New York and its snooty galleries—not to mention snooty gallery owners—was better than this? He wasn't sure what to say to that. So he said nothing.

She didn't seem to notice how uncomfortable her words made him feel. "I need to find a way to hold on to that sense of achievement and bring it back here. I need to feel that way about myself before I'll be any good to you. Do you understand that?"

He nodded slowly. He did understand that she needed to be happy with herself before she could be truly happy with him. What he didn't understand was why she felt it took going back to New York before she could be happy.

~ ~ ~

Gina grinned at Cassidy as the cab pulled up in front of the gallery. It felt good to be back in the city, good because she knew she was only visiting and didn't have to stay here. "Are you ready for this?" she asked.

Cassidy grinned back. "More than ready. Let's go take this town by storm."

As she pushed her way in through the doors, Gina couldn't help but notice how different it felt to be coming back here than it had to go back to the valley. Everything felt familiar there. Right. *Here* she looked around and felt like a stranger. It was hard to believe that this place had been central to her life for so many years. She stopped when she saw Kaitlyn waiting for them in the reception area.

"Gina! It's so wonderful to have you back."

Gina had to wonder how wonderful Kaitlyn really thought it was. The two of them hadn't had any contact since that awful weekend. She'd spoken to Liam briefly about the show and he had been all business. It was as though she were simply one more of his photographers. He was polite, but it seemed hard to believe that they'd been about to get married. "It's good to see you." It wasn't really a lie. She did want to satisfy her curiosity as to whether Kaitlyn had managed to make Liam see that she loved him—and make him love her, too.

"And Cassidy! I haven't seen you since Palm Beach."

Cassidy nodded. "That seems like a different lifetime, doesn't it?"

Kaitlyn nodded. "It does. So much has changed." She looked at Gina. "For all of us."

"Oh my God! Cassidy Lane!"

Cassidy squealed when she saw Ian. "Ian Rawlings! You dirty old bastard!"

Gina had to laugh at the way Cassidy threw herself at Ian and he spun her around. She'd never have described Ian that way, but it seemed he and Cassidy had a very different relationship. She watched as the two of them disappeared arm in arm into his office, then turned back to Kaitlyn. "Wow! I didn't realize they knew each other so well."

Kaitlyn shrugged. "They go back a long way. Do you want to come through? Liam won't be back for a while yet. I want to go over the arrangements for the opening with you."

"Sure." Gina was relieved not to have to face Liam immediately. Perhaps Kaitlyn would fill her in on how much had changed with him before he got back.

Once they'd gone over all the details for opening night Kaitlyn straightened up and looked Gina in the eye. "So how are things working out with your cowboy?"

Gina smiled. "Very well, thank you. How about you? Did you and Liam get together?"

Kaitlyn shook her head. "Not yet. It's taken him a while to get over you. I'm not sure he has."

Wow! Gina hadn't expected to hear that. "I'm sorry."

Kaitlyn smiled. "No, I'm sorry. I've wanted to call you so many times to apologize for that weekend. I was horrible, but only because I was desperate. I could see my future slipping away and I knew you didn't love him."

"Please don't apologize. It's like you said at the time. You did us all a favor."

"Who's doing favors? I'm not sure I can afford those at the moment." Liam stood in the doorway smiling at them both.

"Hey!" Gina was pleased to see a genuine smile on his face. "How are you?"

"All the better for seeing you." He surprised her by coming in and wrapping her in a hug. She didn't miss the look on Kaitlyn's face or the hurt in her eyes. Maybe there was something she could do to help the two of them along.

"How about we let Kaitlyn finish getting everything ready and you come have a drink with me?"

Gina turned to Kaitlyn, but she was already on her way out of the room. "Okay." She could hardly turn him down.

Sitting in the bar on the corner as they had so many times, Gina studied Liam as he tapped out a text. He was a handsome man, in a pretty way. She knew for sure she preferred rugged. When he got done he looked up and smiled at her.

"So how've you been? Are things working out for you and the moody cowboy?"

She smiled. Relieved he was being open and friendly. "They're working out well, thank you. I'm hoping that Cassidy and I will make enough money so that I can keep my dad's place going, but other than that everything is great there."

Liam frowned. "Do you need help? I hadn't thought about that. You were struggling to keep the place afloat when you were here."

He wasn't such a bad guy. Imagine him offering to help. "Thanks, but I think with this new line Cassidy and I have planned I should be fine."

Liam made a face. "She's not my favorite person as I'm sure she's told you, but if you're in business with her, I doubt you'll have any financial worries."

Gina had the same feeling. She just wished they could hurry up and make it a reality so she could relax and get on with building a life with Mason.

"Can I ask you something?"

"Of course you can."

"Are you glad we're over?"

Oh no! What could she say?

He smiled. "Don't worry. I'm just doing what I do. Trying to analyze the situation."

She smiled. She should have remembered. He wouldn't take it personally. He would want all the facts so he could make an assessment and draw conclusions. "Honestly, I am. I'm relieved for both of us. We were good together for a while, but we weren't right for each other, and I think over time we would have made each other miserable."

He nodded. "I agree. We were good. And at the time I thought good was enough. But it's not, is it?"

She shook her head, surprised at his openness and insight.

He smiled at her. "I've been doing a lot of thinking since we broke up. I think I was kind of an ass to you, and I apologize. I never meant to be."

She had to smile at the earnest look on his face. "You weren't an ass, Liam. We just weren't well suited. You probably thought *I* was an ass a lot of the time and I never meant to be either."

The little smile on his face spoke volumes, but he was too much of a gentleman to agree. "Another thing I've realized is that I don't want good. Good isn't good enough. I want great."

"You deserve great, Liam. You really do."

"You've found great with the cowboy, haven't you?"

She nodded. She truly had. And she wondered why she hadn't been making the most of every minute of it. "We were great years ago, and that doesn't just go away. It's taking a little readjusting to accommodate the people we've become, but yeah, what we have—what we are together—is great."

Liam nodded. "Then you do everything you can to keep it. Don't put anything else ahead of it, will you?"

Wow! "Thanks, Liam. I don't intend to lose it again. But what about you?"

He gave her a sheepish look. "I don't want to offend you, but I think I found great a long time ago, too. But I was too scared to go after it. I'm *still* too scared. What if it doesn't work out?"

Gina smiled at him. "No risk, no reward. How many times have you said that about the business?"

"It's different when it's just business, isn't it? All you stand to lose is money."

She guessed that was easy to say when you could afford to lose the money. She had a feeling that there was no risk involved in going after what he wanted. His next words confirmed it.

"Kaitlyn has been with me for years."

Gina couldn't help the grin that spread across her face. "I agree. And you've wasted far too much time already. Go for it, Liam. You two are perfect for each other. I think you've found your perfect right there."

He looked stunned. "You knew? That I felt that way?"

She was able to shake her head honestly. She hadn't known that *he* felt that way, but she sure as hell knew that Kaitlyn did. "I didn't know. But I'm begging you to tell her."

"You think she..."

Gina grinned. "That's for the two of you to discuss, but I suggest you do it right away. I'd love to see a happy ending before I leave."

He looked so doubtful. "You really think she...want me?"

"Come on. Let's go find her."

"But shouldn't I wait? Take time, figure out the best way to do it? Think about how it can all work?"

As she dragged him to his feet she shook her head. She realized what she was telling him was the advice she needed to hear herself. "Just go with it. When you find great, the details will sort themselves out along the way. What you don't want to do is risk losing it. You're totally practical, and I think some of that wore off on me over the years. What we both have to do now is trust that by throwing ourselves fully into what we want, the practical will take care of himself." She grinned at him as she pulled him out into the street and started heading back toward the gallery. "How does that sound?"

He grinned back. "Scary as hell, but it still feels like the right thing to do."

"Then, let's go do it."

Chapter Twenty-Three

Mason looked across at Chance. "Are you sure about this?"

Chance nodded. "You might not like the idea, but think about the alternative. If April stays here and he beats on her, one of us is going to end up going to jail for beating on him—or worse."

Mason nodded. When he'd told Chance what had been going on with April and Guy, he'd had a hard time stopping him from going straight out to the Preston place to beat the crap out of him. Once he'd calmed down, he'd insisted that they needed to come up with a plan to get her out of there. Mason had spoken to April. She was still afraid of what Guy might do. Apparently, he believed that Gina leaving town had something to do with what April had told her. Mason was happy to let that ride. It gave them some time, before he started laying into April again.

Chance didn't even know April too well, but the thought of a man hitting a woman had him well and truly riled up and ready to even the score. April had said she'd love to leave the valley. Leave Montana even if she could, and she was ready to take the risk of just taking her son and leaving.

Chance had offered to drive them down to California. He still had some family there and had spoken to his sister. She'd managed to line up a place to stay and even a job for April while she found her feet.

The plan was to wait until Guy went out for the evening. April said he left at seven and rarely came home before two in the morning. If they picked her up and got straight on the road, they'd be out of state before Guy even knew they were gone.

They were sitting in one of the old ranch trucks out on the edge of one of the hayfields. Chance nodded when he saw Guy's SUV pull out. "There he goes. How long do you think we give him?"

"At least fifteen minutes to make sure he's not forgotten something and coming back."

Fifteen minutes later, Mason called April.

"Can we go now?" she sounded desperate.

"Yep. Get Marcus and your bags, we'll be there in just a few minutes."

Mason couldn't even feel nervous while they loaded April and her son into the truck. He was finally putting right something he'd felt guilty about for years. It was his fault that April was with Guy and it was up to him to get her out of here. Part of him wished Guy would come back and discover what was going on so he could just beat the shit out of him. But as Chance had said, that wouldn't help anything.

Ten minutes later they pulled up next to Chance's big black pickup. He'd left it at the bottom of Mill Lane so Guy wouldn't see it. Once they'd transferred the bags and Marcus, April came to Mason.

"I'll never be able to thank you enough. Or to repay you."

"He shook his head. There's no need. I'm just putting something right."

She nodded. "I loved you back then, you know."

Ouch. He didn't know. "I'm sorry." He didn't know what else to say.

She smiled. "I'm not. I'd never have been any good for you. You need a strong woman. You need Gina. A woman who can stand on her own two feet. You need her standing beside you, not someone like me. You and Gina are perfect together and I wish you all the happiness in the world. You're a lucky man to have found a strong woman who wants you, not a weak woman who needs you. I hope you realize that."

Mason stared at her. He sure as hell hadn't realized that before, but now that she said it that way, he did. He'd been wanting Gina to be the weak little woman who needed him, but why? Just to feed his own ego? She *was* strong, and he did love that about her, so why had he been getting impatient with her and giving her grief about it? He looked at April. "I'm starting to. You take care, April. I hope someday you'll meet the right man. A man who'll be good to you and be what you need."

Chance came over. "Well, she's not going to meet him around here. So can we hit the road and get her to a place where she might?"

April hugged Mason. "Thank you. Tell Gina, thanks for everything, too." She turned and followed Chance to his truck.

Mason sat there for a long while, watching Chance's pickup turn into a tiny speck before he started up the ignition and pulled away.

Why did it take April to tell him what he hadn't been seeing? He'd been resenting the very things about Gina that made him love her—that made her even more perfect for him now than she had been as a kid. He needed to let her know that. He needed to tell her that he supported everything she was and everything she wanted to do. He didn't need to hold her down, to make her small, so he could feel big. He wanted to be what she'd kept asking him to be—an equal partner. And he needed to tell her that—now!

~ ~ ~

Gina stood with Ian and Cassidy. The opening was a huge success. The contrasts in subject matter of her Brazilian shots were creating some interesting conversations. She loved when her work provoked people to think and talk. They were selling well, too. Much better than she'd dared hope. Ian dug her in the ribs. "So, little Miss Matchmaker, I would never have dreamed that you would be the one to get those two to finally see the light." He jerked his chin to where Liam and Kaitlyn were standing in a quiet corner, gazing adoringly into each other's eyes.

Cassidy shuddered. "They deserve each other."

Gina had to laugh at the look on her face. "They're right for each other. I'm happy for them. Liam and I had an interesting conversation and we helped each other to realize a few things."

Cassidy raised an eyebrow at her.

"You helped me, too. To realize that I've been so busy trying to prove that I can make it on my own, that I don't *need* Mason, that I haven't allowed myself to admit how much I *want* him. He's more important than anything else in the world to me, yet I haven't thrown myself into it wholeheartedly because I couldn't let go of my stranglehold on control."

Ian laughed. "So what are you going to do now?"

"I don't know yet, but as soon as I get home to him, I'm going to make us a priority." She looked at Cassidy. "I want to just spend some time with him. Find ourselves a place to live. Put him first. It won't affect the work though."

"Hey, I've been the one telling you to put him first. I know we're good, what we're doing is going to be great. And it's like I said about financial stress, it shows through in your work. I want you as happy as can be, because that will shine through in your work as well."

Ian nodded sagely. "You listen to her, Gina. The woman is genius."

Cassidy slapped his arm. "Quit it, Rawlings." She looked over to the reception area and laughed. "It looks like you won't need to wait until you go home to show your cowboy how much you love him, Gina."

Gina followed her gaze and felt her heart start to race. Mason! Oh my God! He was gorgeous. Seeing him standing there—in a tux no less—took her breath away. She had no clue what he was doing here, but she didn't care. All that mattered was that he was here.

He turned and met her gaze. He smiled that smile of his and she knew. She knew that any doubts were behind them. He was everything. Everything else in the crowded gallery melted away as she made her way to him. She smiled when she saw him nod and start toward her to meet her halfway.

"Hi, babe."

"Hi."

He wrapped an arm around her waist and pulled her to him.

"Thanks for coming."

He winked. "I wanted to show you my support."

"Do you mean that?"

He nodded. "I finally figured it out, G. I love you. I love who you are. I was getting caught up in how I thought things should be between a man and a woman. I was being stupid, because if they were that way between you and me, you wouldn't be you, and I love *you*."

She wrapped her arms around his waist and smiled up at him. "And I love you, cowboy. I got so caught up in proving myself. I was so scared of losing me. I forgot that part of who I am is what you make me."

"We're what we make each other, G. Each of us is strong enough..." He smiled. "...and stubborn enough by ourselves. But we're better together."

"We are. So can we just get on with our life now?"

He nodded. "As long as you mean you get on with your life, I get on with mine, and our life is born of that. I understand now that it wouldn't work any other way. I get it, and I wouldn't want it to be any different."

She reached up and pecked his lips. "You've got yourself a deal."

He reached into his pocket and went down on one knee before her. Suddenly, the room around them came back into focus. Everyone was staring at them and started to gather around.

He smiled up at her and took her hand. He held out a box with a ring inside it. She felt tears prick her eyes when she saw it. No diamond for her. She'd told him when they were kids that someday she wanted an engagement ring with a Yogo Sapphire, mined in Montana.

"Gina Delaney, will you finally marry me?"

She nodded and felt the tears begin to escape. "Yes! Yes, Mason I will."

The crowd around them erupted into applause. Mason stood up and slid the ring onto her finger.

"You remembered?"

He grinned and kissed her lips. "I've had that thing waiting for you for eleven years, babe."

Shane appeared out of the crowd and hugged her. She hadn't even realized he was here. "About time, too, sis!"

She hugged him back. "Finally, we get to make it official. You've always been my brother."

Cassidy stepped forward and took her hand to admire the ring. "Congratulations, Gina. It's beautiful." She grinned at Mason. "I would never have guessed Montana men would have such good taste."

Shane put an arm around her shoulders. "Why would it surprise you, sweetheart?"

Gina laughed as Cassidy shrugged him off.

Liam and Kaitlyn were next to congratulate them. Liam shook Mason's hand. "I wish you both the very best." He smiled at Gina. "And I believe you've found it." He pulled Kaitlyn to his side. "I know I have."

Gina hugged them both. She was happy for them, too.

~ ~ ~

Once they'd claimed their baggage back at the Bozeman airport, Mason grinned at Shane. "Would you mind taking Cassidy home? I have a little surprise I want to show Gina."

Shane beamed. "Of course."

Cassidy rolled her eyes at Gina. "Have fun. Call me tomorrow." She scowled at Shane. "Straight home, mister. No, I do not want to have dinner or a drink or anything else."

Shane grinned back at them over his shoulder as they walked away. Gina had to laugh as he tried to put an arm around Cassidy's shoulders and she shrugged him off.

"So what's this surprise?" she asked Mason as they walked back to his truck.

"It wouldn't be a surprise if I told you, would it?"

An hour later they pulled in at the barn. "Are you going to tell me yet?" she asked.

"Nope, I'm going to show you." He took her hand and led her out back, down past the round pen and across the little bridge over the creek.

She couldn't figure out where they might be going. The only thing out here was Beau's cottage. Mason led her to it and unlocked the front door. "You know I want you to be you and I don't want to make decisions for us, all by myself, but I can't stop being me anymore than you can stop being you."

She gave him a puzzled look, not getting where he was going with this.

He looked uncertain as he met her gaze. "Say no if you want to."

"To what?" she laughed. She still didn't know what he meant.

"Well if you want it, this place is ours. I know I'm impatient, but I want you to live with me, make a home together."

She looped her arms up around his neck. "Mason, you are my home. Always have been always will be. I love you, I love this place. Let's do it."

He tipped his hat back and smiled the smile that melted her heart. "In that case, welcome home, babe."

And she knew she finally was;

A Note from SJ

I hope you enjoyed your visit to Montana and spending time with the Remingtons. Please let your friends know about the books if you feel they would enjoy them as well. It would be wonderful if you would leave me a review, I'd very much appreciate it.

You can check out the rest of the series on my website www.SJMcCoy.com to keep up with the brothers as they each find their happiness.

Chance has finally talked me into giving him his own three book spinoff. Look out for it in Spring 2017.

In the meantime, you'll see glimpses of him in my Summer Lake series, too. If you haven't read them, you can get started with Emma and Jack in Book One, Love Like You've Never Been Hurt which is currently FREE to download in ebook form from all the big online book retailers AND early in 2017 the whole series will be available in paperback as well!

There are a few options to keep up with me and my imaginary friends:

The best way is to Sign up on the website for my Newsletter. Don't worry I won't bombard you! I'll let you know about upcoming releases, share a sneak peek or two and keep you in the loop for a couple of fun giveaways I have coming up :0)

You can join my readers group to chat about the books on Facebook or just browse and like my Facebook Page

I occasionally attempt to say something in 140 characters or less(!) on Twitter

And I'm always in the process of updating my website at www.SJMcCoy.com with new book updates and even some videos. Plus, you'll find the latest news on new releases and giveaways in my blog.

I love to hear from readers, so feel free to email me at AuthorSJMcCoy@gmail.com.. I'm better at that! :0)

I hope our paths will cross again soon. Until then, take care, and thanks for your support—you are the reason I write!
Love
SJ

PS Project Semicolon

You may have noticed that the final sentence of the story closed with a semi-colon. It isn't a typo. <u>Project Semi Colon</u> is a non-profit movement dedicated to presenting hope and love to those who are struggling with depression, suicide, addiction and self-injury. Project Semicolon exists to encourage, love and inspire. It's a movement I support with all my heart.

"A semicolon represents a sentence the author could have ended, but chose not to. The sentence is your life and the author is you."

- Project Semicolon

This author started writing after her son was killed in a car crash. At the time, I wanted my own story to be over, instead I chose to honour a promise to my son to write my 'silly stories' someday. I chose to escape into my fictional world. I know for many who struggle with depression, suicide can appear to be the only escape. The semicolon has become a symbol of support, and hopefully a reminder – Your story isn't over yet

Also by SJ McCoy

Remington Ranch Series
Mason (FREE in ebook form)
Shane
Carter
Beau

Coming next
Four Weddings and a Vendetta

Summer Lake Series
Love Like You've Never Been Hurt (FREE in ebook form)
Work Like You Don't Need the Money
Dance Like Nobody's Watching
Fly Like You've Never Been Grounded
Laugh Like You've Never Cried
Sing Like Nobody's Listening
Smile Like You Mean It
The Wedding Dance
Chasing Tomorrow
Dream Like Nothing's Impossible

Coming next
Ride Like You've Never Fallen

About the Author

I'm SJ, a coffee addict, lover of chocolate and drinker of good red wines. I'm a lost soul and a hopeless romantic. Reading and writing are necessary parts of who I am. Though perhaps not as necessary as coffee! I can drink coffee without writing, but I can't write without coffee.

I grew up loving romance novels, my first boyfriends were book boyfriends, but life intervened, as it tends to do, and I wandered down the paths of non-fiction for many years. My life changed completely a few years ago and I returned to Romance to find my escape.

I write 'Sweet n Steamy' stories because to me there is enough angst and darkness in real life. My favorite romances are happy escapes with a focus on fun, friendships and happily-ever-afters, just like the ones I write.

These days I live in beautiful Montana, the last best place. If I'm not reading or writing, you'll find me just down the road in the park - Yellowstone. I have deer, eagles and the occasional bear for company, and I like it that way :0)

Made in the USA
Lexington, KY
31 August 2017